THE CALL OF ALLIES

HIDDEN HEROES SERIES BOOK 2

SARAH BLYNNE

SARAH BLYNNE WRITES

CONTENTS

To anyone who ever wanted to be a hero

THERE IS ONE WHO
DISTURBS THE SEA,
WHO, NEAR THE
HOLLOW OF A CLIFF,
SPARES THEMSELVES
TO A DEGREE.

THERE IS ONE IN
MASTERY OF NATURE,
WITHIN THE GREEN, THEY
BLEND IN WITH GREAT
MEASURE.

THERE IS ONE WHO
CALLS THE STORM,
CLOSE TO THE OCEAN;
A SPARK OF HOPE IS
BORN.

THERE IS ONE WHO
CURBS THE FLAME,
BY A MOUND OF
STONE, THEY
DODGE THE EYES
OF FAME.

LASTLY, THERE IS
ONE WITH THE
GREED OF A THIEF,
ONCE GONE, THE
WORLD ONCE
AGAIN LIVED IN
RELIEF.

CHAPTER 1

QUILL

We don't have a solid plan. It's unsettling.

Havanna told me she had a convincing argument if the Descendants decide not to join us to kill the Dormant King, but she never told me what that argument was. She's the one taking the lead on this excursion; she's got to have an answer.

She tried to reassure me that this journey would be worth it, but I still went to bed last night feeling uncertain. The only proof we have of where the Descendants are is a centuries-old poem. On the other hand, I would choose going on this precarious journey than going back to Arbol Village. All that's left there are my abusive parents and judgmental villagers.

On the positive side, my travel companion is gorgeous.

I owe it to her that my life has purpose, and that she's given me an adventure, just as I wanted when I ran away from home. She gave me a chance to prove my parents wrong. My powers are useful. *I am useful.*

But that's as far as I will allow my thoughts and emotions for her to go. We get along great, and I will gladly admit I'm flirting with her. But I have too much baggage. The kind of baggage no girl would want in a romantic relationship. It's best to leave it as Descendants who are friends.

At the moment, I'm mounted on my Bennaru, Koa, and Havanna's on Bolt, and heading to Macaphin Village—where we presume the Water Descendant is living—and remain silent with our own thoughts. I catch a glimpse of Havanna from the corner of my eye, her shoulder-length brown hair flowing behind her in the breeze as our horses trot along the sandy shore, and her all-black outfit that somehow keeps her sweat free. The ocean water moves with the breeze, twinkling and fading with every passing ripple. Waves splash against the pebbles on the shore, sounds that could lull me to sleep. Birds ride the ripples and waves without a care in the world, completely unbothered with its movements.

"Are you going to let me in on whatever plan you have?" I ask in an attempt to ease the uncertainty.

"We need to find a hollow in a cliff." She flips open her map. "The poem says the Water Descendant spares themselves near the hollow of a cliff. I have a feeling Voda Cave is where we need to go."

"A cave?" I respond more to myself than her. "Doesn't seem like a very good place for a Descendant to hide."

She shrugs. "Caves can be hidden. So perhaps look for something blocked by moss or rocks or something."

"And what if we don't find anything like that?"

"Then we search the village." She shrugs again. "Look for clues. For example, if their appearance somehow makes them stand out from everyone else."

I swallow the groan in my throat. "This search might take a while."

"I know. But I know we'll find them. The Dormant King is going down. I don't care how long it takes."

One thing about Havanna I have learned is that she will do whatever it takes to accomplish her goal, even if it means sacrificing her life. If she could do it by herself, she wouldn't even involve the other Descendants.

Facts are facts. She's a walking death curse.

Up ahead, a circular structure indicates the entrance to what I assume is Macaphin Village. With my thumb held up to measure the size of the arch, it reaches just below my first knuckle.

"The biggest tell will be something covering their right hand," Havanna continues. "If no one else is wearing anything on their hands, then it's a solid lead."

"And what will you say to this 'lead'? Are you just going to go up to them and say, 'I know you're a Descendant, do you want to come and kill the Dormant King with us'?"

Havanna winces at my sarcastic suggestion. "Well, I definitely wouldn't say it like *that*."

I chuckle softly. "How else are you going to bring up the subject? We can't just go up to them and reveal our identities."

"Of course not. We have to investigate. Talk to them in a way that comes across naturally. Just leave it up to me."

"Hmm, I don't have full faith in that very vague plan. I believe that if we suspect we've found someone, we use Transmission to communicate."

"Why?"

"Because if we exchange looks, onlookers will suspect something." I bring my fingers to my temple. "We need to practice."

"Practice what?"

Without responding, I send a message to Havanna's mind.

Practice flashing my good looks.

Havanna flinches in shock, her breaths coming out in rapid puffs. She's genuinely scared, reliving a terrible experience.

"Are you all right?"

"I'm fine. It's just so similar to how the Dormant King communicated with me. It's not as creepy when you do it, though."

"I'm told my voice is sultry and seductive," I reply with a wink while she rolls her eyes and giggles. "Now, try sending a message back to me."

"I don't even know how to begin to try that."

I pause to think of the best way to explain it. It was second nature for me, but it was harder for my older brother, Indigo, to understand how to respond.

When I was a child, Indigo and I practiced Transmission for hours. When my parents thought I was guarding him from danger at all times, we were separated deep in the woods testing my powers. Neither one of us had much guidance on how the recipient could respond to mental messages. Father told me the powers he passed down to me were useless. Therefore, he taught me nothing. That left Indigo and me no choice than to take it upon ourselves to figure it out.

Once he found a technique that worked, he told me how he did it.

"I had to keep your message in the forefront of my mind. I thought about what I wanted to say in return, and the fact that I wanted to talk to you. Then, somehow you heard me."

Once he got used to his newfound skill, we decided to test how far my messages could span. So, we spread out within the forest to test it. It was around the two-mile mark that Indigo's responses sounded muffled. The distance was similar to an active beehive directly next to my ear.

Indigo was always the peacemaker in the family. Our parents loved him most, so he felt he needed to maintain peace with them. Then he felt he needed to fill the void in my self-worth with encouraging reminders, even when he was dying in my arms from a Dormant's icicle.

"You . . . worthy. You . . . good person. No matter . . . what anyone says."

As horrible as it sounds, I wish the Backers had gotten my parents, not my favorite person.

Some days, I still expect to hear his voice in my mind. Telling me where to meet for target practice, or where I can meet him to hunt for supper. Oftentimes, I used it to complain about our parents.

Nonetheless, he's gone, and he can't talk to me at all.

"When I talk to you," I begin to tell her, pushing aside the sorrow of my brother's death, "think about what you want to say in return. While you do that, tell yourself you want to talk to me. Focus on what you want to say, and that feeling of wanting to respond."

I concentrate once more and send her another message.

Talk to me.

Havanna's eyes are shut tightly, so much so that the corners of her lids crinkle. The two fingers on each hand are pressed against her temples in concentration.

Can you hear me?

"It worked," I say with disbelief and chuckle in excitement. I can't believe Indigo's tactic worked for her too.

Havanna breathes out in relief. "That took a lot of mental energy. Let's practice so I don't have to focus so much every time I need to talk to you."

Our Bennarus continue along the shore at a steady pace. Havanna and I send silent messages back and forth that, to anyone else, would just make us appear mentally ill with random bouts of laughter in between. Our facial expressions without speaking actual words prove to be amusing for the last couple miles of our trip. Our conversations range from what we think the Water Descendant will look like, which ultimately leads to what we think makes the opposite sex attractive.

He has to be handsome, Havanna admits. *And have a kind heart. And not be afraid of the fact that I'm a strong fighter.*

So, someone like me?

For the love of Halivaara, Quill!

Well! Who else do you know that meets that standard?

A grown man?

Ouch. Remind me to never ask you to stroke my ego.

You don't need anyone to help you with that.

Eyeing her as slyly as I can, I see a hint of a shy, sheepish smile on her face, making her entire countenance go from serious traveler to cute girl.

Is she . . . blushing?

I was joking about her thinking I'm attractive, but I never expected her to blush and be shy about it. I suppose she's had limited experience with men compared to the . . . negative experiences I've had with women. I've had more time to be acclimated to this topic than those who have been in hiding all their life.

You're right. I can stroke my own ego.

I'm glad we sorted that out.

We move on to other subjects after that. Havanna gets the hang of talking to me mentally, to the point where she can send a message without having to close her eyes or contort her face to make sure she's doing it right.

The closer we get, the more I hear the sound of rushing water. Not just rushing, but *gushing*. The kind of heaviness that causes divots in the sand.

A massive waterfall pours from a high cliff to a small, rocky pond below. From there, a stream trickles along the expansive beach and flows into the ocean.

I turn to Havanna, her body stiff and face downcast. "And there it is. The cave."

"How do you know?"

"Voda Cave is right outside Macaphin Village, where we are right now." She sighs heavily in disappointment. "The poem says the Water Descendant lives near the hollow of a cliff. A cave." She points ahead of her. "That has to be it. There's no way we can get through that waterfall. It's too big."

The sheer sadness in her tone is hard to ignore. As a Descendant and fellow ally, I have to try to make this better. I have to. I did not run away from home just to reach a dead end.

"Chin up, Zappy," I say with all the playfulness I can muster. "We haven't even looked inside the village yet. Let's at least try that before we cry ourselves to sleep tonight."

My attempt to lighten the mood doesn't make her smile, but she nods, so I suppose that's a win.

Before we get too close to the structure indicating the village entrance, we find a place to hide behind the protruding rock formations along the cliffs that run along the coast. Koa and Bolt shift to a hummingbird and a mouse and climb up to our shoulders while we walk along the beach the rest of the way to the village.

The structure is actually an arch constructed of banana bunches, the ground spotted with the old and over-ripened fruit. We step under it, officially setting foot in Macaphin Village.

Small, polished, wooden homes with peaked roofs line the shore on one side and the rock formations are on the other, creating a sandy walkway in the middle. The Macaphins, barefoot with the white dust of the sand coating their feet, wander about the village, caring for a variety of tasks. One family is cooking in cast-iron pots outside their huts, and just ahead is a group of muscled men tying pieces of wood together. Behind some other homes are women picking fruits and vegetables from small gardens and carrying them in woven baskets. Little children splash around in the water on the beach with glee. The tiny waves that roll in are practically translucent.

"I suppose we're searching this place while trying not to look like Backers or suspicious outsiders?" I quip.

"Yes."

"All right then."

We trudge through, keeping an eye on everyone surrounding us. I'm completely mesmerized at seeing people so unlike what I'm used to from the forest, not to mention how different their clothes are. The women here are stunningly beautiful; I can't help but be enamored with each one. Their jewel-toned sarongs and woven straw hats ripple with the wind's current, and matching shirts tightly hug their upper bodies.

A woman walks past us, hips swaying side to side. Her shirt is cropped enough to reveal her toned torso and smooth, light brown skin. She smiles at me with perfectly white teeth that are a magnet for my eyes. Only for a moment, though, because another one walks past Havanna, and she's just as hypnotizing. She winks at me with a flirtatious smile, bottom lip rolling under her teeth.

Women actually like me here.

That is an understatement. They think I'm irresistible.

The women back in Arbol Village hate my guts. Autumn, a single mother of an archery student of mine, forced herself on me and stole my first kiss. When I rejected her offer of a relationship, she told the whole village I was sleeping with my best friend, Nyx, which was far from the truth. To get away from my parents, I'd sneak to Nyx's house and sleep on the floor in her bedroom, then leave early the following morning to avoid wary eyes. Because the village believed in chaste relationships, this was bound to ruin us if anyone found out. No one would believe us if we denied it.

Unfortunately, I got caught by the last two people I wanted to find out: my parents.

That was the breaking point for my father. Indigo had just died at the hands of Backers and we were all still grieving. They called Nyx some horrible names, and my father did something he managed to hold off doing my whole life. That backhand across the face stung, but not as much as their wholehearted rejection.

I had nothing left. My brother was gone, everyone in the village hated me, and Nyx surely didn't need me around to ruin her reputation further.

I left with a promise to never return.

Once I reached the Tormal Cliffs, I saw Luna Island out in the ocean. On a clear, sunny day, there were lightning strikes. I knew something was different about that. The only thing that could potentially make lightning happen in that kind of weather was the Lightning Descendant, so Koa flew me to the island to investigate. Choosing to leave the only home I ever knew was the first step toward the adventure of changing my life; little did I know meeting Havanna was the next one.

The thick scent of roasting fish and fruit roams straight to my stomach. I haven't eaten anything since the Conna Mondaña in Cal–léa; I could stand a huge plate of food right now.

Havanna is doing an awful job of hiding our reason for being here. Her squinted eyes study each and every villager from head to toe. She spends so long in her visual interrogation that villagers are starting to notice us.

Cut it out.

What? Her tone comes back snarky.

Your face. You're looking at everyone way too hard.

I'm trying to look at people from a distance!

Well, it's becoming obvious to them. If you don't want to get escorted out or attacked, we might need to find a different tactic.

What do you suggest?

A grumble in my stomach gives me the answer.

I'm starving. An eatery is a good place to spy on anyone coming and going.

Waves splash against the beams holding up a huge hut; it's obviously an eatery, and from the size of it and the smell of roasted herbs and meat, it's hard to miss. People come and go. Constant, obnoxious laughter and clanking dishes make up most of the noise inside. Not having the common linen pants or jewel-toned skirts—not to mention equipped weapons—makes us stand out and collect odd looks from others.

The closer we get, the stronger the unidentifiable herbal scent is. Wondering what it is, we step inside and the answer blurs our vision.

Every single person is smoking a six-inch-long green stick and looking extremely giddy. All the women have their hats off, letting their hair down and absorbing the scent they're buried in. There's enough of it to make one think they're stuck in a cloud. A waft of fresh, cooling, spicy smoke blows into my face. It unexpectedly proves to be a refreshing scent.

Another beautiful young woman, who can somehow see us through the thick cloud of smoke, greets us and leads us to the balcony on the back side of the eatery. Her sashaying hips with every step and her exposed lower back distract me from everything she says as she points out the view of the shoreline beside us. When I finally look up to thank her, I suck in a breath at just how gorgeous the view is. The ocean isn't bad either.

To our surprise, she hands us two sticks of what the others are smoking. "Would you like a Bamboo Rolly?"

Havanna and I exchange a confused expression. "What is it?" she asks.

"It's a bamboo stalk filled with ingredients used in the Tonic of Tranquility, but in the form of sticky paste," she explains with a hospitable smile, "pulverized Calming Canna, Cooling Mint, and overripe banana peels. We mostly use them in settings such as these to ease social anxiety and promote relaxation." She adds with a flirty wink in my direction, "A very well-received item among the village."

I take the greenish-brown stick she offers us and examine it. It's incredibly sturdy; the ridges on it look like sections of this plant were glued together. The inside of it is stuffed with a brown resin with a refreshingly spicy and fruity scent. I don't know about Havanna, but I have never smoked anything in my life. The only thing that created smoke in my village was the pile of garbage we lit on fire once a week. Putting something in my mouth to smoke is a new concept for me.

We've been hiding our whole lives, mostly by force. So much of this kingdom and its culture has been left unexplored. There's no harm in trying a Bamboo Rolly.

Why not? I could use something for my muscle tension.

"You know what?" I hand the stick back. "Light it up."

"This one too," Havanna agrees.

The woman takes the Rollies to a lit torch just under the roof and uses the flame to ignite the sticks, then hands them back to us. I have to look at the other customers to see how it's supposed to be used, just to make sure the right end goes into my mouth.

I bring it to my face with my thumb and forefinger and close my lips over it. The smoke collects in my mouth and slithers down my throat. I pull it out and attempt to blow the smoke, but end up coughing instead. My mouth feels cool and spicy with a hint of sweet fruit. I click my tongue to experience the full taste.

"Can you ease into conversation yet?" Havanna asks, forming a small O with her mouth and blowing the smoke. A natural-born smoker, if there ever was one.

"Possibly," I reply with a couple more coughs.

After two more hits, I find myself getting the hang of smoking. So much so that I end up chuckling out of nowhere.

"What's so funny?"

I shrug, the giggles nonstop. "Nothing is funny. But everything is funny." If Arbol Village made these, I may have been able to stay longer. "I shall order the entire stock of Ocean Hake this place has." I thump my fist.

She giggles. "Perhaps you shouldn't have smoked on an empty stomach."

Playfully, I squint and pretend to be confused. "Who are you again?"

When the beautiful woman comes back, I order a giant platter of Ocean Hake with a pile of Winterbulb jam. Havanna does the same, saying something with a faraway look about Winterbulb reminding her of home. Perhaps the Bamboo Rolly is making her sentimental.

"Keep an eye out," she reminds me, her eyes becoming unfocused.

"Yes. Keep an eye out."

She giggles at nothing, acting as a chimney with all the smoke tunneling out of her mouth.

"Now why are *you* laughing?"

She gazes at me thoughtfully. She tries to focus on me, but her eyes avert to other directions. "You're a very attractive man," she admits with abnormal boldness, putting the Rolly back in her mouth. That explains why she blushes around me.

I smirk with all the confidence I have. "Tell me something I don't know, Zappy."

Our food arrives and I can't shovel it in any faster. The sweet and savory flavors of the fish explode in my mouth, and I keep forgetting why we're here. I'm much too focused on being present and reveling in the effects of smoking and eating. My head spins as I turn my head side to side, feeling heavy as a boulder. The eatery and ocean scenery follow me in a panoramic view, similar to the effects of drinking a few glasses of Corn Whiskey. Something about smoking is making the effect stronger.

On top of that, this is by far the best food I have ever had in my life. Arbol Village mostly lives off of fresh bread, Mushroom Coffee, and Midnight Pig.

I'm fine never having Midnight Pig again.

I can't get over how amazing supper is. I want the flavors to stay in my mouth forever. I can even taste the familiar smooth and salty sensation of butter with each bite that dissolves on my tongue.

"You eat like it's your last meal," she points out. "What's with that?"

"It's just so amazing," I reply with my mouth full. "I want a lifetime supply of this. And the Conna Mondaña."

She quirks a brow. "How about I get you a lifetime supply of all the food in the entire kingdom?"

"I will never say no to that."

She leaves the now-shortened stub on the wooden table and takes in the appearances of the villagers. How she's able to do that is beyond my thinking ability. I'm enjoying this all too much.

"They have to be here," she whispers, the giddiness dissipating. "They just have to be."

My arms feel heavy as I hold up a finger. "We haven't been here that long. We need to keep looking. And you need to not get us escorted out of here while doing so."

"Fine," she groans. "I'll try not to."

"I would appreciate that." I look down sadly at my empty plate. "Wait. Who ate my food?"

Havanna sighs and shakes her head. She finds me entertaining; her subtle smile says it all.

Once we leave with slightly wobbly legs and more laughs, we turn left to walk through the rest of the village.

"I think we should sit," she suggests. "The Rolly was a bad idea."

My lips form a stupid, happy smile. I don't remember the last time I felt this relaxed. Or this silly. I should have asked for a whole pack of those things.

"Suit yourself. This is great."

She finds a spot on the beach, just far enough away to avoid the water. She reaches up to grab my shirt and tugs on it. "No. You sit with me."

I cave to her request when she tugs hard enough to make me lose my balance. My fingers dig into the pillowy soft sand and I kick off my boots and socks to bury my feet too. The heat of the sand is a comfortable beach blanket, warm enough to put me to sleep.

I lie all the way back until all I see is a bright blue sky, and spread out my arms. Havanna leans back with me, eyes closed and hands intertwined on her stomach. The tiny puffs of clouds create unusual forms that make my imagination run wild.

I point at a cloud. "I see a pig."

"I'm so proud of you," she says with a sleepy smile.

We spend about half an hour in this position, occasionally pointing at the sky and making odd comments about what we see, just until we feel our limbs again. Then we return to our search.

Our path is immediately blocked by an olive-skinned man with curly, intensely black hair, and a muscled, broad body. He wears the same clothing as the other men in the village and holds a gray trident upright. I know I'm strong and I know my way around a staff and bow, but this man could take me down in a heartbeat with his huge arms.

"Welcome to Macaphin Village," he greets us with an accent that I can only describe as colorful and emphatic, the vowels in the words elongated and pronounced. "I am Sharifa, chief of the Macaphins. What brings you here?"

I have a feeling more than one person alerted him that complete strangers are in their village, smoking and laughing. He likely believes we're Backers, but telling him we're Descendants isn't a good idea either. He may be a Backer himself, or one who has trouble controlling their tongue. Right now, it's safe to assume he's just like everyone else we're trying to hide ourselves from.

I turn to Havanna for the answer. Coming here was her plan, after all.

"We're just travelers," she answers without missing a beat. "Neither of us have been here, and it's beautiful."

Sharifa nods and listens to her explanation, his light shirt and linen pants billowing with the breeze. He folds his arms across his chest, his bicep and forearm muscles rippling with the motion. It's hard not to be jealous of his physical fitness.

"Very well. Before you continue your sightseeing, may I do a quick inspection?" He motions to both of our bodies.

Again, I turn to Havanna, the whip-smart one out of the two of us. Based on her knitted eyebrows and quivering lower lip, even she is surprised with this request. I have sheaths of knives wrapped around my legs; no wonder he wants to check everything out.

But I would have to take them off. And possibly my pants. I may have a sculpted body that makes the women here drool, but I don't want men gawking at it.

"Clothes on, correct?" I ask warily.

Sharifa snorts, which turns into a bout of hearty laughter. Havanna and I exchange a glance, confused on what is making him laugh. Soon enough, we join in weakly, but it's mainly out of nervousness. He doesn't seem very threatening, but neither of us want to question someone of authority.

"I just need to look at your equipment," he clarifies once the laughing dies down. "It's to make sure you don't have anything—" He narrows his eyes and lowers his voice. "—dangerous."

"Hmm," Havanna hums. "Do what you need to, but if you take my sword or his bow, we *will* fight you."

The chief steps back and frowns, taken aback that Havanna has the gall to threaten him, a man who has the muscles to single-handedly throw us in the ocean. His displeasure has me slightly afraid that he's going to take her up on her offer.

"She will, but I won't," I quickly add.

He hums, satisfied that I broke a tense moment with humor. Without another word, he circles both of us, starting with me. He lifts my pack to inspect my quiver of arrows with my sleek, impeccable bow, then pulls out one of the knives sheathed around my legs. With his mouth turned down with the impressiveness of my equipment, he puts the knife back. Then he takes my pack off and riffles through it, making a mess of everything inside of it. Once he's satisfied, he moves on to Havanna, who is currently glaring at him with the fire of a thousand suns. I pretend to be admiring the view of the ocean as I run a couple fingers through my hair to shield my now green eyes, and send a message to her.

You need to relax.

The sound of shuffling sends my gaze back to her, whose angry countenance has turned softer as she stares straight ahead. Hands placed on her hips, she lets the chief lift her shield, unsheathe and sheathe her sword, and sort through her pack on his knees.

Somewhere during his inspection, he finds something that makes him freeze in place.

The tablet with all the Ancestors on it. It slipped both our minds that she had that on her person.

My heart beats against my chest in rapid succession. Either this encounter is tense, or I'm feeling different effects from smoking the Rolly.

Regardless, this is not good.

He rolls the case over in his hands, both mesmerized and per-plexed with the artwork in the stone. We both watch as he does so, to be prepared for any threats. Sharifa may be good at hiding his intentions; anything can happen. A tough lesson I learned when Backers killed my brother.

To our surprise, he's careful to put the tablet back in her pack, and then rises to his feet.

"Enjoy your visit," he says with his handsome, pure-white smile.

Havanna and I glance at each other in surprise at his casual demeanor.

"All right," Havanna draws out.

"If you haven't done so already, I highly recommend you go to our entertainment cabana." He points to a few huts down from the eatery. "The girl who runs it hosts a variety of fun activities. I'm sure she would love to show you how to play some card games."

"Thank you, Chief Sharifa," Havanna says with a dip of her head.

He dips his head in return with what I'm assuming is a knowing grin. Was the tablet in Havanna's pack evidence enough of who we are? Did he figure us out?

We trudge through the sand to the cabana, void of all visitors. A wooden sign above the steps is a painting of three upright rectan-gles spread out and a hand holding them. I suppose they are the cards Sharifa was referring to.

Havanna and I stop in our tracks at the same time. Standing outside the entrance of the cabana on a wraparound porch is a light-skinned, barefoot young woman, probably our age. All of her hair is tucked inside a straw hat that's as wide as her shoulders. If her frowning light pink lips are any indication, she's bored out of her skull and pissed at everyone and everything.

She's just different enough from the other villagers to make her our target.

"I think we finally have a lead," Havanna whispers. "We should go talk to her."

"And say what?"

"We pretend we want to play a game. Talk to her without revealing any important information about who we are, just in case she's not the right person."

I release a deep sigh. "All right."

We move closer to the cabana, but with steady, careful steps. The girl sees us and her expression doesn't budge. Instead, she folds her arms and looks off in the distance.

She must *really* love working there.

"Look at her right hand." Havanna leans close to me to whisper, her body vibrating with excitement that she's trying so hard to contain.

Sure enough, on her right hand is an elegant, golden bracelet with a small chain that wraps around her middle finger and another one that circles around her wrist.

I turn to face Havanna, who can barely contain her smile.

We may have found the Water Descendant.

CHAPTER 2

HAVANNA

Just when I was starting to worry that the Water Descendant wasn't here, the chief of the village leads us directly to her.

He seemed to know what the tablet was in my pack, based on the recognition and awe I saw on his face. When he grinned at us as he directed us to this cabana, he knew what we were *really* here for.

Here she is. The Water Descendant.

I'm jumping to conclusions, though. We don't know for sure yet, but the Bamboo Rolly aftermath has worn off enough for me to realize we have yet to find anyone else who sticks out the way this girl does. The golden jewelry on her right hand being the biggest sign. No one else was wearing anything on their right hands, and nothing so dainty and beautiful.

But that permanent scowl makes her very unapproachable. Perhaps it's just the way her face is.

"Now what?" Quill asks softly as we approach the steps.

I give him a side smile. "Watch and learn," I whisper, then address the grumpy girl. "Hello."

"Hi," she responds in a sullen way that perfectly reflects her expression. Now she's staring—no, she's *glaring*—at me, and my palms begin to sweat under my gloves.

"We would like to play a card game." There's a tremor to my voice.

Her eyes rake me up and down and she finishes my examination with her lips curled into a snarl. Upon seeing Quill, she finds it in herself to briefly smile and bite her bottom lip, just as every other woman has since we arrived. It intensely irks me.

She clears her throat and returns to her sullen demeanor. "Fine." She turns to go into the cabana and waves for us to follow her. Quill gives me an unsure glance before we head inside.

There are a handful of wooden tables and chairs scattered in random places, none of which have people seated in them. A host stand sits in the back, and behind that are three lanes to throw handheld balls into numbered slots.

"Have a seat." She motions to a table as she heads to the host stand. Upon closer inspection, a patch of leather covers her palm and connects to the chain on her wrist and middle finger.

She *has* to be the Descendant.

"Can we use those lanes back there?" Quill asks.

"No. Sit."

We look at each other, taken aback by her rudeness. How does she operate this place with that attitude? Does she hate everyone, or are we the exception?

Quill hides his face and pretends to brush his hair behind his ear to avoid the girl seeing his eyes turn green.

We're in for a treat.

She returns with a deck of cards in her hands, shuffling them as she sways her hips, playing it off as innocent, but indeed knows what she's doing.

This game of hers wasn't the one I was expecting to play.

I sneak a peek at Quill. With the way he's currently tapping his fingers on the table, he doesn't seem to be paying attention to her, but perks up as she gets closer.

My stomach curls when I admit that she's beautiful. So much so that it gives me overwhelming insecurity. I admitted under the influence that I find Quill attractive, but he never said the same of me. Perhaps his view of good looks is in the form of this girl. He may very easily end up having feelings for her, giving me no chance to earn his affection.

This is the moment Jael would tell me to get a hold of myself. Unwelcome grief sets in as I think about how much I long for her to smack me upside the head. Or threaten to throw my feet in the fire as she rubs them.

I really wish she were here for me to confide in.

She's the biggest reason I dragged Quill into finding the Descendants and to end the Dormant King's reign. She, along with Aria and the rest of Ketra, are the biggest reasons I have to get this girl on our side, if she's truly the Water Descendant.

There are little things that cause me to further believe she's the one. All the women inside the eatery had their hats off and yet, she's left hers on. The only reason I can come up with is that she has something to hide.

"My name is Karuna and I'm your dealer today," she announces in a severe monotone.

"Oh, we're all playing?" Quill asks, then motions between me and him. "I thought it would be just us two."

"No," she states with a punch. "Is that a problem?"

He clears his throat with an uneasy chuckle. "No. That's perfectly acceptable. Just the two of us would have been boring anyway."

I shoot him a glare, rolling my tongue over my teeth. Karuna just simply stares at him, then rolls her eyes as she tosses cards in front of us. Quill hides his face from her view.

Just go with it. I'm trying to get her to warm up to us.

From the looks of it, it's going to take all the powers Halivaara can give for that to happen.

That may be true, but we still need to tread lightly. We can't blow our cover in case she's not a Descendant.

I know. I have a plan.

Karuna deals the entire deck of cards, splitting it up between the three of us. The cards boast different elemental symbols: a lightning bolt, a flame, a water droplet, and a leaf, all in a glossy finish that makes them slippery in my hands.

These are all the symbols of the Descendants.

It's plain as day. She's exposing her identity with these cards. That is the stupidest thing she could do.

"This game is called Liar," Karuna says, maintaining the same monotone voice. She picks up the cards in front of her. "You put a card face down in the middle and announce what element you're putting down, and how many. If you think the player is lying, you *must* say 'liar' before the next player's turn. If the player was indeed lying, they have to take the entire pile. If they were not lying, then the person that called liar takes the pile. There are eight cards of each symbol, so that should help you to determine if the player is lying or not. Make sense? I have no desire to explain the rules again."

It takes all the self-control I have to avoid snapping at her rudeness. As Quill said, we need her on our side.

"No, it makes sense," I answer in a clipped manner.

"Excellent," she says in a way that is less than. She takes three cards and slaps them in the middle. "Three flames."

I spread out the cards in my hand, counting how many flames I have. There are only three, so it's possible she's telling the truth.

"You go." Karuna motions to Quill.

He puts six cards on top of hers. "Six leaves."

I have one leaf card and Karuna might have the eighth one. What's the likelihood Quill has so many of one?

"Anyone want to call liar?" he goads us, arms spread and wiggling his fingers in invitation.

Karuna grunts in response, staring at the pile. I suppose she's not going to do it.

Quill quirks his eyebrows at me, daring me to call him out. It's early in the game, so if I'm wrong, I only need to pick up the nine cards that make up the pile.

Screw it.

I point at him. "Liar!"

With a teasing grin, Quill shoves the pile in my direction. Oh well.

I shuffle the cards in my hands, purposely stalling on taking my turn. I need to get this girl to open up in a very roundabout way. For all I know, she may have been raised to lie and do it convincingly. All I can do is try.

"So, Karuna," I begin, pretending to figure out what cards to play, "have you always lived in Macaphin Village?"

"Only my whole life."

All right, so she wasn't sent here from another place to escape Backers, as I was.

I lay down some cards. "Four water."

I'm actually telling the truth with this move. With the way no one calls me out, they must know it too.

As Karuna shifts through her hand, I sift through more questions in my mind. "Have you worked here for a while?"

"A couple years."

"What's it like?"

Her face shifts thoughtfully. "It pays well," she says in a more conversational tone. Finally. "It can get boring. I already know everyone in this village. I know each and every person that comes and goes. It's the same thing over and over again. Three leaves." She lays down the cards. "I suppose that's not such a bad thing, though. It helps weed out the villagers from . . ." She turns to me, dark and threatening, her tone suddenly ominous. "Completely suspicious strangers."

A very clear way to let one know that we are not trusted. She's made it very clear from the moment we walked in here.

I think she has us.

She does, I reply to Quill. *I'm going to get to the point. Even if it leads to a brawl.*

Quill lays down one tree card, giving me the opportunity to keep Karuna talking. We don't have time to play games. I give myself a chance to back out, but I push through.

"Well, has anyone thought you were a stranger here?"

Karuna goes rigid, her eyes twitching as she stares at the cards in her hand. Her fingers tighten around them until they turn white. "What is *that* supposed to mean?"

Stop talking, Havanna.

I ignore Quill's plea. I've already offended her, but we need answers. "I suppose you could be taken as a stranger too," I explain with a nervous voice. "You look different from everyone else in the village, from what I can see."

Karuna's cheeks turn red while the rest of her face remains stoic. Quill stares down at the table.

Congratulations. You just pissed her off, and you're being much too obvious.

And you're not?

"I suppose you're right," Karuna answers, her eyes locked on mine. She neglects to play any of her cards. Her cold, furious eyes burn me alive. "Pardon me."

She gets up and walks to the host stand with her hip-swinging gait. I notice that Quill looks at her for a brief second before turning his attention to me, his lips clenched in concern.

Nice job. She probably thinks we're Backers.

I didn't see you coming up with anything to ask her!

You were the one with the plan! From now on, you're taken off question-asking duty.

Then, it all happens in a blur.

Something stabs Quill's chair, just missing his arm.

It's a sharp blade that appears to be a playing card. It's dug deep into the wood, meaning whoever threw it is a skilled thrower.

I turn to the direction the weapon came from and see Karuna holding another playing card knife, ready to kill.

"Give up the act," she growls. "I'm not going down without a fight."

CHAPTER 3

ANARA

I had them pegged the moment they walked in.

They both carry weapons, but I suppose that's common for most travelers. And not only do they dress much differently from the rest of the village, they keep whispering to each other. Right in front of me! It's so obvious that they have ulterior motives.

They could *not* have been dumber.

I'm positive they are Backers, so I told them my name was Karuna. If they left and came back, asking the villagers for a girl by that name, no one would have a clue who they were talking about.

The moment the girl started asking me more personal questions, I definitely knew something was up, so I started hinting at the fact that I didn't trust either of them.

At. All.

When she started implying that I was a stranger in my village, I took it as a smart tactic on the Backers' part to get me to reveal myself. My reaction was purely due to her accusation hitting so close to home. I'm practically a stranger here. I've lived in Macaphin Village my whole life and I have zero friends. A fantastic excuse for my constant scowl and general crappy attitude. I'm never allowed to leave, according to Sharifa and his wife, Masina. So, of course I hate my life.

Irritated and scared, I threw a knife disguised as a playing card at the man. He may be attractive, but being a Backer cancels that out pretty fast. I just wanted to have fun teasing him a bit.

I whip out another playing card knife. The girl thrusts her hand out, eyes turning gold, and my knife stops in midair.

Wait. Did that just happen? Did I imagine that?

My knife just . . . *stopped*. I blink a few times with my jaw hanging low.

She's not a Backer. She's a *Descendant*.

Before I have a chance to react, the guy stands and thrusts his hand out, his eyes turning green.

He's a Descendant too.

All is well. Calm down.

The voice in my head causes me to gasp and struggle to breathe. Did he just . . . speak to me mentally?

My legs wobble beneath me and I barely make it to a nearby table when I collapse into a wooden chair, skidding it along the floor. I can't believe this is happening. I never expected to meet Descendants at any point in my life. Our Ancestors never found each other, so I didn't expect to be any different.

"You're. . . Descendants," I state breathlessly.

"I'm so sorry," the girl says with compassion, as if that makes this encounter any better, "we didn't want to scare or alarm you."

"Nice job," I deadpan.

"Before we say anything else," she starts, "we have to know. Are you really a Descendant?"

They used their abilities on me. I already know they're Descendants. I can tell them I am too. "Yes," I answer quietly.

"Is there a way you can prove it?" the guy asks.

I narrow my eyes at the idiot. "Why do I need to prove it? I told you I'm a Descendant."

"Just to be sure," the girl responds. "Please. If you want, we can go somewhere more private so no one sees."

There's no one in here except us three, but the front door is wide open. I could easily prove it without a care about who notices. Sometimes I wish I could just show the Macaphins that this is why they have to make sure I'm protected at all times, as commanded by Sharifa. They don't know, so they don't understand the logic.

"Fine," I grumble and stand. "Follow me."

I grab a small glass bottle of water I have at the host stand and lead them to the very back, where the lanes are, and bank to the right. There's a closet where I keep cleaning supplies, and it's the only place that has no windows. Absolutely no one will know we're in here. We're in close quarters, but I have enough room to make this work.

I pour out the water, some of it landing on the floor before I rev up my Upsurge ability. Hand aimed at the puddle, my palm tingling where the water droplet mark rests, I wiggle my fingers, causing it to rise from the ground and from within the bottle. It contorts to my will, elegantly swaying in the air. Water runs through every inch of me, including my fingertips; the sensation wraps around and circulates under my skin, even if water never emerges from my body.

The Descendants watch in mesmerization, their eyes following the water's movement.

They're about to find out that that's not all that's involved in Upsurge.

Just to see their reactions, I spread my fingers, the running water sensation converting into an icy-cold current in my veins. Frost covers my fingertips while the water starts to freeze, mimicking my hand formation as the ice splits into five sharp icicles. Then, with a swift flick of my arm, the icicles shoot out and stab into the wall just above their heads.

The Descendants jump as the icicles zip past, startled with the sudden movement. Something about that, making people fear me and my power, brings a grin to my face. It's a sick evil that I own proudly.

I sigh and fold my arms. "So now that you know who I am, how did you find me?"

"From the poem," the girl answers. "You have a poem and a map, correct?"

My eyebrows scrunch. "A poem?"

"Yes. 'There is one who calls the storm, close to the ocean a spark is born.'"

I maintain my expression. Now I know what she's talking about, but it doesn't answer my question. "All right," I drawl, "what does that have to do with me?"

"There's a line in the poem, 'there is one who disturbs the sea, who, near the hollow of a cliff, spares themselves to a degree.' The poem is about us Descendants, and that line is about the Water Descendant. Which, we now know, is you."

It's all coming back to me.

When my parents disappeared, they gave Masina the poem and map so she could show it to me so I could remember where I came from. Since I have to live in a cave behind a waterfall due to the humidity I need for my body, she feared the parchments would be ruined with the moisture I'm surrounded with, so she kept it safely stashed in a drawer in her bedroom. I haven't looked at it much since. I didn't think it meant anything to me, but they're the only mementos of my deadbeat parents.

Out of spite, I wanted to throw the items in the ocean when I was thirteen. My parents left me behind, yet they want me to keep *their* legacy going? They want me to do *them* a favor? Please. Perhaps when Vulca Mountain freezes over.

Masina insisted on keeping it in her possession in case I want to pass it down to my children someday. Even when I responded to her with heavy sarcasm about having children, she gave me a death glare, and that was the end of the discussion.

"Oh yes, that poem. So special. Everyone should have one," I reply with the same sarcasm I used on Masina when I was a teenager. I made her life miserable during that time.

I can tell the girl is getting annoyed with me by the way she closes her eyes and releases a breath to calm herself. In another life, I would care . . . but this is the life I was dealt, so I really don't.

I haven't in years.

"I need you to be serious and answer the question," she says, seemingly holding back the desire to snap.

"Very well. Yes, I have it."

"Well, the stanza about you places your location here in Macaphin Village."

So that's what the poem is for. I never knew that. Perhaps it was wise of Masina to have me keep it all this time. However, the Ancestors did a terrible job of using that as a message to our whereabouts. That realization makes me roll my eyes.

"As if they couldn't have been more conspicuous," I reply. "Then I suppose it's safe to tell you that my name is actually Anara. I use the name Karuna with strangers in case they're Backers. Throws them off, you know."

"I'm Havanna and this is Quill." She motions between them. "I'm the Lightning Descendant and he's the Land Descendant."

"So, what are you guys doing here?" I ask with a shrug. "I doubt you came here because you simply wanted to befriend me."

"Well, um," Quill begins, but turns to Havanna with uncertainty. "Perhaps we shouldn't have this conversation here."

"Is there somewhere other than a closet where we can talk?" Havanna asks.

"What for?"

She hums before she replies, "Let's just say it involves a common enemy."

A common enemy? The only enemy we all have in common is the Dormant King and his Backers, but surely they can't be here because they want to unite and fight him. That would be a reckless and idiotic move. At the same time, Havanna has made plenty of idiotic moves since she arrived.

But what else are they here for? Whatever it is, it was important enough for them to find each other, then travel to find me.

"Fine," I say. "Go to the waterfall outside the village and I'll meet you there. I just need to close up here."

They nod, then move to exit the closet. Quill goes out first, but Havanna takes a moment to turn back to me and ask, "Are you actually going to meet us there? Or are you going to ditch us and make us look dumb?"

I scoff. "Please. You don't need any help with that."

That comment did me no favors in winning her over. Her eyes burn into mine, ready to throttle me. It's a look I've come to recognize too well in this village.

"I will meet you there," I emphasize. "Go."

Rolling her tongue over her teeth, she follows Quill outside. Once they're out of sight, I race around the cabana to clean the tables and grab the rusty key used to lock the squeaky door.

"Anara?" I hear a familiar voice call my name.

Sharifa and Masina enter. Masina's dark brown hair sways with her every step and the sun illuminates her red highlights. With my pale complexion and nearly white hair, of course I'd stick out like a broken tree in this awful place, hence the hat I never take off in front of anyone.

I hate this thing so much.

Sharifa throws a thumb over his shoulder. "Who were those people?" he asks, less concerned than he usually is when strangers come to the village. In fact, he's far from concerned. The quirk in his lips says it all.

Instead of answering out loud, I motion for them to follow me to the closet. Whenever Sharifa or Masina needed to talk to me about something serious, this was the spot we went to so no one else could hear.

I let them enter first, then I close the door behind me. "They're Descendants."

Sharifa cheers to himself. "I knew it! I just knew they had to be!"

"How?"

"They both wore gloves and they have an artifact of the Ancestors," he says. "I had a feeling."

"So," Masina begins, somewhat excited, "does this mean . . . the time has come?"

I don't share Masina's excitement at this moment. I'm terrified.

I live in a constant battle. I want nothing more than to leave this place, but I was raised to listen to my guardians. And my guardians told me I had abilities that could get me killed if anyone found out about them. What choice did I have than to heed their warning?

They also told me there would be a time when the Descendants would unite and kill the Dormant King. Well, that day has finally arrived. Yet, I feel *nothing*.

"I'm not sure," I answer. "I have to talk to them first. I'm meeting them at the cave after I close up here."

Sharifa waves his hands toward the closet door. "Well what are you waiting for? Go!"

I release a nervous breath, playing with the dainty chain on my hand. "If it is time . . ." I say softly, "I don't know if I can go."

Sharifa sighs with pain and empathy showing on his face, his lips a straight line. He grabs my shoulders, rubbing his thumbs along my pale skin. "Anara, I know life here hasn't been easy, and you've created a hard shell over your heart. You've been desperate to leave, and under the circumstances, neither Masina nor I could let you. But the door has opened now and the freedom you have always wanted is waiting for you. You have the best opportunity to make the choice that will change your life."

"It is a risky choice," Masina says, taking Sharifa's hand and intertwining their fingers, "but I—we—have no doubt that you will accomplish your destiny." She gives me a sly smile when she adds, "Besides, you're advanced with the trident. You will be fine."

"Advanced with the trident" is a gentle way to say I'm flawless. Sharifa spent countless hours with me to make sure I was proficient in the weapon Masina gave to me. It was the perfect height for me to carry whenever I needed it.

Her reference to fighting back is more than likely about how I learned to respond to bullies. I had to use words instead of my trident or my abilities, much to my displeasure. Watching my victim writhing in pain was a secret dream of mine. But, violence in the village is not tolerated. As the adopted child of the chief and chieftess, I had to lead by example.

Sharifa motions to the door with his head. "Now go talk to them. Have supper with us when you have finished. Just make sure—"

"I know, I know, don't be obvious when I walk in," I cut in with an eye roll. I've been doing this my whole life, I don't need the constant reminder that my home is behind a waterfall and not in Sharifa and Masina's hut.

There are some good things about living in a cave, though. The humidity is great for my skin. Besides the sound of the waterfall, which I can tune out, it's quiet. There's no risk of anyone coming in to steal my possessions. On that note, it also means no one can bother me without my permission—and help—to enter, giving me all the solitude I want.

Once Sharifa and Masina leave, I finish putting the playing cards away, but the sound of flapping feet brings my attention to the floor.

Wave, my Bennaru, looks up at me and croaks, the bubble in his throat expanding and deflating.

"All right, Wave," I say, bending down and opening my palm for him. "Let's find out what they want."

CHAPTER 4

HAVANNA

The impact of the heavy waterfall on the rocky pool below sends mist and droplets in my eyes and face. Constantly wiping my skin of the moisture makes no difference.

Quill must notice, because he motions over his shoulder. "Here, stand behind me. I'll protect you."

I accept his offer while I attempt to hide my smile, my heart making a pitter-patter rhythm at his flirtatious remarks. He must have won over many girls in his village simply by flashing his charm. He's making it harder and harder for me not to lean into romance.

As long as I don't fall in love, I'm allowed to be attracted to him.

With his tall and bulky frame, he provides enough coverage to make sure I'm not impacted by the water. Such close proximity to him gives me a chance to take in his scent, a mix of manly musk with the salt of the ocean. A scent that warms me all over.

Evening has set in now. Families have retreated to their huts to enjoy the sunset with their supper. That's when we finally see Anara trudging through the sand to meet us.

"Cover me," Anara commands as she steps onto the rocky pond.

"What?" Quill asks.

She rolls her eyes, her lack of patience blatantly clear. "Stand around me so no one sees."

Quill and I exchange a look, but we do what she says. Her hand aimed at the waterfall, her fingers touch her thumb in the form of an O. Slowly, she separates her thumb from the rest of her fingers. Her eyes turn a stunning bright blue as the waterfall splits in half like a curtain.

I was right. Voda Cave is behind it. No one would have suspected a thing as long as she hid here.

Anara walks through first, then we follow closely behind. While she slips off her hat, something leaps off her shoulder and disappears on the rocky floor, out of sight. Her nearly white hair falls down to the middle of her back. Keeping the hat on at all times makes more sense now. The shocking lack of color draws our attention.

My boot slips a bit at the entrance from the growing algae, and the humidity hits me in the face like a rock. Quill grasps my hand to make sure I don't fall and my heart pitter-patters again.

We follow her around a rock wall where we find the most unusual living quarters. What I presume is a bed made of a large pile of dried seaweed molded together sits on the other side of the wall, with a stone bench on the other side of the bed. Next to the bench is what appears to be a stone shelving unit with clothes in it, but wrapped in some kind of clear covering, presumably to keep them dry. Then I see bulbs of yellow light scattered all over the small space that have me freezing in place.

They're Twinkle Fireflies locked in blocks of ice. Her source of light in this otherwise dark cave. Makes me wonder how she spends her life here, away from the rest of the village.

It breaks my heart that they're in a frozen state. No doubt Anara finds them as useful and soothing as I do, but they mean more to me than just simply being tools.

"Are those Fireflies alive?" I ask, pointing to the bright blocks of ice.

Anara narrows her eyes. "Of course they are," she answers in a condescending way. "They can only form light when they're alive. Preserving them in ice doesn't kill them."

A loud croak and the sound of flapping feet on the other side of another rock wall distracts me from the Fireflies. A green, bumpy frog rounds the corner and leaps in Anara's direction. She's completely unfazed by it as she sits on the edge of her seaweed bed.

She motions to the creature. "This is Wave, my Bennaru."

Wave stares at us blankly with black, beady eyes, questioning our arrival. That changes drastically when Bolt and Koa hop off our shoulders to greet Wave, recognizing that it's safe to trust their surroundings. He exudes happiness with his nonstop croaking and hopping against all the walls of the cave.

The scene brings me joy. I started this. I'm not only reuniting the Descendants, but our Bennarus get to see each other for the first time in centuries. Bolt and Koa couldn't separate from each other when Quill and I met, and it was adorable.

"Fine, let's get this over with," Anara groans, my delight dissipating with her voice. "Tell me why you're here."

She points to the rocky bench by her bed where we take a seat. Quill glances at me expectantly, giving me the cue to take the lead.

"Well, what do you already know about the Dormant King?"

Anara lets out a sardonic laugh. "That he's evil and deserves to die?"

I will celebrate the day when she can answer questions in a conversational manner. If I had the Transmission ability to initiate mental conversations, I would tell Quill he needs to pipe in.

I shrug, relenting to her attitude. "Good enough, I suppose."

"We already established that you're here because of a common enemy, which is the Dormant King," Anara adds exasperatedly, "so what do you need me for?"

"We're trying to find the other Descendants in the poem," Quill finally contributes. "Assuming that the Fire Descendant is still alive, all of us need to fight the Dormant King. Together." He clears his throat. "Which means, we need you to come with us and help us fight."

Anara chuckles. "Let me get this straight. You come into my village, interrogate me to find out if I'm the Water Descendant, *then* you ask me to break out of hiding to go to war against the most powerful being in the kingdom?"

I nod subtly and Quill nonchalantly confirms with a "yes."

"Do you even know where he is?"

I shake my head in shame that I didn't think that part through. "No."

Anara laughs even louder, blatantly mocking us. "This is the most ridiculous thing I've ever heard! You are both idiots. We're going to die before we even get started!"

Part of me is perfectly fine with not traveling with her. She's rude, negative, and enjoys belittling others.

But we need her. Quill and I can't do this alone. With her abilities, she will be a major asset to our goal. She holds the power of water at her fingertips; she has the capacity to do some severe damage. Since her Ancestor banished the Dormant King, she's rendered even more valuable.

"Let me ask you something. Do you really want to be in hiding for the rest of your life? Because, from what I could tell at the cabana, you're not all that thrilled with your current arrangements."

Anara straightens up, her eyes turning downcast, as if I struck a chord. I must be right.

"I don't want to hide forever," she resigns, "but I also don't feel like being a burden to anyone else. My whole life has felt that way." She goes back to her sarcastic self when she adds, "It's a *wonderful* feeling."

Her response is loaded with things she has yet to tell us. She doesn't clarify what she means, but I don't want to pry for that information yet. She doesn't respond to personal inquiries very well.

Quill pretends to rub his eyes while he communicates with me. Anara doesn't need to see that he's talking to me, or she'll conclude we're saying bad things about her.

You may have to level with her. Get personal.

He's right, and it pains me. He's the only one besides Queen Calista who knows my entire story.

I brace myself to delve into my life and to choose my words cautiously.

"I know how that feels," I tell her, the lingering emotional pain threatening to pinch my throat. "That's how I felt after Backers raided my home village. My parents sent me to Ketra with a promise to come for me. They never did. I felt like a stranger for a long time, especially because I couldn't use my abilities."

Anara's eyes are on me as she listens intently.

"I was tired of hiding. So one night, I decided to take matters into my own hands and I used Strike. And that's how the Backers found me."

"Why am I not surprised?"

It's a punch to the gut, but there's no sense in arguing that. I have to keep trying to appeal to her heart.

"They killed Jael. The chief. The woman I learned to see as my mother figure and mentor." I wipe my eyes. "The whole village blamed me. My best friend was angry. I lost everything." I clear my throat, swallowing back the tears that threaten to sting my eyes. "I had no reason to stay. Everyone hated me, and my presence just felt like a weight to the rest of the village. So I decided it was time to leave. To avenge them and Jael." I sit up a little straighter to exude confidence. "I promise you, you will *not* be a burden to us. If anything, you would be a huge help."

Anara's gaze shifts curiously from me to Quill.

"I came because it was better than being in my village." He shrugs casually. "Oh, and Backers killed my brother."

Something about that comment causes Anara to tilt her head back and release an obnoxious groan. "All right. That's a really cute story, but we're two different people. I'm sure the other Descendant will feel the same way. It's probably best that you stop wasting your time in being the leader of this ridiculous, asinine mission of yours."

Ridiculous? Asinine? She has no idea who she's talking to and what this means for all of us.

My anger spikes to the maximum level and I spring to my feet. I've had it with her attitude. I refuse to allow her to dismiss our destiny as a waste of time after I just poured my whole backstory to her, which was not easy.

"What is your problem?" I shout. I don't care if anyone hears us at this point. "Why do you insist on being so horrible and cruel?"

Anara furiously bolts to her feet, looming over me in a menacing fashion. I hear Quill stand as well, no doubt waiting to be a mediator between two fighting girls.

"Listen, you Electric Doofus," she growls, "you don't know what my life has been like. Everyone is forced to protect me, but of course they aren't allowed to know why, so my existence is an inconvenience altogether. And with the way you and I are getting along right now, it's safe to say that my coming with you will make zero progress in fighting the Dormant King." She points to the direction of the waterfall and punches out, "Back off and get out."

Her hurtful words and tone do little to help me keep the tears at bay. I don't know what exactly made her so cold, but there's no need for her to take it out on either of us.

I fully reject the urge to break in front of her. I need to show her I'm strong-willed, and she will *not* be seeing me cry.

"Anara," Quill says in almost a scolding way, "you don't need to be so—"

"Leave," she emphasizes. *"Now."*

I swallow hard and breathe out a shaky breath to indicate the hurt. Perhaps it will guilt her into changing for the better. "If that's the way you want it, fine."

I stomp toward the waterfall. Bolt and Koa shift to smaller forms to accompany us. Then, I realize there's no way either one of us can walk through that much water and I have no choice but to talk to the piece of work that is Anara.

"Can you help?" I snap at her.

"Walk through it. Won't kill you."

With the way Quill's breathing increases, he's reached his limit with her too. How he's handling this with such grace, though, is beyond me.

"Except that it *will* kill her," he responds defensively. "She's the Lightning Descendant. If you haven't already learned, water and electricity don't mix."

I stare up at him with pure admiration. The way he's defending me makes him so much more attractive. My heartbeat speeds up and I forget for a brief moment that I was ever angry.

No. I need to stay angry. I can't let Quill break my focus. I don't want romance. I *know* that.

"So, if you don't mind," Quill adds, motioning to the waterfall, "it's the least you can do."

Anara, to my surprise, wears an expression of guilt. She tries to hide it, but it shows ever so slightly in the downturn of her lips.

"Hurry up, Wet Wench."

Quill isn't right next to me, but I can feel him freeze at my insult, then glance at me with quirked eyebrows. Anara shares the same expression, but it quickly falls when she stretches her hand out, doing the same finger–separating motion she did when we first entered.

The waterfall splits in its curtain–like elegance and we walk between the space. The immediate relief of the cool night air hits me in the face, a welcome reprieve of the heavy humidity of the cave.

This war will be much more difficult if she refuses to come. As much as I want to drag her out of that suffocating cave and force her, I know I can't.

"'Wet Wench'?" Quill asks while walking away.

"She had it coming." I fold my arms and hug myself tightly, somehow hoping that it will help me be in control of my emotions. I look away from him and find anything else to keep my eyes on so he doesn't feel uncomfortable. "I just can't believe how unkind she was. So . . . callous."

I hear him step toward me and feel a large, masculine hand on my shoulder. "Don't let it bother you too much, Zappy," he says in a voice so soothing I feel my heart bubbling in warm affection again. "Perhaps she's right and it's best that she doesn't come. We tried, and that's all that matters."

"Yes." I sigh and nod, enjoying the way his thumb rubs along the sleeve of my shirt.

"All we can do is move forward and hope we have better chances with the Fire Descendant. Yes?"

I manage a weak smile in response. "Thank you."

"Of course." He pats my shoulder and hitches his pack. "We're friends. We're allies. We have to stick together. Just repeating what you told me."

Yes. We're friends. Of course. As long as he keeps saying that, I can keep my heart from constantly sinking in disappointment .

All we can do is move on.

CHAPTER 5

ANARA

I didn't think I would get so defensive. Havanna's story resonates with me, and I don't like it at all.

She's not me. I doubt she was bullied to the extent I have been. I doubt she lacked support from friends or loved ones. I doubt she was left to fend for herself when no one else had her back.

Ultimately, my decision and forcing them to leave is based on the fact that I know our personalities will clash. I'm already vehemently disliked in my own home; it's not going to be any different when I go with them. I'm not going to be of any use. Even while we hold extraordinary powers, literally in our hands, there's only three of us, possibly four if the Fire Descendent is still around. The Dormant King and his innumerable army of Dormants and Backers add to the problem.

I'm well aware that I hurt Havanna's feelings. She comes across as a tough warrior on a mission, but after I unleashed on her, the way her lips quivered and her eyes shone with tears told me I went too far. I felt even worse when Quill came to her defense.

I can't help it. It's who I am. Bitterness, anger, and insults are all I know.

Wave sits at my feet and peers up at me, his gleaming little eyes abnormally large with that twinkle he has when he's begging for something. His throat expands as he croaks at me.

I tilt my head at him as he glares back. "I take it you're mad at me?"

He flicks his tongue on my leg when I least see it coming, and does it repeatedly. A big sign that he's annoyed with me.

"Ew!" I rip my foot away and squirm. "You *know* I hate that."

He responds with a simple croak.

"Fine, fine, I get it. But you understand, don't you?"

He stays silent. Just those eyes boring into me and making me feel guilty.

I sigh and rub my temples. I don't know what I'm doing. I don't understand myself; there's no way Wave will either.

All the years I've wished to leave the Macaphins behind, the opportunity finally falls into my lap. Sharifa and Masina practically showed me the door, although a bit too enthusiastically. And that was before I even talked to Havanna and Quill.

I rejected my only chance.

Why?

"I'm going to Sharifa's," I tell Wave. "Come with me?"

Without hesitation, he hops onto the palm I hold out for him, then leaps up my arm to rest on my shoulder. He's my only friend, as sad as it makes me to admit it. Even if he disagrees with my choices, he's always stuck by my side, as is the duty of a Bennaru. He protected me when I waited till nighttime to go to the beach and practice Upsurge until my headaches nearly blinded me. He shared my joy when the headaches finally went away. He witnessed the moment I got rid of invading Niminims with a power I don't really know much about. He watched me as I learned to sew and became so talented that I was able to make my own clothes. He was with me when I finally decided not to be sad about the environment I live in, and instead decided to harden my heart.

The sand is cold on my feet, the slight breeze bringing goose bumps to my skin and blowing my wavy hair sideways. I didn't bother to put my hat back on. I'm done caring about not exposing myself.

The smell of charred fish and sweet spiciness wafting around Sharifa's hut makes my stomach rumble. He sits by a cast-iron pan over a lit fire, and Masina sprinkles sea salt on the Ocean Hake.

"How did it go?" Sharifa exclaims as soon as he sees me approaching.

I plop myself on a rock that serves as a seat close to the pan. "They asked me to accompany them . . . to fight the Dormant King." I brace myself for their reactions as I finish my thought. "I told them I'm not going."

"Why?" Masina asks. "You've been so desperate to leave this village for so long. You have a chance to, and you said no?"

I shoot to my feet and point at both of them. "You of all people know why. I'm nothing but a nuisance here, especially to you both. That's not going to change if I join them."

Sharifa sighs and turns back to the fish. He doesn't deny it, and that stings more than I expected. It was only out of a sense of duty that they decided to raise me, and they had a hard time with it. I'm not surprised.

I give them credit. Because of them, Backers never found me. I stuck out in so many obvious ways: never taking my hat off, covering my right hand with dainty accessories, my pale complexion, living in a cave. Yet, thanks to them, I've managed to dodge the Backers, along with any suspicious eyes in the village.

Almost every time travelers came through the village, before Sharifa had a chance to inspect them, he urged me to go back to Voda Cave to hide in case they were Backers. Once everything was clear—which sometimes varied between a few minutes to a few hours later—he'd send Masina to the waterfall to play a two-note tune on a flute to let me know it was clear for me to come out.

A couple of times, there really were Backers. The biggest tell was when they denied Sharifa permission to search their things. Or the handle of their weapons stuck out of their packs and it was clear it belonged to the enemy.

Again, it was only out of a sense of duty, otherwise they would be responsible for getting a Descendant killed. No one wants that hanging on their shoulders.

"Anara," Masina begins softly, "our homelife has been less than ideal. You've become much more abrasive over the years. But we know you. The *real* Anara. You are strong. Independent. Loyal. Honest. You have a heart, as hardened as you've made it. You stuck it out by staying here, as painful and unbearable as it has been."

She leans toward me and reaches for my hands. It's been unusual for me to experience affection. It's borderline uncomfortable. But I let her take my hands in hers. This may be the last interaction we ever have.

"Anara, Sharifa and I release you. Just as you've dreamed. You have a duty to fulfill, and there's not a single doubt in our minds that you will succeed."

I know Masina is right. I could have left a long time ago without saying anything to anyone, but I knew that had more bad consequences than good, so I stayed. My fate was sealed, and I had to accept that. Villagers gave me plenty of chances to get into physical altercations with their harsh words, but I chose to use even harsher ones to get my point across.

What are the bad consequences of going with Havanna and Quill? Besides the possibility of dying, none. So what's the problem? No one here will care, except the chief and his wife.

The Macaphins hate me. In a way, I'll be happy I won't have to be a card dealer to people who constantly call me a spoiled princess or say "your highness" every time someone hands me something, or just passes by me on the beach. Sharifa has directed everyone to make sure I'm protected for classified reasons, against cultural belief. The Macaphins only revere people of importance, whether they're royalty or an authority figure. Because I'm neither of those things, no one feels I deserve special treatment. The situation has left me feeling like a burden. I kept to myself and responded to snide remarks with sarcasm and rudeness as a defense mechanism. Eventually, that molded me into the person I am.

Sharifa and Masina tried to get the bullying to stop, to no avail. In all honesty, they didn't try hard enough. Their sense of duty to their people and their culture prevented them from fighting for me wholeheartedly. Because they were tasked by my biological parents to raise me, I feel even more unwanted. Not just because they raised me and trained me in the ways of the trident, but because clearly my parents didn't want to care for me either. Their solution was to leave me here while they jumped ship. How's that for being a total nightmare for everyone?

I may be seventeen years old, but I'm at the point in my adolescence where I don't give a crap about what anyone thinks of me anymore.

"It's time you fulfilled your destiny as a Descendant," Sharifa adds. "Once you do, you will be so glad you took the opportunity to prove to yourself that you are *not* a burden. They need you, otherwise they never would have made the effort to find you. Doesn't that mean they don't view you the way you view yourself? Doesn't that mean they want to give you a chance?"

He makes a fair point. The more I let his words sink in, the more I regret sending them away.

"Here," Masina says while handing me the fish on banana leaves. "Eat, then decide."

CHAPTER 6

QUILL

"Well, this blows."

I decide to check my stock of arrows in my quiver as Koa carries me on his back with Havanna on Bolt beside me. I don't like the low numbers I'm seeing.

"I need more arrows. Since we're close to Arythica, we could see if they have some."

"I suppose. I would be surprised if the richest city in the kingdom didn't have those kinds of supplies." She peers over at my quiver. "How many do you have?"

"Eight. Unless you have another way to hunt for our meals."

She shrugs. "I used my electricity a couple times. Worked well for me."

I snort. "Wait a minute." I hold up my hand as I do everything I can to swallow down laughter. "You've . . . electrocuted your supper?"

"It's not like I had archery skills to fall back on!" She flaps her hands. "I used what I had. And it still tasted good!"

I flinch at her confession. She knows her way around a sword and shield; I assumed she had training in a variety of other weapons as well. I was willing to teach archery to the children in my village because I believed it was a vital skill to have, whether for combat or for feeding a family.

I open and close my eyes tightly. Thinking about those children pains me. I hate to admit to myself that I actually miss them.

Perhaps Havanna can be my new student.

"One of these days, you need to learn the ways of the bow," I comment while wiggling my finger at her. I play it lightheartedly, but I'm quite serious.

"I've tried for years. I never got the hang of it."

I wink. "That's because you've never had a strong, extremely handsome man teach you."

Havanna rolls her eyes. "Sure. We can go with that."

"In all seriousness, I'm happy to teach you," I reaffirm my offer. I really want her to agree to this. That way, I can still get close to her as a friend without making her think there's more to it. I can't give her that impression.

Although, I don't let just *anyone* touch my bow.

Havanna gives me a half smile. "Thank you. In that case, let's head to Arythica. You're going to need an Ice Stone anyway." She points at Olavar Lagoon just ahead. "First, I want to explore that area."

Olavar Lagoon is a relatively large body of water hugged by a ring of sand. Fishing boats are scattered along the border; some of them have decayed into nothing while others seem to be used frequently with their pristine condition and nets sprawled over them.

"You want to go in the water?"

She gives me an incredulous look. "No, Forest Dweller. I just want to see it. I've never seen a body of water like this."

"Forest Dweller," I repeat to myself, letting it sink in. It describes me perfectly. "I like it. I knew you'd find a nickname for me."

Havanna giggles as she hops off Bolt's back. She camouflages in the dead of night with her black clothes, the only source of light being the moon glistening on the water. I do my best to follow her footsteps in the dark with the sound of moving sand and crunching over palm tree fronds. The closer we get to the lagoon, the more I can see her silhouette.

"Too bad it's nighttime," she says. "I can't see if there's anything in there."

I motion to the boats. "Well, there're fish. Hence, the boats."

"Thank you for explaining that to me."

"Happy to help."

Havanna chuckles as she kneels right at the lip of the water. Ever so gently, she skims the tips of her fingers along the surface in a reminiscing way. "Feels nice." A hint of yearning is evident in those two simple words.

"How about this . . ." I suggest, taking a bandana out of my pocket. "Can you dip your face in the water as long as you immediately dry it off?"

Havanna chuckles, assuming I'm joking. "My face?"

"Yes." I hand her the cloth to use. "Enjoy."

She takes it from me reluctantly. Her fingers slide along the material, studying it in fascination, but the weight of uncertainty of the risk sags on her shoulders.

"Just try it," I coax in my seductive, soothing voice and take the bandana from her. "I'll save you if you start drowning."

"That won't be necessary, but thank you."

She leans forward toward the surface, her hair falling around her face in a brunette curtain. She stops herself and ties her hair behind her, then leans forward again. First, it's just the tip of her nose and chin that goes in to get accustomed to the sensation before she plunges the rest of her face underwater. Bubbles rise on the sides of her head for a moment before she lifts herself up. She gratefully accepts the bandana and hurriedly dries her face while catching her breath.

"So? How was it?"

A smile breaks through and she chuckles happily. "It was . . . wonderful."

I softly sigh in relief. I was partially worried about being responsible if she was harmed with this risk. "Do it again. You should try opening your eyes this time."

Havanna leans back. "Underwater?"

"Yes. You might be able to see what else is in there."

She shrugs. "Very well."

I take the damp bandana from her and squeeze it out in an attempt to dry it out quickly. She plunges her face underwater again, which is followed by a muffled squeal.

I urgently crawl closer to her and place a hand on her back. "What? What's wrong?"

She lifts her head, water dripping onto her clothes and taking a hollowed breath from her mouth. "Why did you make me do that?"

"What are you talking about?"

"That stung!" she shouts as she roughly wipes her face off with the cloth. "Ugh, it hurts."

Guilt knocks me square in the chest and sends me back onto my heels. Then, the realization hits me and I laugh out loud.

"What is so funny?" she snaps. "You think my pain is funny?"

"No," I reply as I force my laughter to die down and clear my throat. "I just realized you opened your eyes in saltwater. That's why your eyes sting."

The pause that lasts a few seconds has me worried she's going to kill me. Thankfully, all she manages to do is smack me playfully on the arm. "Are you serious?!"

I scoot back along the sand with my hands raised. "Honest mistake, I promise you."

"Quill!"

She leaps toward me and tackles me, slapping me all over as I keep laughing. I end up on my back and she rolls onto my stomach, which leaves me with her face dangerously close to mine. My lips tingle at the sight of her own pink ones, begging me to close the space between us. Our heartbeats speed up, in sync, her eyes softening upon gazing into mine. The electric tension sparks between us, pleading for one of us to close the space. I could be the one to do it. I could just kiss her and get it out of my system.

No. I can't. I can't do that to her. She deserves better than me.

I clear my throat and turn my head to the side. "Perhaps we should head off to Arythica," I suggest as gently as I can.

She breaks out of the reverie she's sifting in her mind and nods. "Yes. We should."

She rolls off me and onto the sand, then helps me to my feet after she comes to a stand. Without any additional commentary or words, we trudge back to our Bennarus in silence. A large, dark shadow of what is unsaid hangs between us, and neither one of us is addressing it.

We journey past Olavar Lagoon until we finally find a part of the cliffs that are low enough for us to climb back onto higher land. Bolt and Koa have to transform into a gorilla and a wolf in order to climb with us. The rocks are not very steep, but it would have been difficult to accomplish on horseback.

A dense grouping of trees greet us the moment we get our bearings from the climb. Small streams of moonlight fight their way through the tight spaces between the trees, barely giving us sufficient light to see where we're going. Koa trots through the wooded forest floor and makes good use of his heightened sense of smell. Bolt stays close to Havanna and sniffs the air around him.

The ambience is eerie. Cawjays call out among the crunching of branches and leaves under our boots. We take our time crossing the section of trees, watchful for anything suspicious or dangerous. I have my bow ready; Havanna has a hand on her sword.

A yelp from Koa scares me out of my skin. I turn to the noise and hope to Halivaara that he simply stepped on something that hurt his paw. Instead, I find that vines have wrapped around his back legs and yanked him upward, making him immobile as his body swings back and forth.

"Koa!" I take off in his direction with Havanna and Bolt following close behind.

Once I reach him, I feel something akin to rope wrap around my ankle and yank me from the ground. I reach out to grab hold of anything I can to keep this thing from lifting me higher and higher. All I manage to grab are clumps of grass and dead leaves. As far as I'm concerned, this thing will throw me in a pit for the forest animals to feast on.

About fifteen feet from the ground, the supposed rope stops pulling and leaves me dangling upside down. I curl my body upward to find one ankle wrapped in a vise by a thick vine. And there, camouflaged among the twigs below, is my bow.

No way to fight off any hungry creatures in this state. How excellent.

"Quill!"

I wave my head side to side and find Havanna also hanging by a vine next to me. Bolt is below us, his gorilla arms and feet bound together.

"What just happened?" Havanna screams.

"I don't know!" I curl up again to try to grab the vine on my foot, but I can't reach it and fall upside down again. I have rock-hard abs and work on them daily; how can I not get out of this?

"Do you have your sword? Use it to cut the vines."

Havanna reaches behind her for her sheathed sword. By some miracle, it's still attached to her. Now we have a way out.

That is, until the sword slips from her hand and falls. She groans loudly, her brown hair forming an abnormal curtain below her head.

"Great. Good job, butterfingers."

"Shut up, Quill!"

"Looks like we're going to die here," I continue casually. "It was fun while it lasted."

"Up yours, Forest Dweller."

Maniacal, high-pitched laughter echoes in the distance. And the fact that it's more than one creature making that noise freezes us entirely.

"What is that?" There's a tremor in my voice.

The laughter continues through the trees, followed by a swarm of black dots hopping and bouncing over each other. It's getting louder and louder, my heart stopping in rigid fear. Even after blinking a couple times, I'm still seeing those dots. It's nothing I have ever seen in a forest before.

But they're getting closer, and I think they're growing bigger.

"We need to get out of here." Havanna's voice rises in panic. *"Now."*

The *whoosh* of flapping wings cascades my face and gives me hope. Koa had morphed into a hawk at some point and managed to escape, and is now trying to chew the vine off my ankle. My body wiggles with the motion of the moving vine, then stops altogether when I hear Koa shriek as he falls.

Now I'm pissed. I don't care what happens to me. *Nobody* attacks my Bennaru.

Havanna's screams mix with the constant maniacal laughter. With these creatures taking over the surface below, it's safe to assume that we're not going to make it. I have to at least try to save my Bennaru.

The vine wiggles again, then sharp nibbles dig into my leg like needles that cause me to shout out in agony. I see the culprit practically chewing me alive: a round, black creature with two legs, no arms, and one eye that takes up most of its body. Its lips are shaped upward into a creepy smile, baring the tiny blades in its mouth.

I would remember if I had seen these mutants back in the forest, because they are by far the creepiest things I have ever seen.

Having broken free of his bonds, Bolt roars and stomps everywhere to get rid of the monsters, but they keep coming in droves. Their noisiness has taken up all the space in the woods. I can't hear or see Havanna.

With their two legs, they grab onto mine with their birdlike toes, razors sliding down the material of my pants. When they get very, very close to my groin, I do everything I can to kick them off. I contort my body in ways that are unnatural, anything to get these demons off me, but they stick to my pants like tree sap.

"Get off! Leave Koa alone!"

I should know by now that yelling is useless.

This is how we're going to die.

One of them has managed to chew all the way through the vine, and I fall onto my back, almost landing on my neck. Pain explodes all over, and that's when the creatures swarm me to go in for the kill.

Heavy, rushing water crashes through the trees and distracts the monsters. A giant wave gushes through, sparkling in the miniscule moonlight we have. I'm positive someone dressed in blue save for a pair of knee-high brown boots is riding atop the crest.

Suddenly, the figure hops off with a blue trident held in both hands, a stream following the movements of the weapon. Midair, the water splits into small icicles, then the person slices the trident in front of them, sending the ice straight into the monsters' eyes.

The wave settles and turns into a still pool among the dirt when the person lands. Then a humongous jaguar appears, emitting a mighty roar as it goes after the creatures around them. The blue person continues to circle the trident around her body and over her head, the silver ribs of her clothing sparkling here and there. Black dots scatter as she sends them soaring, her almost-white hair turning with her movements.

Anara.

With her hand, she takes some of the water she came with and forms a giant icicle half as tall as a forest tree. She sends it in Havanna's vicinity and slams it down repeatedly, hard enough to make the earth quake. The monsters shriek on impact, telling me that whatever Anara is doing is working. Then she splits the formation into five pieces and shoots it at a group of the creatures close to Koa with a triumphant yell.

As I'm kicking the stupid creatures off me, Anara throws her trident like a spear and stabs three of them in a row. I can finally get up, but an awful pang radiates all over my legs that makes it hard to move, and the ache in my back is impossible to ignore. My clothes are torn from my ankles to my hips and stained from my bleeding injuries. Anara runs at great speed to retrieve her trident, then picks up my bow and tosses it to me so quickly I barely manage to catch it.

"Thank you."

"Whatever. Just help me kill these things."

I suppose she hasn't had much of a change of heart.

"What are they?"

"Niminims. They're smart and a huge pain."

I manage to find a Pineapple Shell arrow on the ground that fell from my quiver, and I'm quick to use it when a wave of Niminims come straight for me. The detonation affects a large number of them, but I can't use more of those arrows right now.

Instead, I reach my hand out to a nearby tree. The branches grow in length and develop sharp tips at the ends, the roots tear themselves out of the soil, and it walks in the direction I command it to. The branches go to work stabbing multiple Niminims simultaneously. I even make it use some of its branches to pick them up and throw them toward other trees.

Anara swings her trident around until she commands the still water to act as a shield. Beads of sweat shine on her forehead with the intense effort of blocking the Niminims that launch themselves at her. They ultimately become trapped and drown.

Havanna, finally recovering herself, creates electricity with her hands and throws it. I get another tree involved in the battle, having it lean forward in swift motions to crush the Niminims, or simply sweep them away. Some have eventually gotten scared and scurry deeper into the woods, their crazy laughter turning into high-pitched squeals.

Anara takes most of the pool of water and forms a wave taller than she is. Then with a push of her hands, the wave crashes and sweeps up most of the remaining Niminims, forcing the water in the same direction she appeared, taking them with it.

Together, with the help of Bolt, Koa, and Wave, we clear out the rest.

Until we find one more that is about to bite Havanna's face off.

Anara is quick to act before it makes contact with her. She whips up water from the ground with her trident and uses it to aim its rope formation in Havanna's direction. Creating three prongs in midair to copy the shape of her trident, it strikes the Niminim from behind. The water loses its shape and falls, still as the dirt that surrounds it. I return the trees to their original state, rooted in the ground and branches shrunk to shorter lengths.

Havanna and I step closer to Anara, catching our breaths and counting our blessings that we survived. Anara reaches for her leg. Attached to the side is a strap holding three small bottles of water, something I failed to notice. She takes one and downs it in two gulps. Wave returns to her side and nudges her hand with affection.

Bolt steps up to Havanna, studying her for any injuries. She has bite marks on her arms that have drawn blood and her clothes are tattered at her ankles. Her grunts and groans indicate her level of suffering.

Koa nudges his snout to my hand and whines. I get to my knees and inspect his wolf form, running my hands over his thick coat. He has a few bites on his legs, one of which is making his paw impossible to walk on. His fur is matted and his eyes are squinted, which tells me he's hurting. I'm even more pissed that those Niminims almost killed my companion.

I lean my forehead to his, mumbling that everything is all right now, stroking behind his ears in the way that comforts him best.

I hope to Halivaara that Arythica has medicine for all of us.

Havanna directs her attention to Anara. "How did you know we were here?"

She sighs and hitches her trident behind her. "This route is the fastest way to get to higher ground. When I heard the sounds of Niminims, I knew something wasn't right. Something or someone needed saving. So I used water from the ocean to get here."

Havanna nods, folding her arms with a smirk. "So . . . you changed your mind?"

She shrugs with a frown, as if she didn't just save us from getting eaten alive. "I thought about what you said, and decided that perhaps you were right." She puts on a faraway look and breaks eye contact. "I may be a burden in Macaphin Village, but I want a chance to prove that I won't be as a Descendant. And to you both."

"Or is it more that you were talked into it?"

"I just saved your dumb behinds from getting mauled by Niminims. You should be thanking me."

Havanna makes a few different facial expressions that signify that Anara has a point. "Thank you." Her response is barely above a whisper.

"That's more like it," Anara replies with a smirk. "Anyway, I want in. If you'll have me."

Comparing what little we know about Anara to what she's saying right now, it's a surprise to both me and Havanna. She's actually showing some humility for the first time since we met her. Perhaps she's capable of being a decent person after all.

There's no way we can do this alone. We almost died at the hands of small, annoying creatures—what's it going to be like fighting someone like the Dormant King?

After Havanna glances at me, I confirm with a slight nod.

"Am I still the Electric Doofus?" she asks Anara.

My gaze switches between the two. I didn't expect her to ask that sort of question, but now I'm oddly invested in the answer.

"Yes. Consider it a term of endearment."

Havanna chuckles while trying to contain her smile. "Then welcome, Wet Wench."

CHAPTER 7

*P*ain *waits for no one.*

I've lived by those words my whole life, but holy Halivaara, those Niminims did a number on me. My injuries sting and ache in every inch of my body and make it that much harder to get a good night's rest in the wilderness. Just as the wounds on my ankle begin to scab over, my boots rub against them and make walking near impossible.

Good thing our Bennarus have the ability to carry us.

Anara explains that the Niminims mainly live in the area we crossed through. Because they don't have arms, they use their legs and mouths to set up traps for their prey, and keep watch until something gets caught in them. That's when they go for the kill.

And they almost killed me. How convenient.

My arms and ankles throb to the point where I have a hard time adjusting myself on Bolt's horseback. Anara offers to fix them for us once we get to Arythica, since she's an expert in sewing. Somewhere in that hollow chest of hers, she *does* have a heart.

Pain waits for no one.

No matter how many times I repeat this to myself, it doesn't make the day pass any faster. My impatience moves me to speak.

"Let's go to a full gallop. I'm about to pass out over here."

"Not a bad idea," Quill agrees.

Anara scoffs. "Weenies."

Yet, she concedes to my request.

The thuds of all the animal feet create a thunderous noise that I use to distract myself from my injuries, along with focusing on Arythica's beauty in the distance.

Arythica is one giant gem that shines bright even in the beginnings of sunrise. One of its castles has a tall, pristine tower that rises high above the city walls with an elegant spire on top. A moat of crystal-clear water flows around the vast city, and a drawbridge spans the water.

After our Bennarus shift to smaller forms, we limp over the drawbridge into the city square. People mull around here and there, waking up with the rising sun. The first thing I notice is not only how clean everything is—the pathways, homes, the box gardens in every front yard and window—but even this early in the morning, people are dressed immaculately. The women's pajamas are silky sundresses with thin straps, flowing elegantly around their legs. A man walks in front of us in what appears to be a blinding-white robe made of extremely soft cloth.

These people aren't just rich. They're *filthy* rich.

"I feel out of place," I say.

"You're *both* out of place," Anara snips. "You look like you lived on the streets and got beat up."

"Thank you," Quill deadpans.

"Oh, you poor, poor things!"

Our attention turns to a woman who, like the other citizens we've seen, is much too formal for this early in the morning. Her dress practically shines alongside the rest of the city with the silvery glitter among silky blue material, and her hair is in a partial updo while the rest of it is curled and flowing to the side.

"You all look terrible," she says with sympathy. "Follow me and we'll fix you up right away."

The three of us follow her, exchanging surprised looks at the stranger's compassion.

"I'm insulted," Anara comments in a low voice. "I look much better than you two, considering the circumstances."

"Again, thank you," Quill says.

The woman leads us under an awning with three long, white cushioned chairs that seem to be made of soft, furry material surrounded by a reddish-colored carpet. A wooden bucket sits at the end of each chair, full of steaming water.

I don't know what this place is, but surely, it can't be an evil trap.

"Have a seat and relax," she directs us. "You will be well taken care of."

And she proved true to her words.

Once a curtain was pulled to separate each chair, we were told to take off our clothes and wrap ourselves in pillowy soft towels. If this isn't the definition of luxury, I don't know what is.

Arythica is the best city to ever exist.

We are pampered, head to toe. My entire body, with the exception of my feet and hands, are wrapped tightly in strips of cloth with Healing Salve on them. My feet are scrubbed intensely clean and are wiped off immediately at my request.

The closest feeling I had to this was when I fed Jael supper shortly before she died. She gave me a foot rub and we talked about men and romance, and she kissed me good night when she left my hut.

It's the last pleasant memory I have of her.

The treatment I receive concludes with a massage to my scalp and temples. I close my eyes, and I remember nothing after that.

All I know is, I'm awake now, it's light outside, my surroundings are very different, and I'm wearing a white nightgown instead of my regular clothes.

In a state of distress, I reach to my left bicep, then breathe out in relief. Whoever dressed me knew to not take off my armband, the only thing I have left of Jael.

The bed I fell asleep on is extremely comfortable, with such plushness I may as well be floating on air. Bolt seems just as comfortable, curled up within himself and his beak stuffed under his wing. The room is made of smooth marble with a vaulted ceiling and a washroom straight ahead of me. This entire room is bigger than my house in Ketra.

I step out of bed onto soft, blood-red carpet that massages my soles. My entire body still aches from the Niminim attack and I have no idea how long I've been wearing these bandages. The white tiles in the washroom show its glossy shine, warming my bare feet in the most refreshing, incredible way. The bathtub is pure white with golden knobs on one end of it. I have no idea why those are there other than to serve as decor.

I have never experienced this kind of luxury in my life.

In front of a full-length mirror with impeccable golden carvings, I peel off the pink-hued cloths stuck to my skin and examine my injuries. The Healing Salve helped greatly, but only provided momentary relief. At least they're fading to simple scars.

One scar catches my attention—the one across my collarbone. That was the night Jael died, when I fought a Backer and he struck me with his glowing blade.

My fingers gently skim the fading line, from one side of my neck to the other. The mark of someone who tried hard to save everyone from her mistake.

Bad memories flash before me: huts on fire, Dormants swiping people left and right, Thaeus rushing everyone to the compound, and watching as the Backer thrust his blade into Jael's torso—the moment I lost everything I loved.

I still have no regrets killing Victor and Darius with Strike. They deserved it.

Are you awake now?

Quill's sudden inquiry makes me flinch, but soon brings a sheepish smile to my face.

Barely.

Finally. We've been awake for hours. You got more beauty sleep than I did.

Great. My need for sleep gave him and Anara time to bond.

Where are you?

Drinking Mushroom Coffee in the foyer with the sweetest cream I've ever tasted in my life. You're missing out, Zappy.

Delightful. Save some for me.

That may not be possible. I may drink all of their stock before we leave.

Three urgent knocks pound on my door as I finish chuckling at Quill's comment. Anara stands on the other side, holding a black outfit with my boots in her hands and her usual disgruntled countenance.

"I fixed your clothes," she grumbles while shoving them at my chest, then lets herself in my room without invitation. "You still look terrible."

"Thank you, and please come in," I mutter while I shut the door. I unfold the clothes and inspect them to see if they were, indeed, fixed.

My pants have no marks or holes on them and my shirt is still perfectly intact. The boots look brand-new with their repaired material and polished finish. The talent she has in this craft really shows.

"My room was bigger than yours," she comments, plopping herself on the bed and bouncing on it, then sees me inspecting my outfit. "What? Checking to see if I screwed up?"

I shake my head and fold the clothes. "No. It looks great. Thank you."

Anara's lip curls in a snarl. "Quill was happy with his clothes too. I know what I'm doing. I won't ever screw up something like clothes and sewing."

I give her an awkward look and make my way back to the washroom to change into the outfit. Everything fits the way it's supposed to.

I emerge with Anara lying on the bed on her back, staring at the ceiling and arms spread wide. She leans up and sees me dressed.

"Thank Halivaara it fits. That looks better than that dreaded nightgown we dressed you in."

I pause, my feet no longer moving as I process what she just said. "*We?*"

"Yes," she drones, as if she's talking to a stupid person. "We didn't want to wake you up from that spa thing we went to. You were snoring away. So Quill insisted that he carry you here, even though I probably could have done it myself. Then the inn owner gave us a nightgown to put it on you." She shrugs. "Quill only helped with taking your old clothes while I dressed you. I was careful to make sure he didn't look."

Quill insisted on carrying me? He helped get me into the night-gown? That seems so . . . intimate. Either I was draped over his shoulder or he had his arms under my knees and back and brought me here.

Imagining it that way warms me to the core. So gentle, romantic, and thoughtful. A magnet for a girl like me.

Except, he probably didn't consider it romantic at all.

"So, are you and Quill . . ." Anara starts, perking up her eyebrows a few times, "in a romantic . . . situation?"

She suspects something. But there is no chance she will get that out of me. As far as I'm concerned, she's not my friend. Just a member of our team.

I scoff to play it off the best I can. "No. What makes you think that?"

She hums. "I don't know. Just . . . the way he insisted on making sure you were taken care of with carrying you. And he seemed to handle you so . . . gently. It was disgustingly sweet."

As much as the desire for romance wants to rear its head, I can't allow it. What Anara is seeing might be a misunderstanding, as much as I desperately do not want it to be.

I don't want romance. I do *not*.

"No. Just friends."

Anara waves a dismissive hand. "Oh well. Who cares." She leaps up from the bed and makes her way to the door, her wavy hair bouncing behind her. "Hurry up and get ready, Doofus. Quill needs arrows."

I don't know how anyone can afford to live here. Everything costs more than a week's wages at the eatery back in Ketra.

Walking through the open marketplaces with the height of the nearby castle shadowing us, Anara and Quill each buy an Ice Stone and stash them to use later. Quill stocks up on a variety of arrows, but grabs a few Pineapple Shells he can store in his pack. I take advantage as well, grabbing enough of the explosive plants to fill the space in my own pack.

Anara and I take our time being enamored with the variety of potions, jewelry, hair accessories, and clothes displayed so proudly. Bottles of all different shapes and sizes, with so many swirls of color that treat a variety of things: skin care, hair care, physical energy, and . . . sexual performance.

Walking away from that *very* quickly.

Women pass us in their poofy dresses made with soft, silky, shiny material with tiny stones embroidered all over. Even their hair is immaculately designed in updos or sparkling headbands. No one seems to feel comfortable. They probably have no idea what comfort is.

I pick up a round glass bottle with thick, translucent liquid closed with a cork. A salty, perfumed scent mixed with fruit tones wafts into my nostrils.

"What is this?" I ask the potion maker.

"I have named that one Swimmer's Repellent," she answers, "made from the insides of a Salty Eel. Very powerful ingredient and a rare potion indeed. Salty Eels are difficult to catch. I only make a few bottles of this every year."

"What does it do?"

The potion maker straightens herself in her seat, proud to delve into the details of her creations. "It prevents a swimmer from getting wet while in the water. And the salty properties keep the swimmer afloat."

My hand instinctively covers my mouth and my heart races in excitement. I have wanted to experience swimming my entire life. The waves, the warmth, and the way water sparkles in the sun or moonlight always draws me in, yet it's my biggest weakness due to the electricity that runs through my body.

At last, there's a way I can experience it without drowning *or* dying. I have the urge to cry just from sheer joy.

"I want a bottle!" I exclaim. "How much is it?"

"One thousand coins, my dear."

Holy Halivaara. There's no way I can afford that. I barely have enough coins in my pouch to keep myself *alive*. Anara scoffs softly upon hearing the price while she continues perusing the exorbitantly expensive potions. Her long, slender fingers wrapping around each bottle with every inspection, her facial expressions voice her inner thoughts on each one.

My face falls while my heart drops. I want that potion so badly. I don't know what made me think I had enough money for it. The tears that were joyous are now ones of disappointment.

"I don't have that kind of money," I whimper. Swallowing the sadness and regaining my composure with a deep breath, I turn to walk away. "I'll meet you outside the city," I tell Anara with a quiver in my voice. "We should get going."

"I need to fill up my water stash. I'll see you when I see you," she grumbles and walks away.

I further observe the elaborate clothing of the citizens while I make my way through the city. I notice the men are dressed equally clean: breeches, wool jackets, stockings, waistcoats, tricorn hats, and buckle shoes. It boggles my mind that they live in those unsuitable outfits. They must spend at least an hour just getting dressed in the morning.

To my left are two large ironclad gates and a cinder-block wall that guard the entrance of the castle. A long, deep-red carpet with gold trim is laid out over the steps and along the walkway, and two people on the other side of the gate catch my attention.

One is a man wearing a golden crown with rubies on his head, a thick red robe trailing behind him. His arm is linked with a young, vibrant woman with a diamond tiara, also wearing a red robe.

These people seem extremely important to be dressed better than the rest of the citizens.

I tap the shoulder of a local standing close to me to ask, "Can you tell me who those people are?"

She smirks, looking me up and down with obvious judgment at my lack of, well, everything. "I presume you have never seen the king and queen before?"

"King and queen?" I turn to the immaculate pair ascending the steps to the castle, a horde of guards flanking their every step. Jael never spoke about a king or queen in Arythica. On the other hand, she never mentioned a king and queen in Sabbia either. I found that one out on my own. Perhaps no one in Ketra ventured out far enough to notice that two regions of Petros are ruled by different monarchs.

"Yes. King Aldous and Queen Avela of Petros. A very powerful pair indeed."

I turn to her with a confused expression. "Petros? What about King Malik and Queen Calista of Sabbia?"

"They rule over the desert only," she clarifies. "Aldous and Avela—pardon me, *King* Aldous and *Queen* Avela—rule over the rest of the kingdom."

In all the years Jael taught me about Petros's history, the subject of royal arrangements ruling the land was never touched on. When

I met Queen Calista and King Malik, I learned otherwise, but I didn't know there were more.

I miss Calista.

Watching the other king and queen fade from view, the woman wanders off, and an idea lights up in my mind. We, as Descendants, have Sabbia's support, but it doesn't hurt to have more authority figures as a backup plan if Sabbia isn't enough. Perhaps they will be of use to us in the future.

"Got distracted?" I hear Anara call out behind me.

I motion to the castle. "I just found out that King Aldous and Queen Avela live here."

"That wasn't obvious?"

"I didn't know," I snap. "Anyway, I was just thinking . . . perhaps we can look to them for guidance if we need more help with the Dormant King. You know, if we need an army or something."

She barks out a laugh. "First, you convince me to help you beat the Dormant King, and now you're already planning our failure?"

"No, but we should always have another plan. Just in case."

"Even if we needed another plan, they are the wrong people to ask for help." She points to the castle. "They have all the riches they could ever want. I doubt they will want to disturb their perfect peace with a fight against a powerful enemy."

Thanks to Anara, I have a new seed of doubt. I don't want to think that she's right, but we also have no other ideas to fall back on.

"You don't know that," I mumble.

"Whatever."

Quill sends a message to me. *Are you both ready? I have all the arrows I need, so I'm back to being the perfect protector for both of you.*

I look longingly at the castle. *Yes. Meet us at the gates to the castle, Forest Dweller.*

As you wish, Zappy.

CHAPTER 8

ANARA

I know for a fact Havanna lied to me.

The way she froze when I asked her if there was anything going on between her and Quill was a clear indication that she is hiding something. Her blushing cheeks and lack of eye contact say more than words can.

She can't fool me.

Whether that is mutual is hard to tell. Quill took care of her in a way that showed a special attachment. Other than telling me how he saved her from a battle with Backers on Luna Island, he hasn't said anything else. We didn't speak much after that. He wanted to drink Mushroom Coffee with what he called the sweetest cream ever and I went into the city for material to fix his and Havanna's clothes and boots. Just before I left, he proceeded to tell me to make sure his pants were fitted enough to show off his toned backside. That was received with a flat "no."

He's an enigma, that one.

Wait. Why do I care? Their problems are not my own.

However, I'm starting to get to know Havanna a little more. The absolute sadness she had when she didn't have enough money for the Swimmer's Repellant was pathetic. I greatly underestimated how much no contact with water bothered her.

I almost felt bad for her. *Almost.*

Especially now, she's so dejected and not saying a word. The silence between us is deafening, save the hooves on the ground and Wave's paws trudging through the grass.

"So, Quill," I break the silence, "what all can your abilities do besides make nature kill things?"

He chuckles. "I use Transform for that. I can send mental messages to people and animals with Transmission."

I nod slowly. "Wait. Is that what you did when you found me at the cabana?"

He winks. "Yes."

"Wow," I say breathlessly. "So, in a way, you can control someone's mind."

"In a sense, yes. I can make animals do whatever I tell them to or communicate with others within a two-mile radius."

Interesting. Now I'm officially impressed.

"However," he continues, "I'm the only one who can initiate a conversation that way, but anyone I talk to has the ability to respond."

My eyebrows raise to my hairline. "How do I do that?"

Quill turns to Havanna, who's a few steps ahead of us. "Zappy, how are you able to respond when I use Transmission?"

The fact that he has a nickname for her is also telling of a hint of romance. Again, not my problem.

She turns to her left to address us, but doesn't fully turn around. "Think about the fact that you want to respond," she grumbles. "Stay focused on the fact that he just spoke to you, then answer the way you normally would out loud."

I address Quill, "All right. Try it again."

His eyes turn bright green as he breaks eye contact.

How about now?

Ignoring the fact that Havanna seems deafeningly disinterested in this encounter, I take her advice and keep his message ringing in my mind, then build up a desire to respond to it. More than that, I build up a need for him to hear me.

How was your Mushroom Coffee?

"It worked!" he exclaims.

Contrary to my regular personality, I end up giggling. Submitting mental messages is so unlike anything I've ever done before. This minor experience makes me even more grateful that I left that idiotic village. Mental conversations are nonexistent back there.

"Great. Let's keep practicing so you can get the hang of it."

We spend some time conversing, which makes me giggle harder with each message he sends. It's not even the content that causes this reaction; it's the unbelievable fact that we're doing this at all.

Meanwhile, I'm getting very dirty looks from Havanna. The occasional peek over her shoulder and accompanying glaring eyes tell me she vehemently dislikes being excluded. Even though we're not even talking about her.

She's much too easy to read.

I personally haven't had romantic feelings for a boy in many years. When I was twelve, I liked a boy named Luca. We played together often, running along the shore and letting the waves crash at our feet, racing each other through the dry sand to see who ran the fastest, and having a tantrum when he won every time.

When I was fourteen, I finally told him I liked him more than just a friend. The way he cringed and told me he didn't like girls made me feel so dumb. I didn't understand how I didn't notice that about him. Then I looked back and remembered he looked at everyone *but* the girls, and I felt even dumber. I wasted so much time with those feelings only to find that I never even had a chance with him. After that, I never found anyone else as attractive as him. He left the village when he turned eighteen two years ago and went off to find a mate in Sabbia.

There goes that fantasy.

I don't know anything about romance now, or what it feels like. All I have to work with is the "little girl" feelings I had all those years ago, and the way Sharifa and Masina treat each other and look at each other with love and admiration. A part of me understands Havanna's jealousy, although I have no interest in Quill. He's not the kind of man I find attractive. She can have him all to herself.

In the middle of conversing with Quill, he makes a suggestion.

Perhaps we should rope Havanna into this. I think she feels left out.

Once more taking care of Havanna and always considering her. Do I *really* need more proof of his feelings for her?

I turn to Quill and shrug. I honestly don't care.

"Watch," he says. "I can include someone else into the conversation, but I still have to be the one to send a message in order for them to respond. For instance, you and Havanna can't talk to each other. It all has to go through me, but you can still hear each other's responses."

"What?" Havanna turns to Quill in shock. "You didn't tell me that."

"It's only been the two of us this whole time." I shrug. "I didn't think it made a difference that a third person could join."

His eyes turn green again and I straighten up in anticipation as he looks at Havanna.

Oh Zappy, Quill calls to her in a singsong. *Turn that frown upside down.*

Havanna peers over her shoulder again with a small, close-lipped smile. *As you wish, Forest Dweller.*

I can hear both of them communicating, even though I won't be able to send a message to Havanna. This is beyond trippy.

Hmm. I see that catching on. I approve.

Anara, you're still the Wet Wench.

She can't respond to you, Zappy.

Oh, all right. Anara is still the Wet Wench.

Wet Wench, do you approve?

A bright idea ignites in me when I, at last, understand what he was saying. We can all communicate, but Quill is the channel we have to run through. This is . . . incredible.

We Descendants are incredible.

As long as she's still the Electric Doofus.

Havanna emits a groan that echoes in my mind. *Fine.*

***

Thank Halivaara we have Ice Stones. The humidity alone is suffocating. How does the Fire Descendant even survive up there?

I have my Ice Stone in my pocket, but Havanna has hers encased in a necklace that resembles the sun. I actually find myself staring at its eye-catching shine from the dull sun that begs to peek through the gray clouds.

We take some time circling the dark gray mountain to find an official entrance or a pathway that leads us up an incline, but most of the rocky terrain is blocked off by metal-spiked wires with steam coming off it from how hot it is.

Definitely not going near that.

Then we feel like idiots because there were wooden signs where we first appeared that lead us in the right direction. However, the first sign is slightly off-putting:

Beware of sleeping beast.

Quill hums uneasily. "A beast?"

I side with Quill. "I don't like the sound of that."

"It's probably just to scare us from going farther," Havanna says with confidence. "If it really is a beast, it's most likely something the three of us can take down easily. Let's just keep going."

That immediately makes me feel doubtful. If this beast has anything related to electricity, I'm dead. I'm sure they will die too, but I only care about me right now.

We force our Bennarus to keep going. At least, that's what I try to do until Wave growls and backs away.

I urge him with a pat on his side. "Go on, Wave."

He hisses and continues retreating, shaking his head.

"Wave, what's wrong?"

Quill and Havanna also attempt to calm their Bennarus to no avail. Koa's and Bolt's desperate snorts and neighs make us very concerned.

"What's going on?" Havanna shouts.

Before either of us can begin to answer, Wave's body disappears from beneath me and I fall flat on my butt on solid earth. As I groan from the impact, I look up and find Havanna and Quill also without their Bennarus. Wave's rubbery frog feet hopping onto my shoulder gives me a clue on what just happened.

"All right." I come back up to standing, wiping the dirt off my paneled skirt. "Our Bennarus very clearly do not want us to continue. As our guardians, don't you think we need to listen?"

Havanna motions to the peak of the mountain. "How else do you think we're getting up there?"

I swear to Halivaara, sometimes I wonder if Electric Doofus has a brain.

"Here's an idea. How about we, I don't know, *fly over*?"

Havanna rolls her eyes and neck. "We're trying *not* to be spotted by Backers, remember?"

"I already risked that when I used the freaking *ocean* to save you idiots! It doesn't matter what we do. Backers are always looking for us!"

"Stop!" Quill intervenes. "We don't have any other choice than to keep going. If we don't want to be caught, and this is the only access point, there's nothing else we can do."

Havanna gives me a teasing look.

Quill is such a suck-up.

My eyebrows rise to my hairline, my hands on my hips. "So you're saying we need to face that beast head-on, no matter what it is?"

"It's two against one," Havanna points out. "We'll be fine."

I turn my doubtful and insulted expression to Quill, who simply shrugs and steps to meet Havanna's side. And, because I'm either stupid or I also am aware that we don't have a choice, I follow their lead.

The beginning of the path is shaded from the overhanging trees and barely gives us enough light to see in front of us. The fortunate part is there's a bright light in the distance to clearly indicate the end of the enclosed path. That gives me some relief.

That relief is quickly diminished when I find the next wooden sign. Quill and Havanna stop on either side of me to read it too.

Sleeping beast ahead. Death imminent.

My uneasy expressions are ignored, yet again. I fail to understand how they don't take the signs seriously, and that perhaps we need a different plan. The question of whether they will listen to someone nicknamed "Wet Wench" hangs in the balance. Nonetheless, I'm at the mercy of these two nincompoops, so we continue onward.

A soft, deep, guttural rumble echoes through the trees. We instinctively reach behind us for our weapons, but Quill holds his hands out to tell us not to move. The rumble subsides, then comes back in rhythmic repetitions.

Breathing.

A deep, grumbling inhale and exhale that signifies the magnitude of the creature it's coming from.

Panic crawls under my skin and sweat immediately coats my face. "That has to be the beast," I whisper shakily. "Havanna, I'm telling you, we need to turn back and figure something else out."

Havanna pumps her hands in an effort to calm me down. "We don't know for sure it's the beast."

"Oh. Well, you might be right. After all, we haven't been warned at all about a sleeping beast from the very beginning! By our own *Bennarus*, no less!"

"Two against one," she repeats. "Now let's go."

I turn to Quill for any sort of validation for my fears. All he does is hang his head and follow after the girl he claims to not have feelings for.

After walking upward a few minutes in silence with just the sound of crunching dirt under our boots, we enter into daylight again, climbing on the path that seems to get steeper and steeper the farther we go. We're surrounded with uneven rocky sand and dark, charred boulders that are taller than all of us combined.

The rumble increases in volume. The beast is clearly huge with the way its breaths blow dust over the ledge.

Then, we find another sign.

Danger—deadly beast ahead. DO NOT WAKE.

Deadly. Death. Danger. All words we have read on every sign on the way here.

We climb over the ledge onto a flat, level path and finally see what the signs are talking about.

It takes everything in me to not yelp at the sight. I have never seen something so frightening and so immensely large in my entire life.

The sleeping beast is deep red in color, curled up comfortably with its massive tail wrapped around its body. Spikes run along its entire spine all the way to the tip of the tail, which appears to be its main weapon with its cluster of sharp, freakishly tall spikes right at the end. Dark brown claws protrude a couple feet from the toes of each foot, and its nostrils are big enough to hold a couple of the boulders around us. The way the eyes are angled displays how bloodthirsty it is.

Quill and Havanna are equally shocked at the monster's size, jaws dropped and eyes bugged out. Breathing in even breaths is proving to be a struggle for them. I pay special attention to Havanna's reaction, since she's the one that made us go on this death journey after I asked her more than once to rethink this decision.

"I'd rather fight Backers than that thing." I maintain my voice to barely a whisper. "There's no way we're getting past that alive. We need to turn back. *Now.*"

She stutters a bit before she remembers to close her mouth and resumes regular breathing. Her quaking hands don't hide the fear running through her. After a hard swallow, she leans to the left, getting an idea of a plan that I'm sure is dumber than everything else she's done before. Even she isn't sure about this. "We can . . . um, climb over that boulder and go around it."

My jaw drops so hard it stretches the corners of my mouth. "You *still* want to get around that? Do you see those claws? The tail? It will kill us before we can even have a chance to kill it! You *do* realize that, yes? You can't possibly be this selfish."

"Excuse me?" Havanna growls through clenched teeth.

"I think there's only one way this will end, Zappy," Quill steps in. "And it's not a good ending."

"Well, we've been talking in front of it and it hasn't even stirred," Havanna points out with a shrug. "Perhaps if we remain as quiet as we are now, we can get away with it."

"Because we're whispering!"

"Even so, if it was sensitive to noise, it would have moved by now."

I inwardly groan. She's so relentless it's getting heavily annoying.

The three of us look back at the monster pensively. Its body rises with a boringly slow inhale, then exhales a long, ragged breath that smells of charred, rotten flesh. Which means it's had its share of victims for meals recently.

My heart races. Wake it up and we're dead. No exceptions. Attempting to go around it will surely get us killed. Others must have tried it and failed; it's not going to be any different for us.

I thought I was doing the right thing by joining the Descendants to fight the Dormant King together, but this is not worth it. I refuse to die this way.

I hold my hands up and back away. "I'm not doing this. You're on your own."

Havanna shoots me a disbelieving look. "You've come this far, and now you decide to bail?"

I pretend to rethink my decision. "I'm afraid so, yes."

Her jaw clenches, eyes narrowing at me. "Fine. Have a nice life."

I motion for her to go ahead with her fatal workaround. She lifts her chin up high, clenching and unclenching her fists, and bounces from one foot to the other. She's dreading this. No matter how hard she tries, she can't hide her feelings.

Quill switches his gaze between me and her, trying to decide what he should do. Ultimately, he crosses his arms and watches her. The pressure is on her to come up with a flawless plan, and he's not following her just yet.

I suppose he's not a total suck-up.

She steps on a groove at the bottom of a boulder to secure her footing, then hops to grab onto a protrusion an arm's length away. She uses all her strength to pull herself upward, muscles shaking and straining with her effort. Her legs and feet hang loose along the boulder to avoid making noise against the rock with her boots, then eventually, she throws one knee at a time on the top of the boulder and hoists herself up. I watch in anxious anticipation, hands sweaty and clenched tightly. I may not want to do this, but I truly don't want anything bad to happen to her.

Satisfied with her progress, Quill steps faintly in her direction. She gestures instructions to him, pointing at the groove at the bottom that she stepped on so he can start there. From here, I can tell he's just as afraid. His boots don't have as much traction as hers.

He steps on the groove and reaches for the protrusion. Havanna leans over and lends a hand that he gladly accepts. Now he has one foot on the groove, one foot hanging loose, one hand grabbing part of the boulder, and the other hand grasping Havanna's for dear life. Their rustling and boots against rock have my body frozen in tension, cringing at the thought of seeing them die right in front of me.

Fortunately, they're making good progress. Perhaps I can join them successfully. I'm light as a feather. They both could help me without making any sort of noise. All they will need to do is grab my arms and yank me up.

But that idea is obliterated within three seconds.

Quill slips.

He pulls Havanna down with him.

They tumble right back to where they started. Right in front of the monster's nose.

And its eye opens.

CHAPTER 9

QUILL

I thought the Niminims were going to kill me. I was wrong.

This is going to kill me.

My stomach drops as an eyeball glimmers in several different hues of orange in the daylight. The color drains from my face, and I may or may not have soiled myself. As I told Havanna, this will not end well.

The monster rises, and holy Halivaara, is it huge.

Havanna and I scramble to our feet as quickly as possible and run back to where Anara is standing below the ledge. We stare as it awakens, frozen in deep fear and a lack of a plan.

Its tail uncurls and straightens as it stretches its thick, pillar-like legs. Footsteps roll the ground underneath in small earthquakes that cause us to lose balance. Then, it peers down at us as if we're its next meal, and emits an ear-piercing roar that makes us all scream simultaneously.

It raises its tail with the fatal spikes above us. I leap to the right and the girls dive to the left just before the spikes slam down into the dirt between us.

Havanna and Anara regain footing as it comes at them with its mouth wide open. I jump to my feet, run as fast as my body can muster, then grab them both by the collar just in time for its jaws to snap shut.

"What are we going to do?" Anara screams.

"We have to tame it somehow!" Havanna shouts back. "Otherwise it's not going to stop!"

As soon as she finishes her sentence, a shadow of the monster's foot darkens the area around us. Havanna reaches her hand out to use Gridlock on it, sweat dripping from her forehead and squinting in visible pain. The foot is coming down on her, oblivious to her strength.

"It's not working! It's too big!"

We split in different directions as a cloud of dirt explodes around the foot. It has one move after another, which gives us no time to fight back.

The spiked tail flies in Anara's direction as she's about to use whatever water she has in her body to form ice, but nothing is working in her favor. She leaps out of the way just before the spikes stab the rock and sends pebbles everywhere.

I have an idea. The one and only idea we have left at our disposal. Otherwise, we need to run back down the mountain away from this thing.

The monster turns its head to me and I'm positive it just grinned. It's confident that it has its next meal trapped.

It opens its mouth and heads straight for me. I'm frozen in place, much too afraid to move as the sharpness of its teeth become clearer.

It's now or never. Wait another second and its jaws will snap close again.

I stretch my quivering hand out and send a message.

Stop. We're not going to hurt you.

Suddenly, the beast shuts its mouth and withdraws its extended neck. Its head tilts in curiosity, similar to the cute way the forest animals do when they're trying to understand me. Like the first time I found out I had abilities, when I was able to calm an Arbol Bear from attacking me and Nyx.

This creature is way bigger than the Bear, but by some miracle, Transmission is working.

You're safe. It's all right. We came to see someone. We're not here to hurt anyone, I promise. So please don't hurt us.

The beast retreats, the earth shaking with every step. Anara and Havanna slowly approach my side and stare in amazement.

"Whatever you're doing, keep going," Anara whispers.

I promise we mean no harm. We're only here to see someone. It's important. Let us through. Please.

It growls in satisfaction and slowly moves over to our right. The wide path it was blocking now opens up to us. It curls back into a comfortable sleeping position and wraps its tail around its body. Instead of resuming its slumber, it keeps its head perked up, orange eyes watching.

Thank you.

It releases a breathy grunt and proceeds to eye the mountain.

"Son of a . . ." Havanna breathes out. "How did you do that?"

I let my tired arm fall to my side. "I just told it we weren't here to hurt anyone, and not to hurt us."

"And it *believed* you?" Anara exclaims.

I shrug. "I suppose so."

"Incredible," Havanna says with a smile. It bodes well for me that I impressed two women at once.

Havanna motions to the open trail. "All right. Let's go!"

"Hold on a minute!" Anara stops her. "Can we take a moment and regain some energy before we run up into the hottest place in the kingdom?"

I chuckle. "I won't say no to that."

As it turns out, our definition of regaining our energy meant lying flat on the rock pavement with our limbs spread out. My chest rises and falls in regular, easy breathing as my heart rate slows. The sight of the mountain summit relaxes me.

Out of nowhere, laughter escapes me. I can't believe we went through all of that nonsense, and all I had to do was talk to it.

Havanna follows suit with laughter. I peer at Anara next to me, who's trying to hide a smile, but she snorts. That turns into her joining us in laughter, covering her face with her hands. It turns into hysterics, and the creature proceeds to fall back asleep, unbothered.

***

From where the resting demon-spawn sleeps, it becomes a moderately difficult hike to wherever we're going.

The mountain is massive and hilly, inclines and declines all over the place. My butt and thighs burn intensely, but in the way that tells me I will have strong muscles after this. I'm still able to maintain my irresistible, manly scent even though I'm sweating with the exertion, despite the fact that I have an Ice Stone on me.

"What are we looking for, exactly?" Anara asks.

"Civilization," Havanna huffs through equal effort.

"How do you know the Fire Descendant is even among a civilization?" she protests. "They could be hiding in a cave or living underground. Kind of like me."

Their bickering is getting ridiculous. I never saw Nyx bicker with anyone back in the forest. That is, until everyone thought we had slept together, then all the women called her cruel and unfavorable names. I'm not used to seeing women converse in this manner.

"Correction," I interrupt with a lift of my finger, "we found *you* among civilization. The poem just happened to mention you being in a cave."

"I *did* live in a cave." Anara raises her voice as she ruffles a piece of paper open. "*'There is one who curbs the flame. By a mound of stone'—*"

"*'They dodge the eyes of fame,'*" Havanna finishes. "I know."

Anara obviously didn't know that the poem was read to Havanna every night when she was little and that she remembers every single word.

"Then don't you think we should be looking for, I don't know, mounds of stone, not civilization?"

"A mound of stone doesn't have to refer to a single rock or boulder," Havanna says. "The mountain could fall into that description too."

"Fair point. But doesn't that mean this search could take days?"

"That's why we're looking for civilizations," Havanna points out in a self-evident manner.

I slow down so I can walk next to Anara. "There are higher chances of being found if you live alone in a secluded area. Blending into civilization makes you look like everyone else you're surrounded with, so you're not as easy to spot."

Havanna seems impressed when she peeks over her shoulder and nods. "That too."

A wooden sign sticks up from the dusty ground, and Anara groans. These signs have yet to have anything good to say. Fighting that monster took a lot out of me too, and I'd rather not have to do it twice. I'm exhausted, and I have never been more terrified in my life.

Except the moment when Father charged at me when he found me coming out of Nyx's house.

And, knowing Havanna, even if there was another creature, she's not going to let that stop her. I can appreciate determination, but to the point of death seems extreme.

"If there is another beast that we have to deal with, I'm going to stab you with my trident," Anara threatens Havanna.

"Why me?"

"Because you're the one that's so determined to get to wherever you need to go, and you drag us with you," she grumbles. "And you would make us fight it, just like that mutant back there."

Havanna throws her head back and sighs heavily. "First of all, I haven't *made* you do anything. Secondly, I'm worn out from fighting that beast. If there is another one, I will see if there's a different way. I promise."

"I'll believe it when I see it."

The three of us approach the sign, and it turns out it doesn't mention a beast at all. An arrow points to the right, next to the words *Mulhutna Tribe.*

Clanging metal, hammering, and rolling rocks echo close by. All I know about the Mulhutna is they mine Ice and Fire Stones with pickaxes and sell them to other civilizations.

"Looks like we're going the right way," I say.

"Well, then let's speed up," Havanna says just before she takes off in a sprint.

Anara growls in irritation and turns to me. "It's as if she doesn't know we're here."

I'm not in the mood to feed Anara's irritation toward Havanna. I can tell she thinks I'm too much of a follower.

A handsome follower, at that.

We catch up to Havanna's pace, which eventually slows down when the path goes from smooth rock to molten lava.

"We're getting close!" she shouts over her shoulder.

Up ahead, a gap between a rock formation indicates the entrance to civilization. Off the side of the pathway is a waterfall of lava with steam emitting from it, with some figures sitting at the edge of the pool it creates with some kind of utensil.

"Humans!" a deep, growling voice bellows up ahead.

That did not sound like it came from a small person.

The three of us stop in our tracks. I get in front of the girls and hold my arms out to keep them behind me. My eyes roam the area for any flying objects, and anything I can use Transform on in case we get attacked. There are only small rocks that will do little to no damage; they might as well be pebbles. All I can use is my archery skills, knives, or Transmission.

The civilization up ahead gathers into a crowd. They appear to hold thick, spiked sticks or pickaxes. From what I can see from this distance, they're much larger than us.

"Humans!" they shout again. "Attack!"

This is not good.

My heart pounds in the walls of my chest. The earth rumbles beneath our feet as they charge toward us. The closer they get, the taller they appear. Nine-foot, red-skinned trolls with gigantic noses run toward us, holding spiked clubs as tall as me over their heads that are covered with thin, wispy, gray hair. Their big, round bellies jiggle over the waists of their knee-length loincloths. Their nasty toenails are the same length as their toes, long enough to grab fish out of a lake.

We are surely going to die, whether it's by their clubs or their massive bare hands.

They've closed in on us. A few clubs begin to swing down on us, but they freeze midair. The trolls behind them bump into their frozen bodies and lose their balance.

I turn to glance over my shoulder to find Havanna using Gridlock on them.

This works to my advantage because I have a few seconds to get them to calm down.

That chance disappears when she moves her hand to the side and the trolls are sent flying into a rocky wall. The others stare in shock at the scene, then turn back to us, their low growls morphing into thunderous snarls that show off their long, sharp incisors. Their hands curl tightly around their clubs, poised for attack. A couple more steps in our direction and they'll have us stampeded.

I have to do something.

I stick my hand out and narrow my focus on them. *Stop. We're not here to hurt anyone.*

They stop and wildly blink. By instinct, their hands reach to their temples, thinking that shaking their bodies back and forth will make the voice go away.

I attempt to coax them to a calming state, as I did with the beast. *All is well. Don't hurt us.*

A few of them become so distracted that they fall to their knees, continuing to shake their heads. Some, on the other hand, refuse to let it faze them. Their eyes turn dark with anger and their breaths become primal, guttural growls.

A few continue with their plan of attack. Havanna keeps focused on the ones she has on Gridlock; Anara has her trident ready, but her stance implies that she's exhausted from the fight with the beast, as am I.

It's to no avail when I keep trying to use Transmission.

Seriously. Stop.

"WE. NO. LIKE. HUMANS!" they bellow loud enough to damage my eardrums.

"DIE, HUMANS!"

Just when I suspect that this is the end of us, the sound of an ear-piercing whistle makes all the Mulhutna freeze.

"ENOUGH!" a woman screams.

Behind the three Mulhutna, a beautiful woman with blonde hair cut to the scalp and tanned skin emerges between them. Like the rest of them, she wears a loincloth that reaches mid-thigh and a large strap of cloth covers her chest. She in no way resembles the Mulhutna, but she's apparently an authority figure of some sort because they're instantly submitting to her will.

However, I find myself wondering how she can handle this intense heat if she's not one of them.

Barefoot, she steps closer to us with a look of pure shock and amazement. Before addressing us, she turns back to the Mulhutna and shouts, "Leave them alone!"

"Chieftess Tena," a Mulhutna says, "they humans. We no allow humans."

"It's all right," she says in a comforting tone. "Let them be. I will handle this. Get back to work."

With low growls of disappointment that they're not allowed to kill us, they turn around and head back. We stare at this savior, stunned that she isn't sharing their attitude about us.

Tena turns back, switching her gaze between the three of us with her mouth partially open and breathless. "How did you get past the Tyranodrake?"

"Oh, that's what you call that killer pet of yours?" Anara says with her signature sarcastic tone. "We should have known."

"Anara," Havanna says in warning.

"We have been safe from outsiders for years because of our guardian creature," Tena informs us, breathless and in shock. "For you all to tame it, and come out unscathed, is a historical moment. There is no other answer, other than you are Descendants."

We all exchange shocked glances, mouths open and unsure how to respond. We don't know if we should confirm, considering that we have no idea who she is, other than the tribe's authority figure.

Havanna leans in between me and Anara to whisper, "At this point, there's no harm in telling her."

She's right. Tena already knows who we are, simply because we got past the beast.

"Yes," Havanna answers, "we are Descendants."

"As I suspected!" she exclaims. "I suppose you are here to meet the Fire Descendant?"

"Yes," Havanna answers a little too quickly.

"Very well. Follow me. I will get you all something to cover your head so your hair doesn't burn off."

My hand immediately reaches for my hair, which is hot enough to burn my scalp. A head wrap might be a wise choice.

We enter Mulhutna territory. The *ping* of pickaxes against rock is near deafening. Pieces of rock fly in all different directions with each swing. A couple individuals sit off to the side on a blanket, drinking from clay cups filled with steaming-hot water, or using it to pour over a sizzling pan of cooked meat. A big heaping pile of it.

"Can you please explain why there's a Tyranodrake at the bottom of the mountain?" Anara asks mockingly.

Tena banks left along the molten lava path, stepping lightly as if she were taking a simple stroll. "It was given to us."

Anara quirks a brow. "I need more details."

Tena chuckles, then puts on a faraway glance. "My husband and chief, Kubo, died during a Backers invasion five years ago. Everything changed. My son was only twelve years old, and the title of tribal chief fell to him. Such a young age to be a leader, let alone a *man*."

She briefly displays a frown and continues, "The Tyranodrake had been lying in wait for centuries in the depths of the volcano. The day Kubo died, the land saw fit to bestow it as a protective gift to the Mulhutna. For the last few years, it has proven successful in keeping our tribe safe while my son grew into the man we needed him to be."

So many lives have been taken by Backers, and the Fire Descendant is yet one more of us that experienced loss. Not a minor one, but loss of a blood relative, or someone we loved dearly. They have caused so much damage, thanks to the Dormant King.

I wish the land saw that Arbol Forest needed a guardian such as the Tyranodrake after Indigo died.

Havanna clears her throat to get past this depressing topic. "If you're a Mulhutna, how come you don't talk the way the rest of the tribe does?"

"I originate from Arythica," she answers. "I maintained my way of speech, and they, theirs."

The path curves around part of the mountain to the right, and that's when the terrain changes to display a livable area. The homes are lined up along a tall, rocky cliff in a U shape. They're either carved-out caves or flat slabs of rock piled sloppily on top of each other to form a hut. The location of the village is a bit odd too. The whole settlement is a few steps away from a ledge overlooking a clear lake. The steam emitting from it sweeps its humidity over our faces to show us what it offers: a nice hot bath.

Within one side of the rocky cliff above the tribe is what appears to be a detailed carving commemorating a member of their tribe. A double-headed axe is slung over the shoulder of the carving, eyes staring off into the hot springs below. He has the signature round potbelly and loincloth the rest of the tribe does. His head is bald while his face is covered with a long beard, and one other feature stands out to me as I examine this impressive work of art.

This Mulhutna doesn't have the deep frown of the other trolls. His lips are in a straight line, but the corners of his mouth curve ever so slightly. He may not be smiling, but the subtle upward swing of his lips makes him not so off-putting.

It's not until we enter the settlement that I see what the Mulhutna women look like. They're freakishly tall, just like the males, red skin, and their breasts are as large as melons that are covered with measly straps of loincloth. Their hair is similar to Tena's in length. They also never smile.

Tena leads us to a cave within the line of stone homes and snags three pieces of cloth in different patterns.

"Allow me to put these on for you." She explains, "There's a way to do it to make sure all the hair is covered."

My hair is already tied back, but she decides to pull off the hair tie and proceeds to wrap my hair. With the way she tugs, pulls, and twists, it's definitely a complicated procedure.

She moves on to Anara, who audibly slaps her hand away. "*Do not* touch my hair."

Tena, taken aback with her rudeness, stiffens with raised eyebrows. Anara snatches the cloth from her and works to gather her hair. Tena backs away and clears her throat.

"Over there—" She points to the Mulhutna carving and leads us closer to it. "—is the Fire Descendant."

Above us, a figure with a mallet and chisel chips off bits of rock, then takes some sort of rough material to smooth it over. If he made this, he's an incredible sculptor.

"Ender," she calls up to him, "can you come down here, love?"

The figure stops and dips his head to look down at us. From this vantage point, he's far enough from the ground that a single jump will break his legs. It's a mystery how he got up there to begin with.

He rearranges the tools he has set on a flat part of the artwork and shifts his feet. He's going to jump down, with nothing to guide him. I debate how wise this idea is until he does it.

We feel his immense size when he lands in front of us. The impact of the shock wave he creates causes us to lose our balance and fall, much to our surprise.

His sunburn-red form springs straight up and he opens his bulky arms wide. Mining has clearly toned his eight-foot-tall body with his impeccable muscles. Unlike the other trolls, his nails are neatly trimmed, thank Halivaara. He wears nothing on his right hand. I suppose he wouldn't need to if the mountain is guarded as much as it is.

"Welcome to the Mulhutna tribe, compos and compas!" he announces with a wide smile and the long Mulhutna incisors.

Tena wears a proud smile as she reaches to grasp his bicep that her hand can't fully wrap around. "This is my son," she says, "and the Mulhutna chief."

"How did she not split in half giving birth to him?" Anara whispers from behind.

The imagery in her question produces a snort out of me. I have to pinch my lips tightly and pretend to rub my stubble to keep from laughing.

Havanna steps up next to me and lays a hand on her chest. "Ender, I'm Havanna. And this is Quill and Anara."

Ender's unblinking eyes completely ignore Havanna and me, and stare hard at Anara. He makes it obvious when his gaze rakes her from white head to her brown boots. While he takes his time undressing her with his eyes, I notice a small gecko scurrying from his knee-length loincloth up to his shoulder.

That must be his Bennaru.

"They're Descendants," Tena adds excitedly, breaking Ender from his trance. Then, to our ultimate surprise, she shows us her right hand, where an etching of a flame greets us. "As am I."

We all stare in awe. Interesting that she failed to explain that her son got his abilities from her and not his father. I suppose that explains why she doesn't wear a head wrap or need Ice Stones to keep cool. She thrives in the heat.

Just as we recover from the shock, Ender leaps and widens his arms again. "Wow! Descendants? This incredible!"

His massive frame approaches us and wraps all of us in a hug, squeezing us so hard we groan and run out of breath. Our faces come in contact with his sweaty—and rock hard—torso.

"Then you truly compos and compas!" he exclaims, clapping his hands after he lets us all go.

"What are compos and compas?" I ask.

"Compo is male friend, compa is female friend." He grabs my shoulder with his long, intensely strong fingers and points to another male Mulhutna. "Emilien right there? Compo." He points to a female. "Regine there? Compa. She's not just compa, though." He motions to his chest, where his pecs are. "She compa with big bombas!"

He laughs so hard at his own joke that he fully bends over. I cover my mouth again to hide my instinct to laugh with him. Anara is rolling her eyes harder than I've seen so far, and Havanna simply seems unamused, arms folded and shaking her head at him.

Ender and I are men. The things we find amusing are the complete opposite from girls. It makes me wonder how Nyx ever put up with me for so long.

"Come," he motions for us to follow him, "let's talk in my home."

With his long, muscled arm, he manages to give all three of us a friendly slap on our backs. He clearly doesn't know his own strength, because we all end up back on the ground. Havanna and I exchange an annoyed look as we lie next to each other on our stomachs with the understanding that this is going to happen frequently.

Ender bends down to help Anara, yanking her back to her feet in one swift lift. His strength is impressive, yet intimidating.

But he cancels that out when he blows Anara a kiss with a side smile, then walks away without helping me or Havanna up. Anara's lips curl in disgust as she rolls her eyes again.

I glance back at the carving along the cliffside. The slight smile on the figure ignites my curiosity.

"What are you working on?" I ask Ender while motioning to his artwork.

He looks back at the carving with the same faraway look his mother had. "Is my aanu," he answers, "Chief Kubo of Mulhutna. He die when I was twelve. By Backers."

The pieces come together. Their chief died at the hands of an invasion, which gave birth to the Tyranodrake, and why the Mulhutna hate humans.

I wish I knew how to relate to him as far as a parents' love is concerned. He obviously loved his father and had a good relationship with him. Growing up with my father, I had every reason to hate him. I still do.

"That's unfortunate," is all I know to say.

"I make that in memory of him," he explains. "He best chief."

Ender directs us to his home, which is the biggest stone home in the village with its wide floor plan and enormous bed with layers upon layers of fur blankets that act as a mattress. He directs us to sit on a slab of smooth stone. He goes to his fur bed, where Tena sits beside him.

All of a sudden, the gecko leaps off his shoulder. Koa, Wave, and Bolt all scurry to meet the gecko and they all tackle each other, rolling around on the stony floor with happy squeaks and chirps. At last, all the Bennarus have united. Now, the Descendants have as well, but the tension in the air is suffocating

"So," Ender begins, "what brings you here? How you find me?"

Anara and I both look to Havanna, the leader in this endeavor. I know very well what to say, but I feel the need to leave this in her hands.

"Do you have a poem and a map?" Havanna asks. "Perhaps one that was given to you when you were young?"

"His aanu gave that to him when he was a boy," Tena answers for him, "but it burned a few years ago."

"All right. Well, the poem gives the locations of all the Descendants. The one about Ender brought us here."

"Oh yes, I remember that."

"I didn't know," Ender mumbles softly.

Tena waves him off dismissively. "You were too young to remember." She straightens her spine, her mouth a solid line in irritation. "And why did you all need to find my son?"

Havanna sighs, directing her attention to Ender. "We need your son's help in fighting the Dormant King."

Ender opens his mouth to reply, but Tena interrupts. "Is he at-large?" she asks in a low voice.

She pays no attention to Tena as she speaks right to Ender. "Not yet. But we want to find him and bring an end to him, the Backers, and the Dormants so we don't have to live a life in hiding anymore."

Tena motions to us. "The four of you against the Dormant King?"

Havanna looks between Anara and me, perhaps for some approval. I shrug and nod. "Ultimately, yes."

"If he is not at-large, why does Ender have to leave?" she questions. "He is the Mulhutna chief. He has a responsibility."

Why else did she think we were here if it wasn't because of the Dormant King? Did she think we were lonely teenagers seeking friends?

Havanna's lips in a tight line indicate that she's losing her patience. Nothing she has said has been directed to Tena, yet she keeps answering for him. I get her aggravation.

"I understand that," Havanna says, her voice cracking, "but this is important. As Descendants, we have a responsibility to put an end to him. We were all bound to meet at some point, yes?"

"As far as I'm concerned, there's no reason for him to leave," she replies. "Yes, you all were bound to reunite, but only if there was a valid reason to." She lays a hand on Ender's bicep again. "He's in a safe place here, and he's happy. Why take that from him?"

As long as she *says he's happy,* I remark to Anara and Havanna. Anara sneaks a glance at me with a slight nod and widened eyes.

Havanna chuckles to maintain her composure. I rest a hand on her knee to tell her to let me take over. She will crack if she keeps talking, and she's terrible at keeping her emotions hidden.

"Ender, what do you think? Do you think you could help us?"

Tena shoots to her feet with a deep glare. "Absolutely not."

Havanna rests her hands on her knees and clenches her lips harder, humming an odd tune to prevent herself from an outburst.

Tena's initial elation upon meeting us has taken a serious down-turn.

"I believe he was talking to *Ender*," Anara says.

Tena's lip quivers while she points at her son. "Regardless, he is *not* leaving. This is a very dangerous thing you want him to do. I lost my beloved husband, I refuse to lose my son as well."

"*Aani,*" Ender says in a commanding tone.

"No. You're not going anywhere. End of discussion."

And with that, she storms out of the home.

CHAPTER 10

ENDER

I lost my aanu when I was twelve years old.

Five years went by quickly. My aani grieves every day, and it leaves me feeling lost.

Aanu had gone to the other side of the mountain with another Mulhutna to head to Arythica with a new supply of Ice and Fire Stones. He ran into a group of Backers just as they left the mountain base. He felt he could take them on by himself because of his brute strength, but soon found he was outnumbered. They killed his traveling partner, then moved to take him down.

Once they did, they followed the path to my tribe.

Aani and my Bennaru, Flame, fought back as much as they could. She used Blaze to throw fire and form a shield of flames around her, and Gale to toss them in the lava while Flame turned into a tiger and mauled any surviving Backers. Aani told me to hide; I ran to find my aanu.

He was on the ground, fighting for his life. Seeing him there, hanging on every last breath, was horrifying. As he slipped away, he reminded me of the advice that he told me many times as a child.

"You strong. You half Mulhutna. If you have chance to use strength for good, to help others, take it. Always."

Then his hand slipped from mine and he was gone.

In that moment, the earth rumbled beneath me so intensely that rocks tumbled from the summit down to the village. A strong, deep cry sounded from the volcano, and the most spectacular thing happened.

An insurmountably huge monster, that we eventually dubbed the Tyranodrake, crawled from the lava and stood atop the mountain. None of us were its master; but it knew where to go. It traveled to the base of the mountain where it served as a protection for all of us. Somehow, the earth knew we needed to feel safe again.

Until the Descendants showed up, no other unwanted stranger had successfully made it here. I have remained safe.

From that day on, not only did I make it a goal to create a work of art commemorating Aanu, but I was determined to hone in my abilities to protect my aani and the Mulhutna. Aanu would have done the same thing.

I was only twelve years old; no one was going to take me seriously as a leader. There was no chance they would look up to me the way they did Aanu. For the first few months of my leadership, they didn't. It greatly bothered me.

Aani helped me to learn how Blaze and Gale worked, and how to control them. There's something meaningful about wielding the power of fire, but I felt that Gale was useless. That is, until she manipulated the steam from the hot springs and made it so powerful that it lifted rocks up to twenty pounds. I was astounded.

The best part was when she taught me how to snap and create a match at my fingertips. It was such a small skill, yet it was incred-ible. It proved useful for many things, including lighting wooden fires.

The moment I used Blaze to quickly roast supper for a family who was tired and starving from a whole day's worth of physical work, the tribe finally started to revere and respect me. That simple act assured them that I could be counted on to provide for them, if needed.

Aani also was instrumental in helping me make wise decisions for the benefit of our race. In a way, she led the tribe right alongside me. Just recently, when I turned seventeen, she made it known that she trusted that I was the best reflection of Aanu, and I didn't need her help anymore.

Now, the Descendants are here before me, and I have a chance to follow my aanu's advice. Yet, Aani insists that this is a bad idea, and I'm inclined to believe her. She takes care of me while I look after the tribe. She cooks me supper of meat every evening, tucks me into bed, washes my loincloth, and prepares my bathing routine every day. It's every man's dream come true. I won't get that treatment with the Descendants.

Aani needs me, and I need her. She needs me alive. The Mulhutna do too.

Although . . . there is a perk to going with them.

It's in the form of a white-haired beauty named Anara.

Leaving the tribe gives me a chance to spend more time with her. She's annoyed with me and I'm thriving on that.

With thoughts of my aanu running through my mind, I want to keep working on the tribute I have for him since he died.

"Great to meet you, compo and compas, but Aani say no," I tell them, rising from the bed. I make eye contact with Anara and wink. "I'll miss *you*, though."

She gives me the most unsatisfied expression. It makes me smile. "Bite me."

"Yum." I lean in with an open mouth toward her arm.

She swats at me while I attempt to bite her, then I manage to simply lick her arm.

"Ew!" She shrieks and wipes off my saliva with her other hand. She eyes me as if I'm the most disgusting creature she has ever laid eyes on, and I love it.

Havanna rises from the rock bench, displeased as she points at me. "All right, hang on. So you're going to stay here and mine rocks for the rest of your life, never knowing what the rest of the world holds for us? Never completing your destiny as a Descendant?"

I quirk a brow. "Uh, yes. I'm comfortable. I take care of tribe, and I don't want to leave Aani. She do everything for me. I like it."

Havanna folds her arms across her chest. "How old are you?"

"Seventeen."

She points at me. "You're a grown man. You don't need your mother to take care of you. You being the tribal chief says enough about how you can lead and take care of yourself."

"I think 'grown man' is debatable," Anara mumbles softly.

That hurts. I *am* a grown man. I caused a shock wave that made them fall over. Then they fell over again when I gave them a simple pat on the back. I have been the chief of an entire tribe for five years. Nothing says "grown man" more than that.

"Perhaps it's time to decide to be done with hiding and do your duty as a Descendant," Havanna says. "Do what your Ancestors never did."

Aani spent much of my childhood telling me about our history. How I shouldn't use my powers in open view of others, how our family has been in hiding for hundreds of years, how the Dormant King has been using Backers to hunt for the Descendants, and that he created the Dormants to further his cause. One fact that was never brought up was if any of the Ancestors attempted to find each other to hunt down the Dormant King.

According to Aani, none of them did. They were deathly afraid of being caught.

I wonder if they had the same kind of life I did—one of comfort, ease, safety. That would explain why no one left their humble abodes to fight.

However, what would Aanu say about this? What would he tell me to do?

If you have chance to use strength for good, to help others, take it.

I want to do this for Aanu, but I also want everything to be done for me.

But something about Anara pulls me in. She's giving me a challenge and I want to be the one to get through to her. The biggest obstacle is to get Aani to understand. There's a high possibility that she will do everything possible to not let me go, even if she has to stoop to manipulation and guilt-tripping. It won't be the first time she's pulled that on me, using Aanu's death as an excuse for everything.

I hold up a finger. "Wait here."

With that, I take wide strides to Aani's cave around the corner. She's most likely grilling meat for her and my supper with the spicy, citrus smell wafting outside the entrance. She knows I love Lime Goose with Mulhutna Peppers, especially the way she cooks it.

She stirs the Peppers around the meat with a clay spatula, and a deep frown to hold back oncoming tears is etched on her face. She has been carrying that frown with her almost every day since Aanu died, but it's deeper this time.

"So," she begins, avoiding eye contact, "I suppose they still request your assistance?"

I nod. "Yes."

"I hope you told them you're not going."

"Aani—"

She rises from the boulder she sits on. "*No*. Do you not remember what happened to your aanu? He was simply—"

I hold up my hand to stop her. "No repeat, Aani."

She lets out a harsh breath and sits back down. Her head is turned away from me as she scoops the Peppers and meat onto two plates. "I miss him," she states quietly with a quiver in her voice. "Every single day."

"I know. Me too."

She hands me one of the plates and I scoop the food into my mouth with one hand. Spicy, sweet flavors explode in my mouth that brings me bliss.

"I just . . ." She pauses to regain her composure, followed by a sniffle and a subtle wipe of her eyes. "I fear that if I lost my one true love, I will also lose my only son. Then I will be left with nothing."

A sob escapes her lips, which she covers with her hand. All I can do is watch her cry while my heart breaks. She gives me a good life here and does everything for me, but I didn't think all of this would affect her to this extent.

"You cannot go," she insists. "You just . . . cannot."

Before Havanna reasoned with me, I would have been in agreement with Aani. Leaving to fight in a war where I may very well die seems like an unwise choice. Who would be dumb enough to leave a life as easy as mine to do something like that?

However, Havanna helped me remember what my aanu taught me from childhood, and that changes everything.

As much as I love my aani, I owe this to Aanu.

"I have to," I choke out.

Aani lifts her face to me, the light of the fire under the pan illuminating the tears in her eyes. "What?"

As softly as I can, I grab her shoulders and lower my head to look into her eyes. "I never been outside tribe. I grown man. I can lead." I pause and try to remember what else Havanna said that made sense, but my mind is blank. "Or something like that."

Her brows narrow in confusion. "What are you talking about? What did those Descendants tell you?"

I shake my head. "Let me start over. Since I was child, Aanu told me always use strength for good. To help others. I can use powers to help Descendants."

She sighs and pinches her lips together. She never likes it when I bring up Aanu, especially when I refer to things he used to say.

"This my chance to use everything I have. To protect kingdom. To do duty as Descendant."

She backs away indignantly, arms folded timidly over her chest and shaking her head in disbelief.

"I must go. For Aanu."

She hesitates and lets my words sink in. It takes a few moments for her to accept what I'm saying with a sad nod. "Then I suppose it's time to give you this."

I have no clue what she's talking about until she goes to the corner of her cave, behind her bed, and grabs something leaning against the wall. I recognize it immediately.

Aanu's double-headed axe.

It takes a strong arm to wield that weapon, but Aanu did it with ease. I never knew what happened to his legendary weapon, and I hadn't seen it since his death. Turns out, Aani had it here this whole time.

She leaves a scuff mark on the floor from dragging it to me. I grab it and lift it effortlessly, rocking it back and forth, then sling it over my shoulder.

Aani eyes the weapon with longing. "Aanu wanted you to have it. He always wanted to pass it down to you when he died."

I arrange the axe upright and run my fingers along the polished wooden handle. The edges of the wide, curved blades are sharp to the touch. Since I was a child, he would sit in the living room and use a flat piece of slate on each side of the blades to maintain its sharpness. He used it as a protective weapon, and if he was sharpening it, it was a cue to stay a very safe distance away from it. At last, I have memories of my aanu that I can carry with me every day.

Aani stands on her tiptoes to caress my face softly, mouth quivering. "I've dreaded this moment for a long time," she admits in a low voice. "I hoped this wouldn't happen in your lifetime. That way, you never had to leave."

I never thought this moment would come either. I never cared if it did or not. As a child, I was made to feel special because I had abilities. Aani told me that the Dormant King sent his Backers to hunt me down because I was special. Hiding was the only way to make sure I stayed safe and no one took my powers. I was perfectly fine with that.

Doubts nag at me, though. Who will cook my food? Who will wash my loincloth? Will I have to tuck myself in at night? How will I bathe if no one gets the water ready for me?

Perhaps I can talk the Descendants into doing those things for me.

Either way, I'm doing this for Aanu. Having Anara there is just an added bonus.

I bend down to wrap my arms around my aani and I let her hold me as long as she wants.

Arm looped through mine, Aani and I walk to my home, where the Descendants await my response.

We take our time getting there, letting her soak in as much of me as she can. As far as she knows, this is the last time we will be together for a long while. Perhaps ever. She will have to be fully in charge as a chieftess. So far, we shared responsibilities, and now the Mulhutna all will answer to her. She will be all right.

The Descendants are lying on the floor on their backs, staring at the ceiling. They shoot upright the moment they hear us entering.

"About time!" Anara snaps. "What did you do, have a picnic?"

Havanna rolls her eyes. "So?"

I nod at them. "I join you."

"Yes!" Havanna exclaims and rolls her way up to her feet. "Thank you so much! You will be such a big help! Perhaps we can head out in the morning?"

Aani seems less than pleased with this entire situation with the way she sighs so heavily.

"Hold on."

One step at a time, Anara swings her hips as she approaches me, finger tapping her chin in deep thought. She comes to a stop directly in front of me, brows knitted, and scans me from head to toe. I bet she's impressed with the amount of time I've spent on my body, and how my extreme height can protect her from anything.

"You've lived in this tribe your whole life?"

The proud grin I was wearing disappears with her random question. "Yes."

"And you've lived in a hot environment your whole life?"

I quirk a brow, wondering where this line of questioning is going. "Yes."

She points at my loincloth. "This is the only thing you wear? Ever?"

Even Aani seems confused with her questions. "Yes," I draw out.

Anara hums. "If you leave with just that, you'll freeze to death, even in mild temperatures. So I have an idea."

"He doesn't leave?" Aani asks with a little too much enthusiasm.

Anara does nothing to hide her glare, and then scoffs. "No. I'm willing to make you an outfit that will not only keep you warm at all times, but something that cushions impact during battle."

"You can make that for him?" Aani asks.

"I can make anything."

"Wait," Quill steps in, "how long will that take?"

Anara shrugs. "A couple days. I just need some crushed Fire Stones and whatever material you have for clothing and padding."

A beautiful woman that can make clothes with different capabilities . . . and she's doing it for me? Surely she's my soulmate. Perhaps I have a chance with her, after all.

Aani seems relieved to have me for a few more days when she gives me a small smile, but also seems uneasy because it still means I'm leaving.

"I like the idea," I say, then turn to Aani. "They stay for a couple days, yes? You cook them Lime Goose and Mulhutna Peppers for supper? Give baths and wash clothes?"

She sighs heavily again, just as she does when she's agitated. Her eyes narrow at me in obvious displeasure, but I don't understand the problem. She's done it for me my whole life, why is it a problem to do it for my compos as well?

"I can cook too, you know," Havanna offers as an attempt to diffuse the tension with Aani.

I clap my hands once and the noise is so loud that everyone flinches. "Perfect! Aani, they stay?"

Her eyes roam between my three compos, then back to me. Her reddened cheeks indicate how much she hates this idea and that it will be nothing but a burden. But, it means she gets to have me a few days longer.

"Very well."

CHAPTER II

HAVANNA

I stare at the map and poem by a fire, about to head out to find the Fire Descendant. Anara and Quill sit on either side of me, staring at the flames. Saying nothing.

Out of nowhere, I feel a gentle hand on my shoulder from behind. Jael.

My heart leaps out of my chest. My mother figure is still alive! She never died after all!

I twist and try to leap up and hug her, but my legs are paralyzed. My body won't let me. My arms reach for her, something that Jael fails to notice as she walks right around them, as wind does as it breezes through tree branches. She stands out of my view; my body begs to follow her, but I remain tense and frozen.

She takes my face in her hands and turns it toward her. She lays a gentle kiss to my cheek, the way she always did to let me know she loved me, without words. I can't see her; she has no face. But I know in my heart, this is the Jael I grew up with.

"You've done so well, Warrioress," she says to me in that soft, alto voice I know so well. "You're going to find him. I know it. I'm so proud of you. For all you've done."

She has no idea how much I need that.

I wake up to a damp, leather pillow in Ender's home, with a headache from suppressing the need to cry. As soon as I lean up, the tears stream down my cheeks, not realizing they were falling.

Quill is right. Recurring dreams of a loved one lost in death will never go away.

I throw the covers off and emerge from the cave, determined to forget the dream. Tena is cooking meat on the side of the home, with Quill watching her silently move the food around in the pan.

This whole arrangement is ridiculous. She's only taking care of us because Ender told her to. I know that is the last thing she wants to do, but she also didn't have to agree to it. Her sullen attitude toward us in general is getting on my nerves. She treats Ender like a child, to the point of not letting him speak for himself. I badly want to tell her to back off, but that won't end well.

I'm already stuck traveling with a difficult person; I'm not in the mood to deal with another one.

Since last night, I've come to realize that the Mulhutna primarily eat meat, and not much else. Not that I mind it. At least they've finally accepted us into their tribe and they haven't plotted to kill us. Which is most likely at Ender's request.

Nonetheless, we have to be here for a few days while Anara makes Ender's clothes. She's going to spend time taking his measurements while he will continue to flirt with her. Quill and I will have lots of alone time together, which gives me excited nerves.

We don't have a choice but to wait here. Ender won't survive outside the heat of Vulca Mountain. We need his strength and abilities.

Quill, Tena, and I sit around the fire that she keeps lit with the flame coming out of her right hand. He and I exchange uncomfortable looks while eating our pile of meat. Tena hasn't said a word to either of us since we sat. She didn't even greet me.

Quill turns his head to the side and nonchalantly shields his eyes. The way he does it indicates they're about to turn green and he doesn't want Tena to see. It's the gesture I've come to recognize when he wants to communicate with me.

Since you're so good at coming up with lies and excuses, can you get us out of here? I'm pretty sure Tena is doing everything in her power to not kill us with her bare hands.

Even that simple message sends my heart fluttering. Having conversations this way makes me feel special, as if this is a special connection that only he and I share.

I need to focus.

I subtly examine Tena's demeanor. Her grip on her clay plate is so tight her fingertips are white, and she's refusing to make eye contact. That plate is going to break anytime now.

We need to finish eating, just to be polite. Then we can say we're going to explore the rest of the mountain.

Simple. I like it.

The gravelly noise of sandals on rocky pavement breaks the silence between the three of us when Ender appears.

"My darling," Tena says ever so enthusiastically. "Hungry?"

Quill looks away again. *That right there tells us everything we already knew.*

"No, ate this morning," Ender replies. A slap to Quill's and my shoulders sends us lurching forward, almost spilling everything from our plates. I'm relieved to not give a reason for Tena to be angrier with us when our food remains unscathed. Ender really does not realize how strong he is.

"You compos should go to the mining area, meet some of the Mulhutna," he suggests.

Nevermind. He's giving us a way out.

Thank Halivaara.

"I suppose we can," I answer.

"Follow path downhill and you find them," he tells us with a pointed finger at the pathway close by. "I need to give Anara my measurements. And Fire Stones."

"Ender," Tena softly scolds, "be a good host and introduce them to the tribe. You cannot just leave them on their own."

I furrow my brows at her. She wants us to enjoy our time among the Mulhutna, but she barely talks to us during mealtime. A hard read, that one.

"Of course, Aani," he says apologetically, and lightly taps our shoulders before letting go. "I introduce you, then I come back here."

Quill and I waste no time in setting our plates down and standing, even though there's still uneaten food. I don't care as long as I get out of Tena's presence.

We follow behind Ender's enormous red frame, his knee–length loincloth swaying with each step as we go downhill. His wide strides and lack of checking back to see whether we're still behind him is a sure sign he wants nothing more than to spend time with Anara and to get this over with.

We finally manage to catch up to his speed as we enter the mining area. The scene before us is very different from what we saw yesterday. Instead of a group of Mulhutna working, they form a circle around two trolls wrestling, pushing against each other using full upper-body strength. Grunts, growls, and chants boom in my ears.

"Anca! Anca! Anca!"

The one I presume is Anca plants his feet deep in the ground and shoves forward with all the force in his legs. His heels create tracks on the rock, his arm muscles quiver and ripple with obvious strain. His opponent shoves back, making Anca slide backward. It's a losing battle for him if he's stuck in the ruts.

We're proven wrong when Anca takes his opponent by the shoulders and tosses him to the side. He beats his chest in victory, just as Bolt does as a gorilla when he's defeated an enemy.

"Compos!" Ender shouts, arms spread out. "What happening here?"

One of the trolls shrugs. "Break time."

"Break time over!" Ender bends down to help the defeated Mulhutna back to his feet. Most of the group disperses but some hang around to examine us.

Ender and the other troll slap each other on the shoulders without making each other fall over. Anca joins the signs of friendship when he slaps shoulders with his opponent and Ender.

"Compos, I introduce you to *new* compos." Ender motions to us. "Havanna. Quill."

They all grunt in some sort of greeting. No handshake. No hug. No shoulder slaps. Just those permanent deep frowns.

Ender motions to one troll at a time. "Descendants, meet compos. Ragnar, Tulek, Kenzo, Hamza, and Anca."

Each Mulhutna nods as their name is pronounced, including Anca, the wrestling match winner.

"They human, but they compos all the same," he emphasizes. "Make them feel welcome. Perhaps they help you while they here."

"I'm sorry, what now?" Quill whispers.

"Human help," Anca confirms.

"Anca among the strongest of tribe," Ender tells us with a sly grin. "He keep you entertained." He turns to jog back the way we came, back to the tribe. "Have fun. I go now."

Excellent. We go from being ignored by his mother to the possibility of being broken in half helping these trolls.

Anca stomps over to his pickaxe, which, quite frankly, is as big as me and Ender combined, the blade about as thick as my thigh.

"First, pick up axe," he says. "Hand to me." With a teasing, ugly-toothed grin, he adds, "If you can. It is heaviest one."

Quill and I switch our gazes between the axe and each other. I wait for him to go first while he waits for me to go instead.

Quill motions. "Ladies first."

I already know I'm going to fail this test. I suppose I have nothing to lose.

Standing straight and feigning confidence, I wrap my hands around the wooden handle. My fingers can barely fit around it, making my grip slippery and weak.

Here goes nothing.

Using all the lifting power from my legs, I pull up on the axe. It doesn't budge. Not even an inch.

Sweat forms on my forehead as I tighten my grip and try again. I use all of my body this time—arms, legs, back, chest—and it still doesn't move. My strength is waning very quickly.

"Lift with your legs, not your back," Quill says from behind me, clearly teasing.

I roll my eyes. "I am."

"Here. Try this."

He steps up behind me. My skin ripples with heat from his touch as his strong fingers grip my hips and shift my stance. It becomes much more overwhelming when his leg brushes up against mine. I take in how intimate it feels to have his hands on me in a gentle caress.

His hands rip away from my hips and he clears his throat, obliterating this moment to awkwardness. I breathe out a gentle whimper that I sincerely hope he didn't hear.

"Try that," Quill squeaks out.

He must have felt something too.

The debate within myself about romance is only getting worse the more we're around each other. I was determined to never have any sort of romantic feelings for anyone after Victor. I was doing great with that goal. Something about Quill is . . . different. I don't detect any hint of deceit with him; although I didn't detect anything with Victor either.

But I know better now.

Shifting my weight, I go for it again. I already know I'm going to fail. Quill's addictive touch has left my knees weak and my hands sweaty. He's going to know he had an effect on me when the handle slips from my grasp.

I quickly wipe my palms on my pants, then grip the handle. I shift all of my weight to my legs and lift. Of course, it doesn't yield.

Even worse, my hands slip and I fall flat on my back. As if I couldn't embarrass myself more.

I lay there and groan, too embarrassed to face Quill once I get back up. But, unluckily for me, he beats me to it when he nudges me with his boot. A smile teases his lips as he peers down with those glistening brown eyes that make it easy to get lost.

"You didn't use your legs."

"Yes I did!"

He chuckles and shakes his head adoringly while holding out his hand. He yanks me back up fast enough that I feel a little lightheaded.

I flinch when his hand reaches out to me. My skin tingles something fierce as his fingers gently brush against my cheek while he combs a strand of hair behind my ear and tucks it in my headwrap. This is the most he has ever touched me, and it jolts my heart into rapid beats. His eyes have a fire in them, a desire. But once he drops his hand, the tension, along with our chemistry, goes with it.

"Your turn," I barely manage to say through the intensity of emotions swimming through me.

He gives me the cocky side smile that I've grown to admire. "Watch how it's done, Zappy."

He grips the handle the same way I did and lifts with his legs. It moves along the gravel a couple inches, but he can't lift it. His arms shake with the effort while his face turns deeper shades of red. Grunting, growling, yelling; none of it matters.

And it gives me my own cocky grin.

With one final grunt, he gives up. He takes a few steps back in tune with his harsh breaths. Anca, who was watching from the side this whole time, lets out a deep, throaty chuckle.

"You humans, so little," he says with a click of his tongue. He grabs the axe and walks away, carrying it as simply as a handheld shovel.

Quill watches him in amazement, hands on his hips and still catching his breath. I keep my cocky grin on him until he feels me watching him and turns around.

"You should have lifted with your legs."

"Shut up."

***

Ender gave me permission to sleep on his bed, which is gigantic and super comfortable.

I saw it and immediately thought of Calista. I felt a little home-sick, so I had to at least ask, just to remember Calista's kindness and generosity.

Missing Calista causes me to miss Jael, and I don't want to go down that hole.

In a far corner, Quill sharpens the knives he keeps wrapped around his legs with a smooth stone. I could watch him all day, but that's not a good idea. My eyes switch to Anara as she sews pieces of material together, Wave sitting on the stone table with her as a frog.

Anara threads so smoothly in perfect stitches. It seems to leave Wave disinterested, as he jumps off the table and joins the other Bennarus in the middle of the cave. Bolt and Koa join in as a mouse and a bird. Soon enough, Koa has Wave's legs clutched in his feet, Wave holds onto Bolt by his tail, and they flutter around the space in a way that makes me giggle.

After a few minutes, Anara stops and swiftly turns to look at me with an offended glare. A common expression for her.

"Stop staring at me," she demands defensively.

I quirk a brow. "I wasn't staring at you. I'm watching you sew."

"So you're staring at me."

I roll my eyes. "At your *hands*. Don't worry, I have no desire to flirt with you, Wet Wench."

Anara chuckles softly. "Good. Because having Ender make moves on me is a lot to tolerate as it is."

"I can imagine," I say with a hint of sarcasm. "I'll stare at the ceiling till supper if that makes you feel better."

She shakes her head. "As long as it's just my hands, I suppose that's acceptable. Thank you, Electric Doofus."

I chuckle and stare at the ceiling anyway. I take this moment to do the breathing exercises Jael taught me.

Breathe in. Hold for five. Breathe out.

Although it helped tamper my desire to use Strike, it helped me relax in other ways. My brain stops racing with uncontrollable thoughts, my eyes feel heavy, and my body feels looser. I suppose Jael had the right idea in teaching me this technique.

My relaxation is interrupted as footsteps approach.

"More Fire Stones," Ender calls out as he plops a white burlap bag on the table where Anara is working. "Pulverized to powder, as asked."

Anara seems less than pleased with his presence as she examines the contents in the bag. "Thank you."

"You think I no bring Fire Stones?"

"Doesn't hurt to check," she mutters.

While they banter, Ender's Bennaru leaps out of the waistband of his loincloth as a gecko and scurries across the floor to the other Bennarus. Koa drops Bolt and Wave to the floor, then grasps Flame's gecko feet and continues to fly in circles.

Anara finishes inspecting the powdered Fire Stones and pours some onto a neatly laid out cloth.

"How are you going to add those to his clothes?" I ask.

Anara sighs, showing signs of tiredness. "I'll use an adhesive on the lower layer of material, add the powder, then attach other material on top to keep it sealed. That way his body constantly stays warm and adds extra cushion."

I nod, impressed. "That's amazing."

"When you have moment," Ender chips in and makes a V motion from his collarbone to the middle of his chest, "can you cut out space here? I want to show muscles. I am proud of chest."

Quill chuckles in the corner while Anara scoffs at the request. She doesn't bother answering him as she goes right back to work. Ender seems to understand her response with a smile and walks away.

"Has he gotten through to you yet?" I ask Anara.

"Ha!" she belts out. "No. Are you serious? That could never work." She stitches a couple more times, then adds, "Can you imagine if I had his babies? I would explode."

Anara's description causes me to snort, which turns into laughter. Harder than I expected. I turn to watch her, and she does something I'm struggling to get used to.

She laughs right along with me.

❊❊❊

It's nights like this that make me miss being in Ketra. When all is quiet, the air humid as a warm summer night, the sun going down and leaving the sky in a dark-blue hue, giving us its last moments of light. This time, I'm not surrounded by soft grass, sand, and palm trees. Ender has taken to his bed, softly snoring away while the rest of us sleep on the floor, cushioned with lots of fur blankets, then covered with more. Getting comfortable is out of the question with how warm this bed is, and the air adds to the difficulty. I'm not going to sleep anytime soon. I'll just have another dream about Jael that will have me awake in tears.

I slowly get out of bed. Bolt sleeps on the corner of the blanket as a mouse, as his eagle form is too big for this space, so I tread lightly so as to not wake him.

The hot spring across from the settlement draws me in with its warmth. The bright orange and red colors of the lava streaming down the mountainside add a measure of light to my surroundings. The crystal-clear water with steam wafting from it makes it even more dreamy. Just to dip my body in there and feel the wet warmth encompass me.

I settle for letting my toes touch the water once I go down the slight decline to the shore. It brings me back to Ketra again, when I would go to my hiding spot in Ketra Falls and dip my toes. This time, the water is so soothing and evokes a sense of tranquility, a soft blanket from the cold.

I wiggle my toes in the lapping water, splashing it onto the tops of my feet. I examine the expanse with the occasional rock structure and immovable boulder protruding from the surface and the shimmering ripples. Everything is so hushed, eerily silent. It's such a peaceful setting.

Until I hear a splash. And not just water lapping around the rocks.

I thought I was the only one out here.

I jump to my feet and walk quickly toward the source of the sound. Now I have to see who's awake in the middle of the night. The swimming noises have converted to heavy pouring; someone is squeezing water, perhaps out of a cloth or sponge.

Someone is bathing.

A shadow on the water and a white arm reaches up, then back down beneath the surface. Just from that, I know it's not a Mulhutna.

I crouch behind a boulder to get a better view of the source of the noise. A beautiful, strong man runs his hands over his arms and shoulders, his back muscles rippling with every movement.

It's Quill.

Only the top half of his body is exposed. That is, until he fully immerses the rest of him, then emerges a second later. With a whip of his neck, he tosses his sopping wet hair behind him and out of his face. With the same rugged fingers that gripped my hips earlier today, he combs his hair back. The indentation of his abs, defined pecs, and flexing biceps have me swooning beyond words.

I have to look away. He's going to come out of the water and see that I've been ogling him this whole time. I do *not* want romance. I may be appreciating a perfectly sculpted work of art, but it doesn't mean I want anything more than that. Even though he's gentle, kind, funny, and a calm presence that I find refreshing. We have great chemistry.

I also don't want anyone else eyeing him the way I do. The women in Macaphin Village were practically drooling over him and I hated it. They may as well have punched me in the gut.

It's doing me no favors to sit here and watch him. All it does is feed my desire for more.

If only I could see his legs . . .

All right. I need to leave.

As silently as I can, still crouching, I turn on my heels. My foot catches on a bump on the ground, causing me to tumble forward. A groan is knocked out of my throat against my will, loud enough for Quill to hear. But that isn't the worst part.

I fall right where he can see me.

"Havanna?" he whispers.

I regain my footing and wipe the dirt off my skin all the while scrambling to find a good excuse for why I'm out here. "Oh. I'm sorry. You were bathing."

He shifts uncomfortably. "Um, yes." A whimper escapes me as he lowers the rest of his body in the water and wraps his arms around his chest. I want to keep staring at his body and imagine what it would be like to touch it. Unfortunately, his actions are in my best interest. "What are you doing out here?"

"I was—" I stumble on my words to save myself from even more embarrassment. My eyes dart to the settlement behind me, then back to him. "I was taking a walk. I couldn't sleep."

"I didn't hear you coming."

"Yes. Well, I'm a quiet walker." My arms instinctively wrap around my chest. This entire encounter is extremely awkward. It's even worse that we're both embarrassed, enough for the tension to explode. "Well, I'll let you get back to sculpting—I mean, bathing. Good night."

I turn and scurry back to Ender's cave, back to the makeshift bed on the floor.

Nighttime walks are out of the question now.

✳✳✳

"Ender, your clothes are ready!"

Anara's announcement slowly brings me out of my deep slumber. I hear the shuffling of large feet and Quill groaning on the other side of the room.

130

I wipe my eyes and lean up to see what's going on. Anara hands Ender a pile of folded clothes that appear to be a mix of black, red, and portions of shiny gray material. He snatches them from her and inspects the outfit by unfolding them and letting them fall to the floor. It's a full bodysuit. The legs and feet are all black with the gray portions that resemble very small snake scales, while the top covers his upper body in more black intertwined with red. A large, bright-red cape hangs behind it by the shoulders.

"Thank you, compa!" he exclaims. "This incredible!"

"Go try it on," she tells him. "I already know it will fit and you will like it, but I want to get a visual. Havanna, Quill, let's leave him alone."

We both groan as we slowly make our way out of the home. I stand and stretch my arms to wake up my body, and roll my neck from side to side.

"We don't have all day!" she snaps, particularly at me.

I glare at her and roll my tongue over my teeth. I don't have a smart retort at the moment and I don't feel like starting an argument.

Sitting around the dead firepit next to Ender's house in silence, I switch my gaze between the pile of charred wood and Quill. I debate whether I should apologize to him for catching him bathing or admit that I wasn't actually going on a walk. Or just pretend nothing happened and never speak of it.

The latter is not a bad idea.

The sound of crunching gravel perks us up.

Ender rounds the corner from his home with a smolder. He slings his massive double-headed axe over his shoulder as the cape flows behind him with the subtle warm breeze. The bodysuit fits his physique perfectly, the material contorting to his movement and defining his muscles.

He looks absolutely amazing.

"What you think?" he asks, turning in a full circle.

I look at Anara, whose jaw is dropped as far as it can possibly go. "Ender, that looks great on you!"

He winks. "I know."

Anara gets up and approaches him to inspect her handiwork. "Wow. I am *good!*"

"You are," he replies softly.

She smirks, but passes right over his comment. "Are you comfortable? Are you warm?"

Quill and I look at each other with quirked brows. This appears to be the first time that she's cared about someone else's comfort.

"Very. Feels just like loincloth. And it's warm. Thank you."

"Great!" Anara squeals. She drags him by the arm back to the firepit and sits him down with us. "So, he won't freeze to death, and we're all together. Can we leave now?"

"We need to know where to go first," I answer.

Anara scoffs. "To kill the Dormant King. Duh!"

I bring my palm to my face and sigh. "I'm saying we need to know which direction to go. We need to have a solid plan on where to go first before we go back out there."

"I'll tell you one thing," Quill starts. "I'm never going back to Arbol Forest. Never."

I understand that. I'm not ready to face anyone in Ketra, and nothing waits for me in Cal-léa. The two friends I grew up with clearly moved on when they bought my childhood home. I'm still furious about that, to the point where I don't believe there is a valid reason for it.

"I literally just left my village a few days ago," Anara says. "I'm happy to never go back again."

The three of us turn to Ender, who only offers a shrug. "No hurry for me," he says. "We can stay here little longer. Come up with plan. You are my compo and compas now. We stay together."

That leaves out Macaphin Village, Arbol Forest, Ketra, and Cal-léa. All the evidence I've gathered about the Dormant King's whereabouts don't lead to any of those places anyway, which bodes well for all of us. I know where we need to go, but we need to have a thorough plan of attack to figure it out.

I race around the corner to Ender's home to search through the pocket of my pants for the poem and map, the only guide we have at this point. Along with the tablet I have of the Ancestors. The Descendants need all the background information they can get.

Walking back to the firepit, it hits me. This is really happening. We found each other. We're united. We're all going to fight this battle together. All these thoughts leave me standing for a few moments, my veins filling with excitement and spreading jitters through my legs.

With a grin, I examine all of them while laying out the parchments. "Very well. It's time to come up with a plan."

CHAPTER 12

ANARA

"Well, Havanna," I say through a sigh, "you're the leader. You brought us all together. Where do we go from here?"

Havanna had us open up our parchments with the poem and map. She allows Ender to use hers as a reference as she talks.

"After talking to researchers, this—" She holds up the tablet. "—represents the banishment of the Dormant King, done by what I'm guessing is the Water Ancestor."

There are four figures dressed in white, each with an elemental symbol above their heads. Then there's a figure with a black hole behind him and a tree above his head. The one with the water droplet has his hand outstretched toward the one with the tree, opening up the hole behind him.

I already don't like where this is going.

"How you know that's happening?" Ender asks.

"Because the Dormant King hasn't been seen anywhere in the kingdom in centuries. It's safe to say that he's in another dimension that the Water Ancestor sent him to."

The second she ends her sentence, I bust out in hysterics. "The Dormant King in another dimension? Do you have any idea how stupid that sounds?"

"I thought the same thing when I heard it," she says. "But once you get the facts, it makes sense." She snatches her parchment back from Ender and shows me the different colored markings on her map. "Many people claimed that they could hear someone trying to talk to them mentally. Just as Quill can do with us."

"He can?" Ender asks in amazement. Quill's eyes turn green as he looks directly at Ender. He jerks back and raises his hands to his temples. "Whoa, that was weird!"

As they chuckle, Havanna goes back to her explanation. "This color means the voice was heard but muffled. This color means it was heard much clearer the closer they got to Luna Island."

"All right . . ."

"The same thing happened to me when I was going to Luna Island. He communicates with the Backers this way. But Backers have never seen him physically. And no one else had seen him for centuries. Some thought they did, but no one had consistent descriptions of him. So the question is, how can he communicate with anyone mentally without ever being seen, unless he's somewhere no one else can access? For instance, another dimension."

I want to come up with a snarky retort, but she actually makes a good point. I know I have never seen the Dormant King, but I have definitely seen the Backers do his dirty work.

"So where does this all lead us?" I ask.

"I'm glad you asked." She brings me the tablet and points directly at the painting of my Ancestor. "Your Ancestor banished the Dormant King."

This was exactly what I was worried about. The Water Ancestor is using Gateway, the ability I've used only a handful of times. I'm still not sure how it works, or why.

I remember the first time I used it. I was practicing Upsurge in the dead of night. Some Niminims were making their way to the village, and I could hear their downright creepy laughter. I recall wanting them to go away, so I stretched out my hand and black holes opened up behind them. They got sucked in and never came back. I didn't understand what I did, or what it was called. Sharifa and Masina were just as confused as I was when I told them about it. I figured those Niminims must have ended up somewhere, I just didn't know where Gateway took them.

"Wait a minute." I hold up my hand. I try to stand, but can't. Dread fills my entire body. "You're saying if my Ancestor did this—"

Havanna cringes. "Yes."

My heart drops. I lose feeling in my legs. How dare she expect something so serious of me.

My palms break out in a sweat that I have to dry off on my knees. I find it hard to swallow. This is much too serious. I'm expected to open the door for the biggest enemy of the kingdom to come back, simply because we want to kill him. Nothing good can come of that. What if we lose? Then the Dormant King and his army will take over the kingdom because I let him back in.

I finally find the strength to stand, and then laugh anxiously. "Nope. Nope. Absolutely not. I didn't expect to be responsible for letting the Dormant King right back into our world. Thanks for the update, Electric Doofus!"

"Electric Doofus?" Ender asks.

"Term of endearment," Havanna answers quickly before turning her attention back to me. "Anara, this is the only way. He has to be brought back to our side of the kingdom for us to even begin to attack. I'm sorry, but if he's in another dimension, this falls on you."

"Hold on. Why can't we just go to his dimension and find him?"

Havanna shifts her weight and juts out her hip. "Do you know anything about the dimension he's in?"

She knows I don't. Fine. I'll play along. "No."

"Do you know how to get yourself into a different dimension and also get us all out of it?"

Darn. She obviously has me bested. "No."

She motions to me. "There you go."

My heart races. This is a lot to take in. I barely know how to use Gateway, and the burden of retrieving him falls on me. I'm the key to starting a war.

I have to sit back down. My hand reaches up to my beating heart. I never expected this to be the case, and I'm having a hard time accepting it.

"I'm sorry, Anara," Quill says in an attempt to ease the anxiety, "but Havanna is right."

I swallow each time I take a breath. Leaving Macaphin Village was my chance to not be a burden to anyone and to get away from the bullying. It was my chance to leave the toxic environment I was raised in. Now, I'm just carrying that burden with me. With a group of people I don't know, but who really need me.

"If that's *my* responsibility, then what? We just beat him up?"

Havanna shrugs. "Basically. Unless you have a better plan. Considering we don't know how powerful he is, we're kind of going in blind here."

Electric Doofus is operating without a brain again. Leave it to me to set her straight.

"Solid plan," I snap. "Just go right into the front lines of battle and die in five minutes. That's brilliant."

"Sounds brilliant to me," Ender pipes in.

I roll my eyes and groan, palming my face. I wait for the moment when I wake up and find that this has all been a dream.

That moment never comes, no matter how many times I open and close my eyes.

"He mainly stays under Luna Island," Havanna informs us, "given that he communicates with people from there all the way to the coast, and that's where the Backers are stationed, that's where we need to go."

"But," Ender intervenes, "if stanza in middle is about Dormant King, wouldn't it make sense go there?"

"No. Because he has to be close to where the Backers are to talk with them. Which means he has to stay at the Backers Fortress on Luna Island."

"Ender has a point, though," I say. "The rest of the poem gave *our* locations. It doesn't make sense that *that* part of it won't do the same."

"See, Anara agrees!" Ender exclaims.

Havanna huffs out a frustrated breath. "I know what I'm talking about. He's not going to be there."

"Actually, Havanna," Quill pipes in. "Remember how you were ambushed by Backers in Sabbia Desert, and that Dormant was summoned to come up and attack? That was only because of the Dormant King being in that vicinity. Who's to say he's not hanging around where the stanza is?"

Her patience is waning with the way she hangs her head and sighs heavily. "Allow me to explain one more time. The voices were heard loudest at the Backers Fortress. He talked to the Backers, at the Backers Fortress. Therefore, he's at the Backers Fortress, on Luna Island. Am I making sense?"

It makes sense to me, but it doesn't quite answer the question we're all trying to figure out, and I want to have fun pissing her off more.

"It still doesn't explain why the stanza is in the middle of the map," I counter.

"Yes! That!" Ender shouts with a finger pointed at me. All his efforts to impress me are only earning him narrowed eyes in his direction.

"Let's back up a second," Havanna suggests with her hands held up. "The position of the stanzas on the map are more like the last-known location of each of us. Mine wasn't accurate because I had to leave Cal–léa as a child, but the rest of yours were correct. And because the Dormant King is in another dimension and no one can know exactly where he is, it would make sense to place that one in the middle. But I know where he is."

"You just said no one can know where he is," I protest, mostly to annoy her.

"I've already given you all the evidence that he's at Luna Island." She emphasizes this with a bounce on her heels. "Come on. I know what I'm talking about. We need to go to Luna Island."

There's silence between the four of us. We all watch each other for a reaction, or for someone to say something to argue with her. Or agree with her. This goes on for a while, to the point where the silence is deafening.

Then it's Quill who speaks up next. "Perhaps it's worth a try to go to the location on the map."

I mentally applaud him for saying something.

"Wait a minute." Havanna points a finger at him, her voice holding back anger. "I told you all the evidence I had about Luna Island, and you believed me. And now you're changing your mind?"

"I do believe you," he says comfortingly that in no way takes the rage away from Havanna's face, "but this also could be a possibility. If we're wrong, then Luna Island will be the backup plan."

Three against one. Havanna loses. And she knows it, because her expression converts from angry to resigned. "Fine. We'll go to the middle of nowhere to find the freaking Dormant King."

"Yes!" Ender's voice booms as he springs to a stand with his arm raised. "I'm ready to bust him up!"

Havanna groans with her head hung over as she plops onto the log seat, arms falling limply over her knees. She's not getting her way and she's pouting like a baby. Boo hoo. I lived my whole life not getting my way. I have no sympathy for her whatsoever.

As long as I don't have to face the Macaphins ever again, I don't care where we end up. But that also doesn't mean I like the plan to have me use Gateway to bring the darkest enemy in the kingdom out of his dimension.

I don't have a choice, though. I agreed to do this. The moment I summoned the ocean to save Havanna and Quill, I was all in.

"By the way," Havanna interjects, "just so you know, I'm delivering the final blow to the Dormant King, whether you all get the opportunity to do it or not."

I narrow my eyes at her and cross my legs. Not only does her statement sound arrogant, but she has the audacity to claim something that isn't hers. It makes the rest of us obsolete.

"And why do you get to do that?" I ask. "Why are we all here?"

Something about what I said strikes a chord, as usual. She straightens up and rolls her tongue over her teeth to keep herself in control while also showing signs of guilt and shame. "Because I need your help to avenge the people I love."

I admire her for openly admitting her weakness, but it sounds selfish that she only wants us here to accomplish her own goal. To be honest, we all want him dead. He's responsible for our life in hiding, and putting our Ancestors in lifelong isolation.

With the next step figured out, we spend some time getting to know each other's abilities so we can all be aware in a desperate situation. I space out when Havanna and Quill talk about theirs and their limitations; I already know what they can or can't do. Ender calls his abilities Blaze and Gale; one manipulates fire and one manipulates air. He's so proud, but it seems so basic. I'm honestly not all that impressed.

Perhaps that's just my first impression.

***

Someone or something is making noise, and it's waking me up.

No one is allowed to wake me up before I'm ready to. Whoever does always gets a tongue lashing, even if it's Sharifa or Masina.

Someone is about to get the same treatment.

I'm used to sleeping with just Wave with me. It was blissful to have the sound of rushing water lull me to sleep. But having others in the room helps one get to know everyone's sleeping habits—Ender snores monstrously loud, Quill mumbles incoherently, and the combined wheezes and snorts of our Bennarus create a high-pitched chorus. Somehow, my brain is able to tune those out. This particular sound is a huff, a sniff, and a whimper, but not in that exact order.

Havanna's movements in her bed on the floor next to me capture my attention. Her back is turned to me as she lifts up her arm to wipe something from her face. I'm still half asleep, but I need her to shut up.

And there's that sniffle.

She's crying.

Her crying woke me up.

That Doofus.

I don't know what she's crying about at this time of night. Perhaps she's getting worked up over Quill, or she's realizing he may not feel something for her after all. Perhaps he doesn't like girls either. I know how that feels.

Or I offended her with something I said, as I have the tendency to do.

When I asked her why she wanted to be the one to deliver the final blow to the Dormant King, she looked at me like I was out of line to ask. Whatever her reasons are, it's more important to her than anything else.

Why am I even trying to figure it out? This is her problem, not mine.

I'm too tired to deliver the tongue lashing.

I pull the blanket over my head to cover my ears. She'll stop eventually. Right now, though, I want to go back to sleep and wake up when I want to.

***

Early mornings are my least favorite.

Yet, here we are, awake at the crack of dawn, getting ready to leave to find the location on the map. Flame turns into a huge tiger, bigger than Wave's jaguar form, and manages to carry Ender's abnormally heavy frame. Wave waits with Bolt and Koa, who have morphed into horses. Tena has her arms wrapped around her son, squeezing the life out of him. Her body shakes as she sobs into his chest and he affectionately holds her as long as she desires. He leans his head against hers as he kisses her hair and rubs his hand up and down her back. The sight warms my heart, while at the same time, it pains me. That kind of relationship has been missing in my life. I wanted it from Masina, but the simple fact that I wasn't her biological daughter was the wall she couldn't overcome.

As far as my biological mother goes, she's dead to me.

Havanna walks in from taking her stuff to attach to Bolt's body. "Move faster," she commands as I'm grabbing my trident and Quill is tying his hair up into a bun.

I scoff in response. "I would move faster if you didn't wake me up in the middle of the night."

"How did I wake you up?"

I march up to her and say in a low voice, "I don't know if you were crying about Quill, but if you were, you need to snap out of it. He's just a boy."

Havanna is visibly angry with her now-reddened cheeks. Sleep deprivation only enhances my unpleasant personality, which doesn't bode well for her. "It wasn't about him, you Wench."

"*Wet* Wench," I correct. "What were you crying about then?"

She averts her gaze to the side and pinches her lips so tight that her eyes close in pain. "Like *you* would care," she mutters with a shaky voice.

Before I get a word in, she turns her back to me.

Any other person with a hint of compassion would be offended by her assumption. With my crappy mood mixed with my usual attitude, she makes a good point.

I follow her lead back to my Bennaru, and my eyes unexpectedly find Ender's. His lips are a straight line, a sign of disappointment. I don't miss it when he very subtly shakes his head at me. Just from that, I know he heard our conversation and thought I should have handled it better. Perhaps he's right. But I don't have it in me to care.

Deep down, I know I should.

Since the Tyranodrake is located at the opening where we came in, Ender leads us to the side of the mountain where the jagged tapestry of Stoneland Hills looms over the path below. I almost forgot about the fact that the entire mountain base is surrounded with barbed wire until we arrived. I don't understand how Ender expects us and our Bennarus to jump over it; it's taller than we are.

Ender leaps off Flame's back and approaches the sharp metal wires. He holds his hand out while his eyes turn a deep red. Fire pours out of the flame mark on his palm that I never noticed before. The wires melt to the point where they split daintily and fall to the ground.

He and Flame cross the opening first, followed by me, Bolt, and Koa. I turn to see what he will do to put it back together.

With his hand out again, he makes a swirl motion with his wrist. A powerful gust of air rises from the ground and lifts the melted wires. While the air keeps them held up, he uses his heat abilities to mend the wires back together. Good as new.

I have to admit, that was impressive.

That is, until Ender turns to look at me directly and shows his idiotic ego with a wink.

"Let's carry on."

We make our way down the mountain. Bolt and Koa are more cautious with their skinny legs and hooves, catching onto grooves in the rock to keep from sliding down the steep parts.

Ender and I are ahead of them, which gives me unwanted alone time with him.

"So, what you think?" he asks, pointing behind us.

"About what?"

He chuckles as if I'm denying I saw anything. "You know. I melted wires. Put them back together. It's great, yes?"

I roll my eyes. "Best thing I've ever seen."

"Is it really?" He shifts excitedly.

This guy really can't take a hint. "No."

With that, I make Wave move faster down the mountain. I want to get away from this overly eager giant.

We reach the bottom where the massive formations of Stoneland Hills cast a shadow over us. Havanna mumbles something to Quill about how she crossed this area coming back from Sabbia Desert. She's only been out of hiding for almost a month, how has she already been to the desert?

Oh well. I don't really care to know.

"According to the map, we need to head that way," Havanna calls over her shoulder as she points to the left. Before we can reply, she kicks Bolt's sides and he takes off in a gallop. Quill shrugs and does the same.

Wave and Flame clearly don't want to fall too far behind because they take off in a sudden run. My breath catches as my upper body is thrown in a whiplash. It's an abdominal exercise just to remain upright.

"You need to let me know when you're going to do that, Wave!" I shout as I latch onto his furry neck.

"Woo hoo!"

Flame zips past me as Ender raises his arm and cheers thunderously. His bellowing and the thumping of Flame's paws fade as the distance between us grows. Now I'm the one who's falling behind.

That idiot didn't even think to stop and help me. Jerk.

Being hidden and cooped up in Macaphin Village, Wave never had the chance to show me what it feels like to run at this speed. There's a certain thrill to it that I've never experienced before. The rush of wind blows my hair in a platinum river behind me, the air beating on my eardrums, eyes drying out, and stomach dropping—it's unsettling while also fun. A welcome distraction from the journey to war.

The bright sunshine peeking through the dark clouds illuminates the wide-open expanse of grassy field beneath us, all quiet save the rumbling of our Bennaru's feet. Gliding Condors—the biggest bird known in Petros—gather in the field with their black and white feathers. They take flight upon our passing and show off their enormous frames, their flapping wings creating large enough gusts for the grass around them to bend to its will.

A Swift Dingo blocks our path, causing us to screech to a stop. It gets ready to leap, baring its sharp teeth and growling. Fortunately, Quill takes it down when he pulls out his bow and shoots it within seconds. It collapses without a fight and lies motionless in the grass.

Conveniently, it becomes our afternoon meal. I'm glad Quill gutted it for us because there is no way I'm touching that disgusting thing. The men should be the one tasked with preparing the food for us ladies anyway.

Ender snaps and ignites a flame between his thumb and forefinger, carrying it like a match. He brings it to the wood and gets the fire going underneath the meat. Then, with both hands aimed at the carcass, Ender pours fire onto the meat to cook it on top. He does this for a couple minutes, all while keeping a relaxed stance. But having it done in this manner is the fastest way to get our food ready.

And, somehow, Ender makes it smell and taste delicious.

We eat in awkward silence. There's only one thing left to do from here, and no one wants to discuss it. I sure don't. There's no way to know what to expect. We don't know if this is going to result in one of us getting severely injured or dying or putting the entire kingdom in danger. The feeling is absolutely terrifying.

I need a distraction.

"All right, this silence is killing me." I throw my hands up, palms open. "Someone please say something positive."

No one says anything for a few seconds until Ender chimes in. "I can burn things. I like it."

Quill snorts. He leaves me speechless in his stupidity. I can't believe we have to travel with him.

Havanna takes his comment and runs with it. "What exactly do you like about it, Ender?"

Ender snaps his fingers to bring the flame back to his fingertips. "They do so many things," he tells us in a reminiscent tone. "Air and fire. Both are essential, but fire dangerous if you let it. It thrilling to take something like that and do anything you want."

He waves his other hand toward the flame and extinguishes it, as if to blow out a match to conclude his speech. He stated my exact thoughts on how I feel about my abilities. Water is essential in many ways, but it can also be dangerous if I let it.

If only the Macaphins knew what I was capable of. They would have learned to fear me because of that, not because I turned into a hardcore brat.

"What about you?" Havanna twists in my direction. "What do you like about your abilities?"

I shrug and motion to Ender. "He took the words right out of my mouth."

Ender nods with a stupid smile. "I knew we meant to be."

"For the love of Halivaara," I mumble.

She turns to Quill next. "And you?"

Quill thinks about his answer for a moment, taking another bite of meat. "I can get really creative," he says thoughtfully with a smirk. "It can catch enemies off guard. I find it very entertaining."

I quirk a brow. "Even when you're about to die? Like with the Mulhutna and Tyranodrake? If I remember correctly, you weren't all that entertained."

"Neither were you the first time I used it on you," he retorts. "It's fun to see how it works on people."

"Yes, that was loads of fun," I deadpan. In reality, it was scary the first time I heard his voice in my head. Now that I know what was happening, and that I can respond, it's amazing.

"You're last, Zappy," Quill says.

Havanna leans over in thought, coursing electricity to her hand. Her fingers move carefully around the sparks that have grown in her palm, watching the round collection of electricity shift and contort with her fingers. "No one can predict what I'm about to do," she answers with humor in her tone. "I can freeze someone in place or use Strike when someone least expects it." She closes her hand, the electricity absorbing back into her body. "It's odd, but I enjoy the feeling of being feared because they never know what I'm going to do."

Quill leans back against a rock, arms spread casually. "In short, we all enjoy having power and control over others' feelings and thoughts."

I cross my ankles and fold my arms, reflecting on everyone's answers. Ender and I enjoy taking elements that we survive on and using them however we want. Quill thrives on making others scared of him. And Havanna likes to leave enemies wondering.

Power and control.

"I suppose you could say that," I say in realization. "Is there something wrong with us if we do?"

Quill laughs as if that's a silly question. "Ha! No. It's fantastic."

"Besides," Havanna adds, "the Ancestors were created with these abilities." She shrugs. "Not our fault they were passed down to us and we happen to like it."

I chuckle. "Great excuses. I'll have to use those to my advantage."

As silly as it sounds, this conversation eases my anxiety.

***

The moment we slow our pace to a trot through a grove of trees, my anxiety returns in the form of a pounding heart against my chest. Vulca Mountain is in the distance behind us now and Siro is a mile or two to our right. Havanna takes the lead with the map propped open on Bolt's neck.

We're in this battle together. As much as that helps, my having to initiate the fight worries me the most.

"I think we're here," she announces nervously.

This spot, in the middle of a grassy field and trees, is an unusual place to find an archenemy. Perhaps he picked this area in the other dimension to make it harder for him to be found.

"When he comes out," Havanna coaches us, "put all your strength into your abilities. We can worry about Backers coming after us later. He will probably use his powers, so we need to give everything we have."

Quill and Ender take their time dismounting their Bennarus. They both stand up straight to exude confidence, but they're also holding a lot of fear in their shoulders. Even Ender seems anxious when he reaches for his axe underneath his cape.

I slowly dismount from Wave, breathing heavily with an oncoming panic. In the back of my mind, I sincerely hope this is the wrong location and that nothing happens. Havanna might be right and the Dormant King actually is at Luna Island.

To prolong the oncoming disaster, I take two bottles of water attached to my leg and drink them both within seconds. It's not a good idea to go into battle without a way to access Upsurge. Without it, my body has no way of using and shaping water the way I need to.

"Anara."

Havanna steps up to me and grabs my shoulders. Her eye contact is determined, and the most sincere I have seen her since she and Quill talked to me in Voda Cave.

"We're right behind you. We're fighting this with you, no matter what happens."

I glance between her, Quill, and Ender, who all nod with the same determination.

I scoff to hide the evident tension seizing my insides. "Don't be dramatic. I know what I'm doing."

Havanna's smirk indicates she's not buying into my facade. I'm not doing a very good job faking a lack of anxiety.

This is really happening. We're facing the biggest enemy in Petros history.

I really don't want to start this war.

But I don't have a choice.

I plant my feet on the ground to brace myself. One hand holds onto my trident, the palm sweating so profusely that it loosens my grip. With one more deep breath, I reach my other hand out. I pretend there is a Niminim in front of me that I want to get rid of. I imagine the ugly pest bouncing on its stick-thin legs and taunting me with its tongue hanging out. The image is glued to the forefront of my mind while my hand hums with a subtle energy, a low vibration that makes my entire body quiver.

A small speck appears above the grass, six feet in front of me. Then it quickly expands into a black hole lined with bright blue, large enough for me to walk through.

Our Bennarus all begin shifting to get ready to fight. Bolt as a gorilla, Koa as a wolf, Wave as a jaguar, and Flame as a tiger, and the bull standing with them in support.

Now we wait.

I turn around to ensure that Havanna kept her promise. All three stand behind me, their eye colors changing. She builds an electrical charge between her palms. Quill has his hand aimed at a boulder, his eyes a beautiful green. Ender claps and his hands turn into the colors of hot embers in a firepit.

They're ready.

And now, with their support, so am I.

CHAPTER 13

It's been at least a couple minutes, and nothing has happened.

Whatever does happen, though, I'm protecting Anara at all costs. Perhaps she won't see me as an idiot after this.

She, Havanna, and Quill are my compos now. I will protect them. But we weren't exactly prepared for what emerged.

A massive bull leaps through and runs straight for Anara with its horns aimed at her. She jumps to the side just in time while the rest of us yell and dodge out of the way. It ignores Havanna and runs straight to the Bennarus behind us.

Suddenly, it screeches to a stop right next to them. It snorts a couple times, treading lightly as it sniffs at them. They stay in their places, but their heads are tilted in confusion, trying to figure out who this creature is.

The vibe changes the moment the bull hops around excitedly, side to side. The Bennarus, neighing and chuffing, close in on the bull and rub their faces against its body. The bull nuzzles its nose in their fur, snorting and happily accepting the love. They all seem to get in each other's way while making sure they all receive affection. It's chaotic in a heartwarming way.

Then a familiar shriek causes us to turn our attention back to the hole. Before we process what's going on, the source of the noise barges through.

A whole swarm of them.

It doesn't stop. Dormant after Dormant pours out, outnumbering us greatly. They flood into a circle around us, closing in in a threatening manner. The Bennarus stop their reunion upon seeing this impending fight, and brace themselves to help us.

Anara hastily works to open other portals to send the Dormants back, but it's a fruitless effort. There are too many for her to focus on, and they're closing in by the second.

We have no choice but to kill them before they kill us.

"Anara!" Havanna screams. "Stop! Just close it! Close it!"

Anara closes her fist and the open portals disappear. She holds her trident with both hands and takes note of the situation.

Quill has arrows ready to pull, Havanna has her sword and shield in both hands, and my hands are hotter than coals. The Dormants have their tentacles ready, baring their teeth. One of them snaps its jaws in my direction in a way that makes me flinch.

I force the fire broiling in my hands to spread to my axe. The flame eats up the handle, all the way to the tips of the blades. The heat becomes so intense on the metal that it erupts in reds and oranges. I swing my newly ignited axe in a circle, enough to make them recoil slightly.

They haven't seen anything yet.

The adrenaline, the feeling of going into battle—and knowing I will come out victorious because of my size and strength—surges through my veins. It's the same feeling I have before a wrestling match with my Mulhutna compos.

"Any ideas?" Quill asks Havanna over his shoulder.

She waits a moment before responding. "Kill them all, and try not to die."

"That's helpful."

Havanna emits a war cry, the Bennarus join in with their roars, and the battle begins.

A horde of Dormants charge at me, their tentacles whipping around in a way hair does when floating in water.

Those monsters have nothing on me, yet they're confident they can take me.

I charge at them with my own triumphant yell that all of Petros can hear, my flaming axe spinning over my head. I jump and twist in the air, swinging my axe down with force. The fiery shock wave sends them off their feet and onto their backs. The grass burns up and only does minimal damage to the Dormants. I take the space of time while they regain their composure to spin in a circle with my axe as a final attack. They shatter into ash that coats the grass.

Dust is everywhere. Quill has control of a boulder that breaks down into smaller, but heavy rocks. It thrusts the rocks at the Dormants, while he uses his other hand to throw knives at others. Their shrieks become louder the more we take down.

Havanna freezes some Dormants in place, which gives me an opportunity to finish them off with fire surging out of my hands. Quill seems to hold his own until a Dormant flings a tentacle and knocks him onto his back. Slowly, it stalks up to him, growling ever so subtly while simultaneously opening its tentacles. I slam my axe down and send a fiery shock wave at it just as he braces for the Dormant's impact. Fire erupts around its body, along with an ear-piercing cry. I take advantage of its vulnerable state to use Gale with the smoke and toss the Dormant in the air.

"Shoot, compo!" I shout at Quill.

Still on the ground, Quill nocks a Pineapple Shell arrow and shoots while the Dormant is still floating. It turns to dust right away.

Anara uses Upsurge to use the water in her body to create icicles. She throws her arm back and forth to stab Dormants with it. They keep trying to corner her as she contorts water to her will. Her trident becomes a tool for control when she forms sharp points with the water and stabs them. But she's getting outnumbered rapidly, and she won't be able to fight them all by herself.

Since Quill is getting back on his feet, I make a snap decision. "Compo! Help Anara! Get ready!"

He seems confused at my request, but readies three Pineapple Shell arrows regardless.

"Run to fire, and jump!"

He still doesn't understand. He even doubts that whatever plan I have will work based on his narrowed brows.

I tested this many times with my compos. I know it will work.

He runs straight for the fire, and jumps. I use the air from the fire to lift him and he shoots the arrows at the Dormants surrounding Anara. Still midair, he nocks one more and hits another group.

A yelp sounds from my left. I turn to see Havanna trapped between two Dormants. One has a tentacle around her ankle and the other has her wrist and neck bound. They tug, pull, and fight over who will go for the kill. Her face turns red and only darkens the longer they choke her. Then it all changes when one of the Dormants wins the argument and she's brought close to its mouth. Another one of its tentacles blooms open with a dark orange ball glowing inside.

I use both hands to pour all the fire of Vulca Mountain on it. Its scream pierces the air, loud enough for the whole kingdom to hear.

Somehow it manages to keep hold of Havanna's body as it teeters back and forth from the impact.

A bigger attack is needed.

I clap my hands and form a large ball of fire and roll it toward the Dormant, leaving a trail of fire in its path. It collides with the Dormant and finally lets go of Havanna's body as it burns. Dust surrounds her once she lands flat on her back.

Quill moves a tree where the Dormants have him cornered. He bends the branches to use as weapons, but there are so many of them that they tear the tree down with their fiery attacks. He acts quickly to involve many more, this time intertwining them by the roots of their trunks to make one giant weapon. Dormants leap toward it, but they get swiped by the branches. Other branches extend and skewer multiple enemies, then throw them to the side.

While he controls nature to his will, I search around me for anything I can use to help. I see fallen leaves on the grass around the trees, enough to make a large pile. I take the opportunity to use Gale again.

I move my wrist in circular motions to create a tornado. The leaves rise from the grass, bending to the mercy of the swirling air around it. While I keep it turning at swift velocity, I move it to the Dormants closing in on Quill. They look up and around them in wonderment at the spinning leaves that block their vision in every direction.

Havanna uses this to her advantage and raises her sword. A spot in the partly cloudy sky brightens and opens up, sparkling with electricity that connects to her weapon. Once she's ready, she spins with her electrified sword. Multiple bolts of lightning strike the Dormants, turning them to dust in one hit.

Their numbers have reduced. Our environment has quieted drastically, but I have an eerie feeling we're not out of the thick of it. They may still be lying in wait somewhere, sneaky as a Swift Dingo.

Out of nowhere, a gasp escapes Anara as a Dormant knocks her onto her back. Her trident lands far enough away that she won't be able to retrieve it.

Time to prove myself.

I run at full speed and in wide strides to get in between Anara and the Dormant that is about to kill her. Her hands refuse to form water, a sure sign that she's dehydrated, and there's not a spot of liquid in sight.

I have to reach her.

I get down to my knees and slide in front of her. I punch the grass with my flame-engulfed fist as hard as I can with a booming yell. A fiery dome barrier erupts around me and Anara. The heat of it causes the Dormant to run the other way, but they're not going to survive what's coming.

The impact of my punch causes the dome to inflate outward toward the Dormant faster than it can run. The dome overtakes it, burns it, and turns it to dust.

Finally, everything falls silent. Dust coats the grass in a thin layer, some of it sticking to our skin in an unspoken war tattoo.

Havanna and Quill stay frozen in place to recover their breaths while watching the thickness of the dust slowly dissipate with the wind. Havanna seems the most taken aback of all of us. The way this journey turned out has been unexpected. We're all paying the consequence of not listening to her in the first place.

Either way, we would have ended up fighting someone or something. And it was an amazing release of pent-up adrenaline. We may not have beaten the Dormant King, but we did win this match.

That alone is a conquest my tribe would celebrate.

I do just that when I beat my chest and howl in victory. Quill and Havanna barely even notice as they watch me, reeling from the events of the last few minutes.

I twist to see Anara, who has yet to recover herself. Her eyes hold a lot of fear, but also with the exact expression I've been yearning to see since I met her.

Pure admiration.

"You," she finally says breathlessly, "you saved me."

My chest swells with pride that she sees me as a savior, not the idiot that won't stop trying to impress her. I swallow any urge to show my excitement and simply speak from the heart.

"Only because you beautiful," I reply with a wink.

She scoffs and pushes herself off the grass. "You had to ruin it."

I suppose that response didn't help either, and now Quill is snickering behind me.

A snuff perks us up toward the Bennarus. The bull that ran out of the hole goes back to nuzzling his new friends while they lick it on the head.

They know each other.

"Wait a minute," Quill says, pointing a thoughtful finger at the scene, "that bull is a Bennaru."

A whole new idea to me. It makes so much sense. I recall how excited Flame was to see Bolt and Koa again, playing together in my home, just as they all are now.

"Whose Bennaru?" Anara shrieks.

"The Dormant King," Havanna answers in disbelief. "If all the Ancestors had one, and the Dormant King was the Power Ancestor, then this must be his."

We watch in mesmerization as the bull hops side to side to communicate with them in its own unique language unknown to us. Havanna has a point of who the bull belongs to. However, Bennarus never leave their owner's side. Yet, this one did.

"And how did we get swarmed with so many Dormants?" Quill asks. "Doesn't that mean the Dormant King summoned them and we found the right location?"

"Not exactly," Havanna replies adamantly. "He would have come out with the Dormants if he was in the vicinity. And if he really wanted to keep his Bennaru, he would have tried to catch him. The question is, what did he do to make him leave?"

"Perhaps he tired of living in dimension?" I suggest.

"No," Anara responds thoughtfully. "Bennarus stay in one place with their owner, no matter what. Whatever happened was bad enough to ditch him. I assume that he created so many Dormants in the other dimension that the Bennaru felt unsafe. After centuries of being there, who knows what the Dormant King is capable of creating."

The bull seems to be listening to our conversation and understanding what we're saying, because it grunts and dips its head in a nod. My heart softens at the idea that this loyal Bennaru felt so unsafe that it came into this dimension to get away.

"Says a lot about the Dormant King," Quill mumbles.

"So," Anara starts, "what do we do with this . . . thing?"

Havanna sighs and gazes upon the bull with eyes full of compassion. "He's a Bennaru. He's one of us now. We can't leave him." She turns back to us with a look that begs for our approval. "He obviously wants nothing to do with the Dormant King, otherwise he wouldn't be here. Perhaps he could be helpful in our fight against him."

Quill sneaks a side smile in her direction without her knowledge, one of affection and pride. It's a look that I caught a glimpse of when they spent time with my other compos back home. It's also a look I saw exchanged between them when they tried to lift Anca's axe when I turned back to see how they were faring.

The moment she glances back at him, he turns away from her. He likes her, but doesn't want her to know it. I've seen this among my tribe. I may know the reason behind his desire to hide it, even if he doesn't admit it outright.

Quill clears his throat and turns back to the matter at hand. "If he's going to join us, he needs a name. Like Kane."

"Kane?" Havanna asks.

"Yes. It's a powerful name."

"It sounds like cane sugar," I mumble.

The other three gaze between me with annoyance and at "Kane" thoughtfully. He stops paying attention to us while he gathers with the others, nudging his head against theirs without poking them with his horns.

"Kane," Havanna says, mostly to herself. "All right, Kane. I suppose you're with us now."

All of us and our Bennarus, plus Kane, depart from the battle area to set up camp in a more secluded area, and come up with the next plan of action.

Anara stays close to my side the whole time, even going so far as to loop her arm around mine for extra security. She never lets go and never makes eye contact with me. Just studies the ground and pinches her lips in a tight line.

I secure my arm close to my body, just so she can feel how physically fit I am. I may appear immature and clueless, but I show up where it matters. Every troll in my tribe would agree.

"Thank you."

Those two words give me a smile of victory.

CHAPTER 14

QUILL

Poor Ender.

Poor silly, helpless, clueless Ender.

For reasons I don't understand, he really likes Anara. Her biting wit and obvious disgust somehow drive him to keep trying.

Perhaps too hard.

He may need guidance from someone who is equally handsome and somewhat of a magnet for women. My experiences haven't necessarily been positive ones, but it helps me to better understand what attracts women the most.

He saved Anara, and the wall she's built has broken down a little by the way she walks in close quarters to him the entire time we search for a place to camp. Just when I think nothing can crumble that extremely thick, hardened heart of hers.

Ender calls us his "compos." It's the least I can do to be his compo too.

We find a good place for shelter next to Douma Lake just before the day turns to dusk. Truthfully, it's more of a pond, but it provides us with a nice supper of Carpies and Spiny Bass that Havanna uses electricity on so I can save my arrows. I give her a hard time about electrocuting our food for us, which makes her blush and smile. She's been blushing frequently in my presence. I haven't known her for very long, but she doesn't appear to be a "girly" girl who is obsessed with boys.

I don't know what to think.

Havanna and Anara work to set up the tents while I prepare our meal at the edge of the lake, a safe distance away from them. The only sounds around us are tiny waves of the lake splashing onto the shore, the birds chirping in a rhythm only known to them, and the distant echo of ruffling material and the girls talking. All else is peaceful, even relaxing.

Ender sits against a tree and watches all of us work, offering zero help. His mother did him no favors by doing everything for him his whole life. No wonder he debated leaving in the first place.

"Ender," I call out in a loud whisper. "Come here."

He rolls his head to the side while letting out a complaining groan. "I no help with supper. Gross."

"Get up, you lazy troll," Anara snaps at him as she lays out blankets inside one of the tents.

"I don't need your help," I assure him, ignoring Anara's comment. "Just come here."

Begrudgingly, Ender stands and walks over to me, obviously thinking this is a burden to him. He plants his butt on the ground and sighs, almost grumbling.

I shake my head and scoff. "Calm down, lazy troll. I just want to ask what exactly is going through your head when it comes to Anara. Why are you trying so hard?"

Ender grins sadly while leaning back on his hands and extending his legs that are as long as my whole body. "I think she pretty," he admits with a casual shrug, "but when I think I got through to her, she give me look."

I know exactly what he's talking about, but I desperately want to hear him describe it. "What look?"

"The one that says she want to be anywhere but with me."

Very accurate.

"She walked right next to you all the way here," I point out to ease the sadness. "Her walls are crumbling a little."

Ender suddenly leans up at the glimmer of hope in my observation. "You think so?"

"Yes. But—" I lay out my hand, palm faced down. "—you have to calm down. You're trying too hard. Instead of trying to impress her by flirting, just ask her questions. How she's feeling, how she slept last night, anything you can come up with. It can be a good start to a conversation. Trust me, I know."

The only experience I have with any of this is with Nyx. We were best friends, but it didn't mean we always had something to say every time we were together. We had to be creative and ask those idiotic, simple questions, and sometimes we'd laugh because it was so awkward. Of course, sometimes we irritated each other. During those times, I kept trying to reintroduce myself into her life instead of respecting the space that she needed once in a while. When I finally listened to her, she came back around.

Except I'm not following my own advice when it comes to Havanna. I need to back off, and I can't.

"You right, compo," Ender replies, leaning all the way down on his back. He rubs his eyes with the heels of his hands with a soft groan. "I can't help it. I have need to try hard, but it don't work. I no know what to do."

I toss the fish guts back in the lake, an action that gains an extremely nauseated look from Ender. "Just think of a question to ask. Like how she feels about gutting supper next time."

His lips curl as his face wrinkles in disgust, then he laughs. I chuckle as I rinse my hands in the water. Even though he's a Mulhutna, he has a charming smile.

But not as charming as mine.

"How about you?" he asks. "You and Havanna . . . friendly."

Oh no. This isn't good. I thought I was doing well with hiding it, but I guess not.

Anara mentioned it in Arythica, and I blew it off and said we were friends. Now Ender, the least experienced one among us, notices it too.

I've never experienced romantic feelings for a girl my whole life. Arbol Village offered no options for a potential mate, nor did I feel any girl would accept my broken self, thanks to my parents. Their harsh words—my powers have no purpose, I only exist to be Indigo's protector, no woman will ever see value in me—have been deeply ingrained. I never bothered pursuing anything with anyone. As hard as Indigo tried to assure me the exact opposite of what they said, my parents came in and reinforced their statements.

It's a vicious cycle. A tough one to break free from.

I keep my response as simple as possible. "I think she appreciates just being my friend. Nothing more."

"Do you think she feels same? Or you put up wall, and hope she gets message?"

He's more observant than I give him credit for.

I do my best to push her away, but then I end up missing our chemistry, and I can't resist touching her when I have the chance. The more time I spend with her, the harder it is to stay true to the mantra I've told myself. In Vulca Mountain, the opportunity presented itself to simply reach out and touch her hair. I just had to stroke her hand, just once. Once I got it out of my system, then

I could finally keep her at arm's length. The more I do that, the more she will understand that I will not give her anything more than simple camaraderie and friendship. That way, I won't have to explain the reason behind my actions. I refuse to get into that, no matter how much she asks.

I owe her so much for changing my life and giving it a purpose. But that's all.

"Are we eating supper or what?" Anara calls out impatiently. "Hungry girls over here!"

My first reaction to her barking at us is to turn to Ender with annoyed eyes. He just smirks, shrugs, and lifts himself up.

I still don't get his logic.

Ender starts the fire, making my task way easier as I cook the Carpies on a spit. Anara just seems bored when she looks off to the direction of the lake, ready to roll her eyes at anything.

Havanna stares at the fire with her hand on her chin and squinted eyes. "I told you all this would be a bust."

Anara groans in frustration and, just as I predicted, rolls her eyes. "Yes, you were right, you are amazing, we bow to you, blah blah blah. Perhaps we can talk about *anything* else besides how crappy you feel."

"Wow," Havanna says. "Such compassion. We almost got killed by a swarm of Dormants."

"And you don't think that's a possibility when we actually fight the Dormant King?" she snaps. "Use your brain for once, Electric Doofus!"

"I'm just saying, Wet Wench," Havanna counters, "that we could have stuck with a more solid plan and we would be more prepared to fight the Dormant King."

"All right, so we took a wrong turn," Anara says. "Who cares? Not everything has to be done perfectly or according to your timetable. There's nothing wrong with exhausting other options first. In case we need to rule out other ideas."

I see it from both sides. Havanna has all the proof of where the Dormant King is, yet we ignored her. At the same time, I, too, wanted to see the validity of the Dormant King's stanza in the middle of the map, and not above Luna Island.

"Why was stanza in middle of the map, then?" I ask, mainly to myself.

Havanna considers this thoughtfully and perks up her head with an idea. Her eyes shift upward while she smiles ever so slightly. "I think I know someone who has the answer."

"Really?" Anara says with sarcasm and disbelief.

Havanna pays no attention to her tone when she looks at me with a sly grin. "Yes. In Killios. I have a score to settle with him. If he cooperates, he can help us instead of trying to get us killed."

Immediately, I know who she's talking about.

I hold up my hand to stop her line of thinking. "Wait, Zappy. He led you to a trap that nearly killed you. Had I not stepped in, you would be dead, remember? How do you know that won't happen again?"

"There's more of us this time," she clarifies, then motions her chin to Ender. "Besides, we have a giant troll. If that's not threatening enough, I don't know what will be."

Ender sits up, eyes brightened in excitement. "You want me to fight enemy?"

"If needed, yes."

To our surprise, he beats his chest with his fist as he does when he's victorious in battle. "I accept challenge!"

Anara sighs in what seems like defeat. "So, instead of going to the Dormant King, we're going to Killios to beat someone up that may not be worth our time?"

Havanna glares at her. "He knows a lot about the Ancestors and the Dormant King. He will be worth our time."

"Enlighten me, Doofus."

She stares at the fire in front of us and sighs. "I went to see him because I knew he had information about the Ancestors and the Dormant King. Instead of helping me, he led me directly to the Backers Fortress where I was greatly outnumbered." Her tongue rolls over her teeth. "I want him to know his plan failed. And we're entitled to what he knows. I want him to know he can't fool me anymore." She looks up and eyes the rest of us. "He won't fool *us*."

"Well then," Anara says with an evil grin, "now that I know that this is all about revenge, I'm all in. Let's go to Killios."

Havanna nods, remaining thoughtful and letting the next step in our plan sink in. "Yes. Tomorrow, we'll go to Killios."

The idea is simple, but I'm very wary. I don't trust Arthur. Using Ender as an intimidation tool may not be enough to get our way. In fact, that may motivate him to bring us to another trap, perhaps a more dangerous one we can't fight our way out of.

On the other hand, if we scare him enough, he may do whatever we want him to.

The rest of dinner proceeds wordlessly in the most awkward way. Anara goes to her tent that she's sharing with Havanna without saying good night. Ender excuses himself soon after, clearly uncomfortable with staying awake with just the two of us. Now it's just me and Havanna. Alone.

Again.

I focus on the dying fire and ignore the itch to start a conversation. It takes everything in me to simply ignore her presence. I block out all the sounds of nature around me to watch the embers try their hardest to keep burning. The wood pops out sparks and the little remnants rise and fall back down.

"So, I have a question."

Uh oh. There goes all the mental effort to block her out.

Instead of coming up with a lame excuse to not talk, I remain polite. "Sure."

She clears her throat. "You mentioned you never want to go back to Arbol Forest. Why is that?"

I breathe out a harsh, irritated breath, and attempt a diversion. "Why don't you want to go back to Ketra?"

She narrows her eyes at me. "I've explained my side, but you never explained yours."

I use a great deal of self-control to avoid emitting a loud groan. It baffles me that she cares so much to learn the ugly parts of me. It's bad enough that Nyx knows all of them; now someone else wants to dig into that part of my life. I need to shut this down right away.

"You don't want to know."

She scoffs in offense. "I wouldn't ask if I didn't."

"Trust me, you don't," I respond in a more biting tone.

Havanna folds her arms defensively. "And how would you know that?"

I shake my head, continuing to avoid eye contact with her. I'm not getting into this. Not now, not ever.

"Because my past is the kind that can easily change your view of me. And believe me, you won't look at me the same way if I tell you."

"Again, you don't know that," Havanna argues, slowly getting more annoyed, "you might be surprised."

My fists open and close to calm the anger rising in me. I breathe in and out of my nose harshly, just to calm my panicking heart. I'm about to lash out at her, and she doesn't deserve it.

I refuse to become my father.

"I'm not talking about this," I tell her with a shaky tone to keep my rage in check. "If you know what's good for you, leave me alone. Just . . . please, leave me alone. Please."

I don't need to look up to know that I've just crushed her heart. Worse yet, I embarrassed her. She remains frozen in place, not even shuffling her feet. It's when she sniffles that I know I ruined any chances of becoming closer, whether it's as friends or more. That in itself causes a crack in my solid heart.

After what feels like an hour, Havanna huffs a frustrated breath and stomps away to her tent. I don't call after her. I don't apologize.

I just sit there. Being the coward I am.

She'll thank me later.

CHAPTER 15

ENDER

I have never been to Killios.

Well, I have never been anywhere outside Vulca Mountain, obviously. But if I have a chance to use my strength for an adrenaline rush, I won't say no.

Havanna and Quill are unusually quiet while we take down our tents. I'm used to seeing them banter, smile, and occasionally flirt. Instead, she's glaring at him and brushing past his shoulder. He doesn't seem confused with her actions at all, just hurt.

What happened last night?

Once Anara dismissed herself, I didn't see the point in staying awake. I didn't want to watch them flirt all night.

Now, the tension is palpable and extremely awkward. We compos must get along. I may be chief of the Mulhutna, but these are situations I know nothing about.

Anara, at the moment, seems more aggravated than she did when we left Vulca Mountain yesterday morning. Her eyes are practically on fire as she glares at Havanna's back and turns to the task at hand.

Quill told me to ask her simple questions, and that might open up a good conversation. He makes it sound so easy, but I'm having a hard time searching my mind for something to say as I slowly approach her.

I want to tell her she's beautiful. That she's amazing when she uses her abilities and her trident. That I didn't stay awake last night because I wanted to stay awake with *her*. That I liked it when she walked next to me on the way here yesterday. If she asked, I would have carried her, without question.

Quill's practical advice fades further and further in the back of my mind.

Anara is forcefully shoving things into a bag when I'm almost right next to her. Her soft grunts and frown indicate she has no interest in talking, but that doesn't stop me.

"I like water."

She immediately stops what she's doing and narrows her eyes at me. "What?"

I'm asking myself the same thing. I wanted to say something about how I liked seeing her use Upsurge yesterday, but it came out awful. My words are jumbled, and it sends my heart into a panic.

I try again when I clear my throat. "I meant . . . how you sleep?"

She sighs deeply, going back to forcing the tent in a bag. "Exhausted. Electric Doofus over there was crying last night. Woke me up and I couldn't fall back asleep."

Havanna crying and being obvious about her anger toward Quill, something might be adding up.

"She woke me up crying the other night too," she complains. "So annoying."

I give her a side smile. "You wake up to anything, don't you, compa?"

She scoffs. "She wasn't exactly quiet about it."

"Did you ask why she cry?"

Anara chuckles in a sardonic manner. "Ha! No. Not my problem. I'm sure it's nothing I can fix."

This is the perfect opportunity to share something with her that can spark a longer conversation. All because my aanu built the tight-knit culture I grew up in that fostered listening and talking things over. That practice benefited the whole tribe.

"Back home," I tell her, "we Mulhutna call each other compos and compas, yes? Because we family. We united. We laugh together, we cry together, we support each other, we mourn together. Everything, together."

Anara folds her arms, her lip curled in annoyance. "What's your point?"

"The four of us must do everything together." I motion to all of us. "We four united. We support each other. Everything, together."

Anara eyes her boots with a world of vulnerability and shame.

"I don't know how to do that," she admits. "I was never raised that way. I was bullied my whole life. So I never supported anyone. And no one supported me."

I knew there was something behind that beautiful wall that explained why she became so ruthless and numb to everything. She didn't have to make me new clothes for my survival, but she did.

She cares. In that hardened shell is a good heart.

"I sorry, compa," I say softly, very gently grasping her shoulder in comfort. To my ultimate surprise, she doesn't seem disgusted by it. "You can break pattern. They no define you. *You* do."

Those may be the deepest words I've ever spoken in my whole seventeen years of life. Anara just helped to express the deeper parts of me, the parts I rarely reveal to anyone. The Mulhutna are not deep by nature, but the human side of me compensates for that.

Her eyes soften as she searches me for guidance. An impressed smile plays at the corners of her mouth that she does well to suppress. "So . . . what do I say? Next time that happens, I mean."

I shrug, hiding the excitement bubbling inside me that she's having a natural conversation with me at all. "No need for words. Just be there. Simple tap on shoulder, hold hand, hug." I can't help but grin when I add, "Since you feisty, she be all right with you no talking."

My chest blooms with happiness and pride when her smile breaks through and playfully swats at my torso before turning back to packing.

I'm having too much fun to stop there. "How you feel about gutting supper tonight?"

She gags in response. "Just kill me."

That gets a genuine laugh out of me, even though I know she's being serious. Quill suggested I ask her, although jokingly. He was right all along. It was that simple.

All I can do is stand there in stunned silence, trying to hide my own smile.

"What does person look like?" I ask Havanna, pumping up my adrenaline by knocking my fists together. "So I can be on lookout."

We're halfway to Killios, surrounded by nothing but a wide-open field of grass. Siro is way off to the left of us and Vulca Mountain is the height of a large hill from where we are.

Most of the travel time has been spent with our Bennarus walking at a leisurely stroll, easing into the break of day. Kane sits on Flame's head as a shrew, completely transfixed with his new surroundings. His squeaks of exhilaration are nonstop.

Havanna's heavy-lidded expression and frown carved on her face haven't changed since we left Douma Lake. Bolt's slow stroll causes her near-limp body to sway side to side. She barely notices it, or cares. "Beard, muscular," she replies in a bored, monotone way and shrugs. "I don't know. That's basically it."

Quill casts a worried glance in her direction. "You've been acting odd all morning. Are you all right?"

Havanna twists to look at him, but says nothing. Just stares at him. Their quiet exchange is unreadable from my perspective; all I can see is the back of Havanna's head. Her silence speaks volumes.

"Fine," she finally replies, but brusquely. "Just didn't sleep well."

A cough breaks through in Anara's direction. "*You* didn't sleep well?"

Havanna's glare switches from Quill to Anara, and I eye Anara long enough for her to notice. My expression begs her to remember what we discussed earlier: show more support than irritation.

She takes the hint when her eyes soften again, and she sighs. "I didn't either. Had a hard time relaxing after the Dormant war yesterday." She nearly chokes on her words when she adds, "Did you?"

Her comment gets a nod of approval from me. She seems satisfied when she returns it with a hint of a smile and turns back to the journey ahead.

"I suppose you could say that," Havanna replies, avoiding eye contact with Quill and keeping her chin held high.

"Did your dreams of my handsomeness wake you up?" Quill jokes.

"You too ugly to dream about," I tell him. Then I bust out laughing at my own joke. I can't help it.

Quill scoffs. "I'm beautiful. I don't know what you're talking about. I *invade* girls' dreams."

Havanna releases a breath that may as well have contained fire. Her eyes match the intensity of her sigh because she looks extremely mad. Quill cringes and shrugs, then turns his focus ahead.

The urge to put myself in the middle of their issues rises in my chest. As a chief, resolving conflicts is part of my duty. Once in a while, a troll would lash out and punch me for getting involved. Physically attacking the chief is highly offensive, to the point where the tribe votes on whether execution is necessary. Aanu believed in giving them a chance to be apologetic before taking such extreme measures; I always made sure to follow his footsteps.

I would have made him proud.

The only problem a chief is never allowed to be involved with are ones between mated pairs. It's believed that those issues are private to them alone. They are most certainly allowed to talk to other compos for advice, but it is required to leave the chief out of it. Even if a romantic argument was thrown in my direction, I had no guidance to refer to on how to handle it. My parents never taught me. Perhaps that explains my poor skills in talking to Anara.

I have no choice but to apply the same rule here—stay out of it. Let them resolve it themselves.

"We should probably go the rest of the way on foot," Havanna suggests. "We don't want them seeing our Bennarus. We're far enough away that no one can see them shift."

We dismount and let them change forms.

"I almost got mauled by a Swift Dingo on the way there last time," she adds. "Be on the lookout."

"How did you *almost* get mauled?" Anara asks in a snarky tone. "Usually you do or you don't."

Havanna rolls her eyes as we walk through the tall grass toward the stone walls that make up Killios. "It jumped at me and Bolt turned into a gorilla and killed it before it got me." She turns to her shoulder and strokes his mouse head. "I would have been dead if he weren't there."

I examine Kane as a shrew as he now rests on Anara's shoulder with Wave's frog form. He willingly ditched his owner, which leaves him with no choice but to fend for himself.

The Dormant King has a whole army of Dormants. He doesn't require any more protection than that.

"Oh, when we arrive, you guys need to guard me," Havanna says, which garners an odd look from all of us. "It's to avoid being recognized," she explains in an exasperated way. "If Arthur sees me, he will probably run. But he won't recognize any of you. So you will all need to surround me as we go in. I don't want them to suspect anything."

"What about me?" Quill asks. "I'm strong enough to protect you."

"Your ego could use a break," she retorts, then diverts her attention to me and Anara.

She goes on to warn us about the two guards that stand outside the entrance. "As long as we tell them we're there to see Arthur and have news about the Dormant King's whereabouts, they will probably let us in."

"But," I bring up with doubt, "we no have news about Dormant King's whereabouts."

Havanna rolls her eyes and hangs her head. "I'm too tired to respond to that. Anara, can you explain it to him?"

Anara turns to me with a compassionate half smile that is a huge contrast to the disgusted expressions of the past. "That's the point, Fireball. We're lying so we can get in."

I never lied much growing up. We, as Mulhutna, are always honest with each other. I'm not going to be the one to tell this lie, but I will follow along. I suppose that's what we have to fall back on.

Killios didn't seem to be that far away when we started walking. From here, it's still a small dot. We've been walking for a million hours. My legs are burning from taking large steps and my feet are beginning to ache. I complained about it once a few minutes ago, but no one responded. I want validation for my pain.

"This walk taking foreverrrrr," I say. "I thought we close!"

Anara leans her head back and groans. "We get it, you don't like walking. You can shut up now."

"We *are* close," Havanna announces. "Calm down. We'll have plenty of time to sit when we catch Arthur and interrogate him. Trust me."

"Interrogation," I repeat the word with anxious anticipation. Suddenly, my complaints become obsolete. "Yes!"

Finally, *finally*, we make it to the front gates of Killios. I'm more focused on sitting than anticipating beating someone up for information. I should be more excited about the latter.

Quill and Anara walk behind me near my arms and Havanna hides between them as we approach the gates. The guards are as still as the pillars behind them that hold the gate up, but finally approach me when we get closer.

"We're here to see Arthur," Quill says as he moves in front of me. All they can manage to do is stare at my height and bulging muscles. I smirk at them, excited that I can instill fear in others outside my race. Make them tremble to my will.

"What business do you have with him?" one guard asks in an accent I can only describe as tall-sounding and odd.

"We have new information on the whereabouts of the Dormant King," Quill answers with such clarity that one would never suspect he was lying. I'm slightly astonished with how well he's playing into this story, with his stoic expression and loose stance.

"Very well," they say, and they slam the butts of their spears on the ground twice. The gate opens. Quill moves to stand behind me again and we enter the camp.

My whole life, I have seen nothing but rocks and stones. It was my understanding that the Mulhutna tribe only built with those materials. But I became awestruck to see the pathways made of rocks carved into perfectly smooth rectangles.

Havanna moves in front of us to take the lead as we follow the pathway that curves to the left. "This way."

"Obviously. This path only goes in one direction," Anara grumbles.

Either Havanna doesn't hear her or she chooses not to respond as we continue onward.

I pay more attention to how weird these houses look than the fact that we're confronting an enemy. I thought homes were only designed into square boxes and flat roofs, but seeing them with roofs pointed upward in triangle shapes simply baffles me.

The path leads us to a large, open area with people in black attire and armbands with emeralds in them. Everyone wields some type of sword or spear, and stands a distance from what appears to be human-shaped, stuffed cloth figures to practice their techniques.

I never learned combat that way. My aanu took a pickaxe and showed me all the ways to use it to get the results I wanted using rocks and boulders. He told me the concept was the same with his double-headed axe, which I liked using the most anyway. The axe accomplished more than a pickaxe did.

Havanna leads us to the biggest house I've ever seen on the right side of the training area, marching up the concrete steps without waiting for us. She has no plans to stop and knock when she unapologetically shoves the double doors open with both hands. The doors slam against the wall and she enters without a care about how this looks to an outsider.

The three of us follow suit, examining the small space. In front of us is a curtained area with a table and a tea set. The kettle steams with recently boiled water, and a teacup is halfway full of a greenish liquid. Two red velvet pillows sit on either side, no one occupying either one. A dining table sits off to the right next to a window, holding a plate with crumbs on it. The room is dimly lit with only a couple lanterns, and is frighteningly quiet, save my clomping footsteps on the wooden floor.

Another door toward the back catches my attention. It swings in and out ever so slowly. I know that doesn't happen for no reason.

Something doesn't feel right.

Havanna takes one careful step at a time toward the curtained area, where Quill is feeling the pillow's material on his fingertips.

"Arthur?" she calls out loudly in a singsong tone. "It's your good friend, the one you tried to have killed by a horde of Backers. Remember? Neat trick, by the way."

I hear a soft shuffling behind the swinging door. With the way they're preoccupied with searching the space, I'm the only one that hears it. Being as quiet as my footsteps will allow, I tiptoe toward the door, to the source of the shuffling, that has now tapered off.

I place my large hand gently on the door and push. It swings open and reveals what appears to be a very narrow cooking space. The tools are much smaller versions of the cast-iron pots and spatulas that we use in the tribe. The silverware is small enough to bend in half with just two of my fingers.

I don't see anyone here. But I'm positive I heard something.

A heavy object hits me in the back of the head. Someone who is really good at hiding is definitely in here.

In all the times I've been hit with the intent of making me unconscious, it's never worked. This person has no clue that it takes much more than a puny pan to make an impact.

I turn to see the culprit, but something wraps around my neck from behind and attempts to pull me to the floor. I grab the object to yank it off, and it feels somewhat familiar.

An arm.

Someone is trying to choke me.

This person is about to see that no one has successfully choked me.

The attacker groans and grunts as he uses all the strength he has to cut off my air supply. It's laughable how he thinks he can win this one.

In comes the beating up I've been yearning for.

I turn with my back facing the wall. His body swings in motion and knocks things to the floor in a noisy clatter. Voices shout on the other side, but I'm too focused on getting this human off me.

I jump backward toward the wall and slam his body into it. He still hangs on, but more loosely now. I do it one more time, just as the others storm into the kitchen with their weapons at the ready. The arm finally loosens from my neck and the culprit slumps onto his stomach.

With little effort, I grab him by the shoulders and peel him off the floor. Letting out my full Mulhutna side, I'm not very gentle when I pin him to the wall so hard that his body makes a life-sized dent.

The man's muscular arms explain why he was able to latch onto my neck as long as he did. His thick beard and extremely dark hair contain spots of silver; thick eyebrows hang low as he struggles within my grasp.

"This him?" I ask.

Havanna puts all her weight on one leg and places her hands on her hips.

"Yes," she answers with a devious smile. "That's Arthur all right."

CHAPTER 16

HAVANNA

What a coward. Hiding from us when he very well knows why we're here.

This is the perfect time to release all the tension I've been feeling since Quill pushed me away last night. I was so angry I cried myself to sleep. Just when I thought there was a perfect moment for us to connect, he ruins it. Pushes me away and leaves me to feel like a fool. Unfortunately for him, he's not going to win my affection back so easily.

Alas, Arthur's going to be the outlet for that anger.

"Havanna?" the slimy betrayer asks in a strained voice.

"Good to see you." I turn to Ender. "If you don't mind, get him on a chair."

"With pleasure, compa."

Ender takes Arthur off the wall and tosses him over his shoulder like a potato sack.

"Wait! Wait a minute!" Arthur shouts in desperation, punching Ender's back. "Can we speak calmly on this matter?"

This is making me so happy.

"Once you're in a chair and everyone has their weapons on you, absolutely."

Quill grabs two wooden chairs—one for Ender to plop Arthur on very ungently and one for me to sit in front of him. Ender grasps Arthur's shoulders to keep him still, tight enough that Arthur winces in pain. Anara holds her trident at his neck while Quill has a hand on one of the knives on his legs.

"Do you really think your friends can keep me from escaping?"

I sit in front of him, cross my legs, and lean forward. "I don't *think* they can. I *know* they can."

Arthur breathes heavily in anguish and frustration, his expression contorted in pain. I'm still smiling that we have him trapped. I can't help it. He tried to have me killed, and now he knows that was a massive failure.

To my surprise, he attempts to rise from his seat, kicking the chair down while doing so.

"Help! Hel—"

Quicker than lightning, Quill unsheathes a knife and holds it to his neck, and the middle prong of Anara's spear pokes at his throat.

"What do you think you're doing, Arthur?" I laugh and motion to my allies. "They can kill you before help even arrives. Which, to be honest, will do you no good anyway."

Quill uses Transform to make the chair's legs wiggle about until it walks a few steps forward, then backward, then freezes back to its original form. Arthur yelps at this movement until Ender shoves him back onto the chair. He sighs in defeat and hangs his head.

"You're so stupid," Anara tells Arthur with a chuckle.

This is going quite well.

"Before one of us pummels you," I begin, "I demand an explanation. I have a hard time believing Jael trusted you. You're a traitor." Arthur peers back up at me with nothing but guilt and harsh breaths. "I also have a hard time believing that you sincerely thought I wouldn't come back to hunt you down."

He twists behind him as much as his neck will allow and observes the other Descendants. All eyes are on him, causing him to shift his body uneasily and whine in panic. His mouth is a straight line as his breathing picks up. Then he eventually resigns to his fate.

"Very well. You have me. I will comply."

"Good." I uncross my legs. "But since none of us trust you, you're going to have weapons on you for a while."

"Understandable." Arthur shifts himself again to get comfortable. "I must say, Havanna, I underestimated you. You managed to find the other Descendants on your own, which is no easy feat."

"Cut the crap." I stand so I'm hovering over him. "Why did you do it? Why did you throw me into a trap like that?" My memory flashes to the moment I knew I stepped into the Backers Fortress, and I was greatly outnumbered until Quill arrived and saved me. Without him, I would have died. I owe him that much.

He's still in the grasp of my wrath, though.

Arthur's face changes, disappointed and ashamed. Just as I hoped. His eyes even shimmer with tears, but I don't count on those being real.

"I had a deal with the Backers," he begins with a quiver. "Backers infiltrated the camp and kidnapped some of my soldiers."

Kidnapping. The method they seem to use most. Just as they did with Lavi's son, if her story is true.

Arthur swallows hard, a sheen of sweat on his forehead. "One day," he continues, "while I was searching for them, I was blindfolded. I was taken to a corner of the camp with no residents. Once the blindfold was lifted, I saw them."

He has me invested in this story. "Who?"

"My soldiers. My *family*. Gagged, bound to a pipe, with Backers holding blades to their necks."

I swallow hard, imagining how traumatic that scene would be. How traumatized I would be if one of those soldiers was Jael.

I push down the bile in the back of my throat. I can't think that way.

"They threatened to torture and interrogate my cadets if I didn't help them in their search. And, to make matters worse, they wouldn't leave until I agreed. If I refused, I would have been responsible for the deaths of my own students. I didn't want to live with that burden. So, as much as I desperately did not want to, I obliged. They told me how I was to act, what I was to say and do. Everything was their plan." He motions to me. "When you arrived, one of the Backers pretended to work as a guard. I told him I found you and asked him to alert the other Backers on Luna Island, and the rest is history."

I remember all of it. Both Arthur and the guard looked at me in a way that sent chills down my spine. I've learned over the years to listen to that feeling, so I left as quickly as possible.

It explains how they knew I was coming to Luna Island. It explains how the Dormant King led me there and communicated with me.

"My sincerest apologies, Havanna. If it wasn't for that agreement, I would have vehemently refused. My students mean everything to me. I am not a deceitful man by nature." He leans forward and says with much sincerity, "If you are to take anything away from this, it is that Jael was right to trust me."

He means to be comforting, but it just pisses me off more. Had Jael known he was capable of betrayal, there was no chance she would maintain any sort of friendship with him. Part of the training in Killios, from what she told me, is to never let enemies use the ones you love to get them what they want. On paper, it seems doable, until it really happens. Arthur was tossed into that situation; their lives were in his hands.

He *had* to give in.

"What happened after that?" Quill asks.

He shakes his head shamefully. "Once they got what they wanted, they freed my men and took off. Not a word." Arthur turns his attention to all four of us. "I was always on your side, and I will continue to be on your side, if you'll let me. I am at your mercy."

My head says I need to believe him. My gut is the total opposite. He seems genuinely remorseful, and I'm empathetic with the choice he had to make.

But none of it may be enough to regain my trust.

I motion to the double doors. "In that case, how do we know there's no Backer standing outside waiting for the news that we're all here in front of you? How do we know you're not making this up? I'm shocked that with your knowledge of the Backers, you fell for one of their well-known tactics."

"Backers know how to use things with a lot of meaning to their advantage." He leans forward and adds, "No doubt you know a little something about that, yes?"

"That's how Lavi did it," I mumble out loud. She seemed innocent, even trustworthy. Then she led me to a Backers trap and she claimed to do it because of her son, whom the Backers were holding hostage.

Arthur's eyebrows knit in confusion. "Who?"

"Lavi," I say, as if he should know who I'm speaking of. "The researcher. She said she knew you, and that's why she was looking for artifacts related to the Dormant King. How do you not remember?"

He shakes his head. "My apologies, Havanna. I was never acquainted with anyone named Lavi."

As if I couldn't hate the woman more.

She lied about having a connection to Arthur and stooped low enough to drag her son into this as the pawn. I still don't know if she even has a son. Lavi may not have been her real name. How did she even know who Arthur was?

I threatened to do her harm if I ever saw her again. I truly meant it.

The only positive thing to take away from this encounter is that more of the puzzle pieces are connecting. We need Arthur's expertise, but not at the risk of getting killed.

"Excuse us," I tell him as I motion for the Descendants to gather by the kitchen door. I keep a close eye on him as we speak.

"I say we trust him," Anara says.

"What?" I whisper loudly. "Why?"

"He may be the only person we can rely on." She turns to Arthur, then back to our circle. "Like it or not, he has resources that we need."

"That was exactly what I thought the first time I came here!" I emphasize with my hands. "He's capable of setting us up for another trap."

"Then we need to pay attention to clues," Quill whispers. "Pay attention to his suggestions. We will know if it's another trap. Especially you, since you also know how they operate."

"What he say," Ender chimes in, pointing at Quill. Of course Ender has no opinion. He's just thrilled to fight anything at all.

I lean over to check on Arthur, who watches us with anticipation. I struggle to make the right decision after making so many wrong ones thus far.

"Besides, he hasn't tried very hard to escape," Quill adds. "He's cooperating now."

"Only because he knows we're capable of doing serious harm." I point at Ender. "And we have a troll."

Ender nods, his face in war mode. Anara's and Quill's desperate eyes rely on me to make a choice. They're the only ones I can trust. As long as we all look out for signs of betrayal, we can allow Arthur in to help us.

I release a nervous sigh. "Very well. Let's talk."

CHAPTER 17

All right. I give up.

Ender has earned my respect.

Most of it anyway.

I've treated him like crap since we met, which ultimately made him try harder to impress me. Well, when I was pressing my ear on death's door, he saved me. He was wholeheartedly willing to get hurt by the Dormant, but that didn't stop him. He didn't even think about it.

Something about that means the world to me. No one, in my entire life, has come to my rescue when I needed it. But he did. Only days after meeting me, he's taught me more than Sharifa and Masina ever could.

I can put up with his antics with that in the back of my mind.

The map is the center of our attention on the table in the curtained area, the five of us circled around it on the red pillows. As Havanna told her side of the story that led us here, I found myself feeling something very unfamiliar: empathy. No wonder she cries at night. She's been through everything.

However, she's doing this by choice, so I'm unsure how far my empathy needs to go.

On top of that, she's awful at hiding her current feelings toward Quill. Whatever happened when I went to sleep last night took a very wide turn. She has treated him with contempt since we left Douma Lake, and he has no sense of the reason why. Even when she recalled the moment he came to her rescue to Arthur, she barely acknowledged the part he played.

Quill must have really screwed up.

I'm not going to get into that. It's their problem to work out.

"Allow me to make sure I understand," Arthur begins after Havanna recaps her version of the story of Luna Island. "The voices you heard were strongest on Luna Island, but because the stanza about the Power Ancestor was in the middle of the map, you ventured there instead? And only found Dormants?"

"Correct."

"And this supposed Bennaru escaped and has accompanied you since?"

Quill flinches. "*Supposed* Bennaru?" He points at Kane in shrew form scurrying around the legs of the table. "That was a bull. That is now a shrew. He is definitely a Bennaru."

"His name is Kane," Ender adds with enthusiasm.

Arthur examines him on the floor. Kane sits up on his hind legs and sniffs in Arthur's direction, tilting his head to understand us.

"Very well. Pleasure to meet you, Kane." Arthur concedes, then turns back to the map and poem. "In that case, this poem sure steered you wrong."

Havanna's eyes scan all of us with an annoyed death stare. "I know," she practically growls.

"Then why is the poem in that messy circle?" I ask insistently.

"Perhaps the stanza was put here to complete the circle, not because the Dormant King was actually located there. Had this been somewhere else on the map, questions would certainly rise."

Havanna tilts her head at me in a mocking way while addressing Arthur. "Oh really?"

I inwardly groan. I know she was right all along; there's no reason to rub it in now.

Arthur raises a pointed finger thoughtfully. "There is one more thing to consider. When the Ancestors went their separate ways, do you think it is likely that they knew exactly *where* the Dormant King ran off to?"

The four of us look at each other for the answer. The only sources of information I have about our history disappeared with my parents. Sharifa and Masina knew the poem was to be kept with me at all times, but they knew nothing of the details of who wrote it or why it was done in a circle. I decided that if they didn't know, it couldn't have been important, so there was no point in finding the answers myself. My Ancestors and their generations lived in hiding. I was following their course of life. Why would I care about figuring it all out?

"I suppose not," Havanna replies.

"Then, perhaps a theory to consider is that his whereabouts were unknown at the time this poem was written, so it made sense to place the stanza in the middle. Otherwise, it may have been written on a different part of the map."

Now *that* was a new idea for me.

Quill, Ender, and I examine each other with a mix of perplexity and confusion. The Ancestors went to all that work to write a poem that ended up wasting everyone's time and effort. Not to mention that we almost died trying to find him, only to find that he was never there at all.

All right. I understand Havanna's frustration.

"Well, then why bother writing anything about the Dormant King at all?" Havanna asks agitatedly. "This just made it harder for us to decipher!"

Ender points at her in agreement. "I with Havanna."

"They sure planned that out well," I grumble, shaking my head.

Havanna tilts her head back and groans loud enough to shake the teacups on their saucers, then leans forward to bury her face in her hands. All we do is watch, speechless, as the agitation unfolds before us. Overly dramatic, in my opinion.

"Doofus, chill," I remark apathetically. "What's done is done. No point in getting upset about it."

She lifts her face from her hands and glares at me with the intensity of all the thunder in her body. "You don't understand. You have no room to talk."

She's right. I don't understand. It was never important to me to do so.

"All is well, Havanna," Arthur says, being the voice of reason in the room. "Now that we know what happened, we can form a plan."

Havanna straightens up and sighs to regain her composure. "Where do you think he is, then, Arthur?"

He cringes the slightest bit. She's not going to like the answer he has for her. "Where he's always been. Luna Island."

Havanna pinches her lips together to maintain whatever reaction she wants to hold back. She says nothing, silently stewing in her own head. It's borderline scary how silent she's being.

"As far as seeing him face-to-face, that is an easy solution." Arthur turns his attention to me, and I immediately seize up. "Anara, is it?"

I swallow hard. "Yes."

"You were the one that used your ability that brought in the Bennaru and Dormants, yes?"

"Yes."

"What did you call it?"

I have a bad feeling about where this is going. "Gateway."

Arthur nods and sighs before addressing us as a group. "I hate to tell you all this, but I'm afraid you need to go to Luna Island as planned." He peers directly at me and delivers the blow I knew was coming. "And use Gateway to bring him back."

"I knew it!" Havanna emphasizes with a fist pounding on the table.

"You can't be serious!" Quill shouts, rising to his feet in protest. "It didn't work out so well last time, and all we fought were *Dormants*! We're going to be absolutely screwed if we have to fight Dormants *and* the Dormant King!"

The panic I felt the first time I had to do this is coming back, heart racing and palms sweating. Once again, the burden of the Dormant King's reappearance falls to me.

Doing it once was bad enough. Twice is asking for a losing battle. That's just an invitation to let in another swarm of Dormants while adding the most powerful enemy in the kingdom to the mix. I barely survived the last fight; what if I don't survive this one? What if Ender isn't close by to save me again? What if my skills aren't enough?

The possibility sends a shudder down my spine.

"Arthur, that island is crawling with Backers," Havanna implores in a tone desperate for his understanding. "If we draw out the Dormant King with them surrounding us, none of us will have a chance."

"Well, of course," he agrees in a way that should have been self-evident to us. "That is a battle you will certainly lose."

"You could have led with that," I say through my clenched teeth.

"Then what do you suggest?" Havanna asks.

"Allow me to use an example." Arthur points toward the kitchen door. "Ender, get me the box of pencils on that shelf there, would you please?"

Ender whines. "I no want to get up."

Deep down inside that idiotic head is a good person, but he can be annoyingly lazy. "Oh for the love of Halivaara, Lazy Troll, be useful!" I scold him, smacking him on the arm.

That action earns me an eye roll as he begrudgingly stands and exits the curtained area. His heavy footsteps pound all the way to the shelf, his heavy huff of annoyed breath equally as noisy as he searches the shelf.

"I no see it," he calls out after a few seconds.

I plant my face in my hands. I don't know what to do with him.

"I can find it," Quill volunteers as he stands. I look at Havanna and shake my head in disbelief, and she nods in a silent agreement.

Quill brings a wooden box back to the curtained area with Ender following behind him. Arthur takes the box and empties the pencils out of it and onto the map. He does nothing to control the little pieces of wood that roll in all different directions in an adventure of their own.

"Imagine that I need to make corrections on this map," he begins, "but it's difficult to work efficiently with all the clutter. So, what do you believe is the solution?"

Before we can answer, he swipes his thick arm across the table and pushes some of the pencils into Havanna's and Quill's laps while the rest softly tap the floor next to Ender and roll endlessly around him. He does absolutely nothing to clean them up.

Jerk.

Arthur raises his arms to conclude this supposed presentation. "Same with Luna Island. You can't focus fully on the Dormant King if you have the clutter of Backers around you."

An uneasy feeling drops in the pit of my stomach. I truly hope he's not saying what I believe he's saying.

"I no get it," Ender says.

"What you're saying is," Quill utters with reluctance, "we need to . . . eliminate the Backers, and the Fortress?"

Arthur's mouth twitches. "That is precisely what I'm saying."

I believe now more than before that this man is on our side. There is no other reason he would go so far as to explain a plan as intense as this while considering how to be effective. He is, however, forgetting an important aspect of this plan.

He's not going to be fighting this battle with us.

"Ah yes, as long as you make it sound easy!" I exclaim. "Are you joking with us right now? What makes you think we will have the energy we need to fight the Dormant King after eliminating the entire organization? We have to be at our strongest if we're going to face him!"

"What she said," Ender says while pointing at me.

It would help us greatly if he contributed something other than words of agreement.

"And this is where my expertise and materials come in." Arthur rises from his seat. "However, I have a few things to do around the camp. Join me in about an hour with the soldiers for supper, then you're welcome to stay here. Get some rest. Tomorrow, we will reconvene. You will need focused minds to accomplish this, step-by-step. You all have been through a lot the last couple of days."

He has no idea.

***

The last thing I remember is falling asleep in a large room that fit the four of us with all five Bennarus getting comfortable in their small forms in the corner. The only sound was everyone's rhythmic, steady snores. Even now, that continues as they sleep dreamily.

Except me.

Havanna, on a small mattress next to me, wakes me up with her sniffles. Bolt as a mouse remains asleep. At least he can sleep deeply enough to not hear her. She's much quieter with her crying this time, but it fails to mesh with the boys' breathing. I can easily single it out.

My initial instinct is to tell her to keep it down and let me sleep. All the nights I cried in Macaphin Village, I received nothing. So I gave nothing to her when she cried during the last couple nights.

But Ender's advice from Douma Lake causes me to see this from a different perspective. He brought it to my attention because he obviously felt that part of me needs improving.

No need words. Just be there.

I take a deep breath. What if she pushes me away? I will feel like a fool and I'll never do it again.

Ender certainly has an answer for that too.

You can break pattern. They no define you. You *do.*

Crap. He's right. This is the first step to breaking that pattern. I think back to how many times I wished someone would step out of their comfort zone and be there for me. Perhaps that's what Havanna needs.

Yet, I'm so incredibly nervous. I still have an urge to have something to say.

Simple tap on shoulder, hold hand, hug.

The incessant overthinking hasn't stopped Havanna's tears. I have to act. It starts with me.

As silently as I can, I fold the covers off my body and lightly step to Havanna's bed. I stand there at the edge as an alternative for sitting on it. Ever so gently, my trembling hand touches her shoulder. She flinches and flips over in my direction, wiping her eyes. I retreat my hand quickly and hope she didn't notice it.

"Let me guess, I woke you up?" she says begrudgingly.

Normally, my natural personality would shine through with a witty yet mean comeback. That's the kind of relationship I have formed with Havanna, and it's my fault.

You can break pattern.

I place my shaky hand on her shoulder again in the most genuine way I can muster. It's clear I have never done this before. It's making me so uncomfortable that I'm sweating, and it's difficult to pretend that I'm not.

Ender has made me want to be a better, more approachable person. I do want to be that for someone, even if I've never been taught how.

Yet, through the muck of uncomfortable emotions, I find the right words to say.

"You can cry all you want. We don't have to talk about it. All right?"

The moonlight through the window illuminates her face. The tears on her cheeks brighten and show her brows scrunched together in confusion. "Are you being sarcastic?"

I lightly chuckle and shake my head. "No."

She covers her mouth. "Thank you," she squeaks out through her sobs.

The knot that I didn't know was sitting in my stomach breaks apart and sends relief throughout my body. She appreciates my effort. It's not going to waste, and I'm giving her something she needs that perhaps one day she will return when I need it.

She holds out the covers for me to slip under. All of this is so unbearable, but I'm cold, so I let her wrap the blankets around my legs as I lean my back against the wall. She buries her face into my leg, cushioned with her pillow, and continues to sob quietly. A world of sorrow and yearning is pouring out in those cries, and it puts a mild crack in my heart that is wildly unfamiliar to me. I'm feeling for these people, and I barely know them. As long as I remember that, I stay in my comfort zone and keep my hand on her shoulder.

She cries until she falls asleep. Then I fall asleep beside her.

And we never talked about it.

CHAPTER 18

QUILL

I went to Killios having a sour taste in my mouth about Arthur. He put Havanna through the wringer. Yet, he's had a sudden change of heart, and he's fully dedicated to helping us.

He's quite intelligent.

For most of this morning, Arthur has fed us a meal paired with piping hot tea that I nearly spat onto the floor before it could give me blisters in my mouth. Conversation has been largely engaging as he asks us questions while writing down our answers on paper. He wants details of our individual abilities, and the limitations that come with them, claiming this will help him come up with a plan that will flow well and will help us succeed.

As the other Descendants talk, Arthur takes me to a section of the training grounds that contains everything an archer would ever need for arrows.

Including Pineapple Shells.

"You're going to need a large supply of these," he tells me upon showing me the full barrel. "This will be the key to taking down all those buildings, coupled with Ender's Blaze."

I take off my quiver and examine the arrows I have left, which happens to be a large supply since my purchase in Arythica.

"I'm very well aware," I say with a knowing wink that makes him sink in regret. As long as that is the driving force behind his assisting us, I don't care how guilty I make him feel.

When I reenter his home, I take some time tying the Pineapple Shells to the arrows I have while Arthur converses with the others. I have a feeling I will be relied on to make those watchtowers crumble.

I have no qualms about that.

I must have been totally focused on my task, because Havanna has been missing from the group for a bit. I may have attempted to push her away, but that doesn't mean I'm not drawn to her. She's instilled in me a protective side that wants to make sure she's all right.

I find her standing in front of the stove with blue-colored steam billowing from a pot. It's an unusual smell that I know is not a meal being cooked.

"What are you doing?"

The pot is the center of her attention as she stirs the contents with a wooden ladle. I already am aware that she's angry with me. The way I treated her the other night was guaranteed to hurt and anger her. She doesn't understand it right now, but I have faith that she will.

"Making Battle Elixir," she answers in a subdued way, still avoiding my gaze. "I still get headaches when I use Strike, but they're getting better. Helps to have this on hand."

"Do you need help?"

"No. I'm fine."

Whenever a woman says she's fine, she's lying. I know this from experience. They just don't admit what's going on because they think their feelings won't be understood, so it's better to play it off.

Havanna is not fine. Her lack of eye contact and curt responses confirm as much. As a man, fixing a problem such as this is an unbearable itch.

I have to ignore that itch the best I can because even though I caused this, I can't fix it.

The least I can do is apologize, even if she will never know the reason behind my actions. I apologized to my parents for everything, hoping that may change their overall attitude toward me. The words are in my throat; I just need to force them out. I'm not apologizing to my parents; perhaps she will receive it differently.

"I want to . . ." I nearly choke. This is Havanna, not the vile, loveless people I left back in Arbol Forest. "Apologize. If I hurt your feelings."

She finally turns to me with eyebrows up to her hairline. *"If?"*

This isn't going as smoothly as I had hoped. Another reminder of my parents.

"Very well. I apologize for hurting your feelings."

Seemingly satisfied, she turns back to the pot. "Thank you."

The itch to further fix this is coming back. The only way I can do so is to explain myself. However, I'm going to keep it vague.

"I suppose I have a hard time talking about that part of my life," I say. "That part of me is still fresh, considering I left that behind not that long ago. I haven't figured out how to talk about it."

Havanna shrugs as she slides a smothering plate over the flames, then slides the pot to another part of the stove. "I suppose I'm more open about who I am and my past than most. I suppose I shouldn't have expected you to give me your life story after only knowing me for a short time."

I shrug. "Probably. Yes."

Her eyes roam everywhere around her except for any part of me. "I hope one day you learn to trust me enough to share that part of you."

With that, she leaves the kitchen.

***

We spent a few more hours forming a plan of action. Then Arthur led us to the training grounds to sharpen our weapons as an extra precaution. He feels that it's a good idea to have our weapons in the best shape. I groom all of my knives until they're sharp to the touch. So sharp that the Dormant King doesn't stand a chance.

Combined with our abilities, this war will work in our favor. Arthur's help is invaluable. Otherwise, we may have ended up dead before it even begins.

Havanna thinks it's best to head to Luna Island as soon as we have a solid plan and understand our roles in it. There is no point in delaying the inevitable any further.

Usually, she and Anara give each other death stares and have nothing positive to say to each other. As we gather our things in the house, I witness Havanna grasping Anara's forearm. Not in an aggressive way, but in wordless appreciation. Anara responds with a small side smile and walks away.

What just happened?

Havanna nods at our host. "Well. Thank you, Arthur."

He nods in return and waves farewell. We exit the double doors and descend the stairs toward the training area where the soldiers practice various forms of combat.

"Havanna."

She turns around to find Arthur catching up to us on the stairs. We all stop to face him as he stands in front of her, vulnerable and in deep regret.

"I truly hope, in time, I can regain your trust." He peers over her shoulder to address the rest of us. "And the trust of you Descendants."

I watch Havanna's reaction to the statement that seems to stem from sincerity and a desire for improvement. She lowers her head and clenches her lips while taking a moment to respond. She wants to trust him, but she's extremely reluctant. Even though he almost got her killed, he did everything he could to make up for it.

That still may not be enough for her.

"And, I hope you know that Jael was an incredible warrior," he adds. "Strongest woman I knew, that one."

She lifts her head and sighs. "You know, Arthur, after all the times I've been betrayed and lied to, I realize the only way to know if you're being genuine is to give you time to prove yourself."

He nods. "Time will tell."

She responds with a final farewell wave and we cross the training grounds back to the camp's main entrance.

"Once we're out of sight from camp, we can mount our Bennarus," Havanna informs us as we traverse through the tall, grassy field. She faces Anara with a hint of empathy. "How are you feeling?"

"Wonderful," she answers with heavy sarcasm. "Just freaking wonderful."

She places a comforting hand on her shoulder. "This is going to go a lot more smoothly," she says in an effort to ease the anxiety. "We have a better plan, and we know what to expect now."

Anara finds no comfort in her words when she busts out in a mocking laugh. "Whatever you say, Doofus."

Her face falls in humiliation and her hand slides off Anara's shoulder. As much as I can appreciate her attempt to encourage all of us, there is still something to be said about the possibility of at least one of us not surviving this fight.

I hope it's not me.

I need to survive.

CHAPTER 19

ENDER

Here we are. Facing our fate from the Tormal Cliffs. With Luna Island just a couple miles ahead in the middle of Agura Ocean. The most amazing, beautiful view I've ever seen. A sight I want to remember as long as I can.

Flame converts into a vulture while the other Bennarus shift into their bird forms, ready to fly us into battle. For the first time, we see Wave in the form of a large macaw. We stand next to our supportive guardians, bracing ourselves for what is to come the moment we set foot onto the deadliest territory in the kingdom.

I can't speak for the other Descendants, but I have been looking forward to this moment. At last, I can avenge my aanu and live by his dying words.

"This sure feels familiar," Quill says. "I was just here a couple weeks ago."

"Welcome back," Havanna comments with a perceptible snarkiness in her tone.

Clearly, the air has yet to be cleared between them. Anara shrugs upon seeing my observing them and simply turns back to the ocean.

"Let's practice Transmission one more time," Quill suggests. "It's the only way we will be able to communicate when we're separated on the island."

"We practiced all the way here," Anara whines.

"One more time," he says. "The more we practice, the better we will be at using it during the heat of battle. We will be multitasking, so we can't make mistakes. Otherwise . . ." Quill places his hands on his hips, dreading what he's going to say next. "Failing to do so might result in death. For one or more of us."

Those words happen to be the ones that strike me the wrong way. I refuse to accept that. We Mulhutna absolutely hate this topic, to the point where the reality of it is denied.

Havanna sighs a shaky breath. "No matter what happens, though . . ." She turns to Quill and Anara with worry, and a little bit of pride. "It was a pleasure to meet all of you."

She's about to make me tear up. And big-boy Ender does not cry.

"Enough of this," Anara snaps. "We have each other. Now let's go take these guys down!"

"Transmission," Quill reminds us.

He brings two fingers to his temple. *Ender, head for the tower on the bottom left, as Arthur showed you.*

I acknowledge his command with a nod, then mount onto Flame's back.

Havanna and I will take the towers on the right, and Anara, head to the one on the top left, in front of Ender.

I respond to him the way he taught me, which took longer for me to learn than everyone else. I focus more on getting the hang of responding than the fact that I want to respond at all. It takes more focus to do the latter.

Wait, what bottom left? I finally manage to ask.

Quill has been patient with me since we've met, but I can tell there are moments where he's holding back from yelling in aggravation.

Just stay behind Anara. You're heading to the tower behind her.

Stay behind Anara. With pleasure.

Havanna straightens up and sighs. Bolt eagerly awaits her as she climbs onto his feathered back. "Right. Nothing else to do now but to go in full force." Her eyes uneasily roam between the three of us. "Are we ready?"

Quill and Anara mount their Bennarus. Anara gulps down a bottle of water in preparation, then grips onto Wave's colorfully feathered neck until her knuckles turn white. "Ready."

This is nerve-racking, but I look forward to crushing my enemies under my axe. Writhing in pain as they beg for their life. I picture my aanu next to me, slinging the axe that I hold now, and winking at me with all the pride he can hold. That wink was the one gesture that confirmed his approval. That I was doing good.

I will earn that wink, whether he's here or not.

I let Blaze engulf my axe in fire, then I swing it over my head with the fire trailing behind it. "I ready!" I bellow from the depths of my diaphragm.

One at a time, our Bennarus leap off the edge of the cliff, flying right toward the war zone.

My heart pounds faster and faster the closer we get to the island. The buildings are being repaired from Havanna and Quill's previous visit, shown by the wooden beams and stacked piles of cinder blocks. The island itself is bigger than it is from the view of the cliffs, but the rest shouldn't be too much to take down.

My towering height alone will hopefully be enough to scare Backers away.

A boom echoes, and soon, a large, metal ball soars in our direction. We dodge it easily, along with a flurry of arrows that follows.

This is going to be awesome!

I let out a war cry. When everyone else follows suit, including our Bennarus, I'm more ready than I ever was before.

Quill shoots Pineapple Shell arrows at a watchtower, and chaos ensues.

Flame banks left toward our assigned destination. From the corner of my eye, Backers sprinkle out of the crumbling buildings, falling with the broken pieces. I lose track of where everyone else goes as Flame swoops lower.

Our homes crumbled the exact same way when Backers invaded our village and killed Aanu. This time, they're getting a taste of their own medicine.

"Flame!" I call out. "We do this for Aanu!"

He caws loudly and I prepare to play my part of Arthur's plan. We swerve in all directions as arrows fly at us. White figures run amok in their watchtowers while one group of them spins a cannon to aim through an open hole in the ruined structure.

Havanna warned us that they used these on her and the cannonballs were so strong that she couldn't use Gridlock on them. I know this well. One cannonball can blast away an entire cliffside.

Flame flies down low enough for me to hop off and do a somersault on the ground, my cape flowing behind me. Blaze courses through my veins straight to the mark on my palm. My hands come together to form balls of fire that I throw to another watchtower. The *boom* it causes sends adrenaline from my legs up to my arms, where I excitedly create more rolling balls of fire in succession. Dust billows from the foundation, Backers fail to escape it on time, especially when Flame shifts to a tiger and attacks anyone the rubble missed.

A crowd of white comes at me with glowing blades armed and ready. Fire engulfs both my fists now, hot and powerful. I punch the ground, double fisted, and send a dome of fire in their direction. More push through toward me, stomping and running over the corpses that fell to my power. Callous and uncaring.

They're not compos at all.

I reach behind me to grasp my axe, sending fire along the handle and to the blades. I swing it back and forth, then spin in a circle. The weight of my weapon drives the force that brings me closer to them and leaves my vision a complete blur. I hear the fearful yells and shouts as my axe makes impact. My progress here is substantial; no one bothers to fight back.

They won't win.

The arrows stabbing the ground near Flame's paws tell me I haven't succeeded in destroying the watchtower completely. While he roars boisterously in their direction, I instead aim my fire toward the windows, just before they launch a cannonball at me.

Backers explode out of the window, but somehow freeze in midair before falling to their deaths. Havanna comes up next to me, holding them in place with Gridlock.

"Send them to the ocean!" she yells. "Deep enough where they can't make it back!"

We discussed this portion with Arthur. Make Gale so strong they have no chance of making it back to the island.

I focus on the ocean and the breeze blowing over the surface of the water. The wind stops and collects in one spot by a palm tree, succumbing to my will until it combines into one extremely strong cloud of air. In the control of my hand, I maneuver it until it rests under the frozen Backers. Havanna breaks Gridlock and lets them fall under the cushion of my working breeze, then takes off back to Quill.

Just as I notice their relieved expressions, it brings a goofy smile to my face as I shove the Backers to the ocean as hard as I can, their shouts of fear trailing off and feet kicking about as if that will help them.

They're too far out to sea. There's no saving them.

CHAPTER 20

HAVANNA

"Remember how we did this last time?" Quill shouts as I approach him from helping Ender.

"You shot arrows and I used Strike," I confirm.

"Exactly." He nocks three Pineapple Shell arrows with a nod. "Let's do that again."

"Just warn me when you tell my Bennaru to pick me up and throw me in a watchtower."

"No promises. Sound good? Good."

I smirk to myself. We work so well together in so many ways, yet he doesn't see it the same way I do.

Backers run amok in an almost humorous way. Their shouting commands at each other echoes down to us; they're panicked and afraid.

Good. They *should* be afraid of us.

Exploding arrows at the base of the watchtower do little to serve its purpose as Backers manage to escape and run toward us in a flood of white.

"Strike!"

My sword and the lightning in the sky become one, my new favorite thing to do. I whip the blade downward, where lightning strikes multiple Backers. I take my left hand and create another connection in the heavens, then throw that down as well, creating another bolt of lightning that hits more enemies. I switch back and forth between my left hand and my sword until all of them collapse.

Quill shoots more arrows at the crumbling building to finish it off. I get creative as Backers tumble out of the windows and use Gridlock on them to leave them frozen mid-fall.

"Quill!" I motion to the Backers. "Save your Pineapple Shells and get these guys!"

He wastes no time in reaching for his regular arrows and shooting in swift, beautiful movements, not once missing his target. I release Gridlock and let them finish their fall.

I twirl in a full circle to find anyone attempting to escape. All we hear are the distant booms on Anara and Ender's side, until flecks of white on the beach catch my eye.

On the north part of the island, Backers hurriedly push a wooden boat into the water and hop into it.

"Quill!"

I point for him to see, which garners an evil grin from him that looks so unbelievably sexy.

"That's really cute."

The rubble from our destruction rises, chunks building atop each other into a large pillar. Arms and legs sprout from the sides and the bottom and it walks in the direction of the boat. The arms lift at an alarmingly rapid rate, then slam down on the boat equally as fast. Shards and splinters of wood spray in every direction. Once the job is done, Quill lets his hand fall, along with the rubble that crumbles into a huge pile.

He turns to me and winks. "You may now tell me I'm incredible."

CHAPTER 21

ANARA

Arthur instructed us to leave absolutely nothing standing, even if all the Backers have been taken. Simply because if there are other Backers throughout Petros, we don't want to give them something to come back to.

I intend to do just that.

"Wave!" I call. "Join the others, and jump in if we need help!"

Wave billows into his beautiful, colorful macaw form and takes flight above the island, joining the other four Bennarus flying in the sky.

Some of the Backers have made their way over to me to fight face-to-face. I have no qualms about that; I can take them.

They circle me, but I swing my trident around my head and hit all of them simultaneously. I stab one in the torso, flip my weapon, and thrust it behind me to get another. Just before I finish off the next one, a Backer slices at me with her blade and I successfully block it with my trident. We get into an altercation that involves me trying to get her with the prongs, and her swinging her weapon at me, with each blow being blocked.

Then, she swings down and puts us both in a locked bind. She pushes her weight onto me. I shove back. All the muscles in my

214

body burn with the stagnant energy. My arms are close to giving in, my legs tired of holding me in place, and I can't help but yell out in pain. Everything in me quakes; the brat in front of me has the nerve to *smile.*

Then I remember a strategy I came up with when I was younger. One that even threw off Sharifa when I trained with him.

Now *I* can smile.

I shove her away from me and come at her, faking her out by pretending to aim for her head. The moment she bends forward, I deliver the final blow.

Finally, I defeat that dirty sock.

In one of the windows of the watchtower above me, Backers work to turn their cannon to their target, straight below them.

Where Ender is throwing fire at any and all structures he sees.

He's too distracted to notice that he's about to be crushed by a cannonball. He saved me; I need to save him.

Time to make good use of Upsurge.

Hand aimed at the ocean, I pour all of my focus into forming the water into a wave. Splashes and crashes of water increase in volume as the wave gets bigger and as tall as the Tyranodrake. I have spent many nights practicing wave formation, then calmly settling it back down so no one suspected a thing; I know I'm good at this.

The wave becomes so large it casts a shadow above the watchtower. I'm careful to form a sharp, knifelike peak, then thrust it toward the watchtower's window in a full stream. It worms around the top floor while I make sure it gets every single Backer in there in one fell swoop, interrupting the preparation of the cannon. Once it's finished, I split it into two streams. I keep one static while I shove the other against the watchtower as hard as I can. The heaviness of the water's volume breaks down its already decayed state, disintegrating to its will. It captures the pieces it left behind, and I return it to the ocean.

With the stream I kept still, I send it toward Ender, surrounding the area he just destroyed. The color of the water changes from a translucent blue to gray from the rubble floating within it, and spots of white indicating that I captured stray Backers. It brings me great joy to see them trying to frantically swim their way out of this massive collection of water I created. Serves them right; they should have known we were bound to fight back at some point.

I swing my hand behind me and send it all back into the ocean where the Backers can rest in peace with the wreckage. Give it a day and their corpses will show up on the beach as proof of our victory.

I used a lot of strength, mental and physical, for Upsurge, and I'm starting to feel it. For the first time in years, a headache forms in my temples. All I want to do is lie in the warm sand and go to sleep. Just as I did many times growing up.

But I can't. My duty is far from done.

There are still some homes and other establishments to raid, but I don't have it in me to use Upsurge again. I barely have it in me to lift my trident.

I hitch my weapon and run to the next closest home, then get down on my knees to avoid being seen. Wave appears as a frog on my shoulder while I peer around the corner of a ruined stone wall and come up with a plan while saving my strength for the real war.

The thing I have to remember: This is just phase one.

Anara, Quill says in my head. *I've sent Ender to find you if you need help. Havanna and I are fine over here.*

I keep my need to respond to him in the forefront of my mind, just in case I have to communicate on a whim. Bolts of lightning flash in the corner of my eye, and sporadic explosions boom in the air. Quill was being honest.

I scurry across the gaping hole in the wall and continue crawling. I hear shuffling feet against a dust-covered stone floor inside, and agitated whispers to follow.

I focus hard to talk to Quill, trying to drown out the background noises. *Send the Bennarus my way. I have a plan that requires their help.*

"Anara!"

Ender runs toward me after loudly declaring my name. I whip my head around to face him and hold a finger to my lips to keep him quiet. He screeches to a halt, kicking up a layer of sand in front of him, then I motion for him to come closer, but to do so stealthily.

For him, that's easier said than done.

"I think there are more Backers hiding in these houses," I whisper as low as I can muster. "We need to get them before they get us." I point to the homes around me. "I just told Quill to have the Bennarus come here. When they get here, I'm going to have them go in before us, and they will alert us if they find anyone. Then we can go in with our attack."

Ender points at half of the watchtower that Upsurge didn't tear down to completion, but got most of it. "What about watchtower?"

I wave my hand dismissively. "It's all right. I took them all down. Bunch of weaklings."

He chuckles at my overly casual attitude. "Very well. How we attack houses, then?"

I blink repeatedly at him. The way he baffles me leaves me speechless, and that is not acceptable.

"I just told you, Fireball!" I say in a forceful hiss.

For the first time since I've met him, he rolls his eyes as a signal that he grasped what I already said. "I know. We use weapons? Or abilities?"

Oh. That I didn't exactly clear up. His question is actually valid.

Tight-lipped, I answer, "Weapons. Unless the situation calls for us to use abilities, like if they start running away or something."

"Yes. Very good."

I smile excitedly at him, more and more grateful that I have him as an ally. "Ready?"

He nods eagerly. "Yes. We go."

His shuffling feet follow me as we crawl to a ruined house, just as Kane and Flame land next to us. They turn into their smaller forms and scurry ahead. A small hole on the bottom allows them to slip through. We round the corner to try to find a front door, if there is one, while also keeping an eye on our Bennarus. Commands being yelled on Quill and Havanna's side overtake the quiet on this side of the island. More lightning bolts shoot down from the sky with bone-shaking booms. Yelps of pain, bloodcurdling screams, and the familiar sound of broken rocks tumbling down follow closely after.

The Bennarus exit the home, then head for the house next door. We follow their lead, keeping low to the ground. This time, instead of venturing around the house, we wait for a signal. Which gives me the opportunity to reflect on what comes after this.

I lean my back against the wall and sit on my knees, staring at nothing. I carry a heavy burden on my shoulders, a responsibility that can't fall on anyone else.

It takes all the hate in my body to admit it. But I'm scared.

"I'm not ready for this," I whisper.

I feel Ender's concerned eyes on me. "Compa, we're in war. Too late to not be ready."

I shake my head. "No. About bringing the Dormant King back. It's . . . scary."

He turns his body toward me, giving me his full attention. "You almost did before. You can do again."

I pick at my fingers and release a shaky breath. His attempt at comforting me is sweet, but does little for my jumbled nerves. "This isn't the same, Ender. It was scary before. In the back of my mind, I doubted that we were in the right area, so I didn't think it would happen. But I still wanted to try in case Havanna was wrong." I chuckle in an unhumorous way, thinking back to all the times I've annoyed the crap out of her. "To be honest, I was relieved when we had to fight just Dormants."

Ender says nothing while his eyes soften in understanding. In this moment, where it's just the two of us, he's proving to be the listening ear I so badly need.

A friend.

CHAPTER 22

Ender

Seeing the pain and fear in a girl who does everything to exude nothing but confidence is moving.

Anara is taking this moment to show how vulnerable she really is, and practically begging for comfort. Exactly as I hoped she would do one day. The genuine sadness in her voice is hard to ignore. When she wrings her hands together so tightly they turn white, there's no denying her anxiety.

"Now, everything has led us here," she continues. "All the proof has led to this . . . place, and it's more real, you know? I will be the one that is responsible for whatever the Dormant King does. And if we don't defeat him, it just means he can and *will* attack the rest of the kingdom." She shakes her head. "I could never live with myself if the fall of the kingdom was my fault."

I was fortunate enough to have Aani my whole life to calm any fears I had, especially when it came to taking my aanu's place. It was an overwhelmingly challenging task to be a newly appointed chief. I was yet a man, and knew nothing about leadership, or about making the right decisions about anything. Aani relied on Aanu for everything; she had to learn it all beside me. I constantly worried about not living up to my aanu's example; an added concern for Aani. I needed him more than anything.

Now, Anara needs me more than she has needed anyone. I can show the chief side of me I have developed over the years.

"Compa," I say in a comforting, soothing way, "I understand. It scary. But, the more real, the closer we are to goal."

Anara lifts her head, listening with desperation. "So, what do I do? Despite your . . . personality, you surprised me with your wisdom the other day."

My mouth turns in a half smile at her backhanded compliment. "You need only do one thing, compa." I motion above us, indicating the situation at hand. "Understand that none of this your fault. Never will be. I no let you feel that way."

Anara smirks. "Taking charge of my feelings, Fireball?"

I nod in seriousness. "Yes. Now, remember one other thing." Anara's teasing face clears and returns to paying attention to me. "You bring Dormant King back, we stand behind you. You not alone. You my compa."

Anara's demeanor finally settles and she smiles appreciatively, something I have yet to see from her. It's as beautiful and bright as the sun.

Her hand reaches out to mine ever so slowly. My heart races in anxious anticipation, my body tensing as I await its destination. Then, her long, strong fingers grasp mine. Her pale hand is so small compared to my giant red one. My thumb runs over her skin, using a miniscule of my strength to hold her.

Quill was right again. She was coming around.

"Also, this Havanna's fault. Not you."

She chuckles, with humor this time, showing her perfect smile that I've come to adore. "You have a point there."

A series of roars from the next house over breaks our intimate moment. We rip our hands apart and rise to our feet when I hear Flame's familiar call, followed by one from Wave. With Bolt as a gorilla, the three of them scour the homes and tear them apart with their strong bodies, teeth, and hands.

Anara and I hop into the house through an open window, only to find Backers exiting on the other side. Just as I'm about to chase them down on foot, Anara has a different idea.

Her trident is in a tight vise in her hand when she holds it back. With an energetic yell, she throws it with all her might. It goes far enough to catch one of the Backers in the back, just as knives fly out of nowhere and stab the rest of the Backers, one at a time.

Quill appears on the scene with Havanna following closely behind him. Anara meets with them to retrieve her trident from the fallen Backer.

We stand in a circle, right in the middle of the island, letting the reality of current events sink in. Dust is thick in the air, mixing with the smoke from my own fiery destruction. Other than the sounds of crackling wood and splashing water on the shore, all is silent. No yells, no running feet, no booms of cannons.

I take a moment to use Gale from the breeze billowing against the palm trees. The dust follows the direction of the air, giving us daylight once again as it moves in one giant brown cloud toward the ocean. At last, our surroundings clear and give us a better picture of what we've done. The Bennarus, all in their large forms, run to meet up with us, nudging all our hands as a way to check on our well-being. Kane, belonging to no one, rubs his nose against us all.

Everything is flatter than it was when we arrived. Every single building has collapsed, with nothing left of the Fortress but debris.

The urge to beat my chest in victory is palpable, but I don't want to celebrate just yet.

"Did we get everyone?" I ask. "It quiet."

Havanna shakes her head at first while lifting her nose in the air to listen for any conspicuous noise. Eventually, she sprints toward the beach. Quill grabs the knives still stuck in the backs of the fallen Backers, pulling out the blades as easily as picking up an ordinary object he just dropped. He wipes them clean with his now dirty gray shirt, then neatly arranges them on the sheaths wrapped around his legs.

"Koa—" He turns to his wolf. "—all of you, check the island. No survivors whatsoever, all right?"

Koa snorts and runs with the Bennarus, the pounding of their hooves and paws receding with the distance.

"Um," Havanna calls to us from the beach, "we're not quite finished."

I hang my head back and groan. We already worked so hard up to this point; I want a break.

We catch up to Havanna and see what she sees. Unfortunately, she isn't wrong.

Rowboats full of white make their way to the coast. The rough waves toss the boats about, with water constantly splashing inside.

Finishing this is going to be easy.

"Hey!" I shout.

They turn toward us, then start to row faster, thinking they can save themselves. They have at least another mile or so before they reach the coast, and they're trying to run from four people with strong powers.

Their fear of us makes me laugh.

"Let's make this interesting," Anara says to Havanna with a smirk. Her eyes, along with the water droplet on her palm, turn blue in preparation. Before she can do anything more, Havanna steps in.

"Actually, can I?" Havanna asks, reaching her hand up with the lightning bolt in her palm glowing a bright yellow. "You might want to save your energy. And I need to use Strike so my headaches will go away."

I felt the same way when I started using Blaze and Gale. The first few times I was getting to know my abilities, my headaches lasted for days. My being big made no difference in how excruciating they became.

"By all means," Anara says nervously, motioning ahead of them.

Havanna summons the bright glow within the cloudless sky just above the boats. The crackles and sparks steal the Backers' attention. Their urgent shouts at each other indicate they know what's about to happen as they seek an escape.

Their end is inevitable, and it's glorious.

Havanna throws her hands down with an energetic cry. The Backers dive into the water, just as bolts of lightning make a direct hit on the boats. The force is so strong that it destroys both of them beyond repair. Broken wooden shards are all that's left of the Backers.

At least, that's what we believe until their white heads pop up from the surface.

"What?" Havanna screams in disappointment.

Anara steps in front of her with a knowing smile. "Don't worry. They're just stubborn. I can take care of the rest."

Havanna steps back and Anara takes charge. Her hands reach out in the direction of the Backers, palms facing up where the water droplet glows a gorgeous blue. On either side of the enemies, a wave forms and grows bigger and bigger. Sweat beads on her forehead, all the way down her neck. The Backers attempt to swim away from their impending doom with their urgent strokes and kicks.

"Can you freeze them for me?" Anara casually asks Havanna. "That would be most helpful."

Havanna smiles at this request. "Absolutely."

She reaches her hand out, eyes turning gold. It's hard to tell from this distance if Gridlock is working, as the waves move in all directions and block our view.

But none of us expected what came next.

"I'll tell you when to let go," Anara adds.

Anara's hands tremble, more so than they originally did. Her fingertips frost over, which causes me to worry she's slowly killing herself, so I step closer to her.

"It's all right," she says softly without looking at me, "I'm fine. I promise."

I turn back to the waves, and I see what she's doing. From the bases, the water begins to turn white. Roots of it sprout in tendrils and work their way to the top.

My eyes nearly bug out of my head.

She's creating ice.

Once the waves are frozen all the way through, and Havanna maintains Gridlock on the Backers, Anara proceeds to lift the glaciers off the surface of the water. Her breathing increases in speed when she causes the ice to rise higher and higher.

"Let go!"

Havanna releases Gridlock just as Anara drops the ice on them, immediately holding onto her temples. The impact causes a tsunami on its own with the waves rocketing up, then back down over the glaciers. The impact is so severe, it takes a moment for that part of the ocean to settle. All we do is stare in amazement at what she just did.

I think I love her now.

"That *amazing*, compa!" I exclaim as I take her petite frame in my arms and spin her around. She goes rigid to my touch at first, but she relaxes and wraps her arms around me too, giggling softly against my chest. My entire body loosens and melts to her affection that is finally showing itself. Her eyes try to appear disgusted with me, but the smile doesn't lie.

All the Bennarus find us on the beach and stand next to their owner with no sign that there is anything more to accomplish. Kane stands outside the group, head hung down and tail swishing side to side.

Poor Bennaru. Without an owner that could give him a better life. And needs to feel a part of our team.

Havanna waves him over to her, an invitation he happily accepts when he bumps his head against her hand. She releases a sigh that tells us our duty here is far from over.

Anara peers up at me, afraid for the next step. For what she has to do. The vulnerability she exposed to me earlier makes an appearance. Nothing I can say will help; I told her all I know, all the facts. Support can't be told in words. It needs to be shown.

She volunteers her trembling hand again, silently asking for my help. Making sure I don't fail to read her intentions, I test her reaction when I wrap a finger around hers. Her other fingers reach for mine, and I let them. My hand encompasses her whole fist, a somewhat symbolic way of telling her I'm here for her.

As of now, I make a decision that means my life. I will always be there when she needs me. Just as I will live up to my aanu's words to use strength for good, I will live up to my internal promise.

She is my compa.

CHAPTER 23

Havanna

I still can't believe it. We destroyed the Backers Fortress.

All these years of hiding from them, fighting them, running from them . . . it's all over. Nothing and no one remains. There are probably still some roaming around in Petros, but the number is no doubt scarce.

It all feels dreamlike.

All of us, and our Bennarus, turn to face the opposite side of the island. According to Arthur, that's where Anara needs to open the portal to ensure we have plenty of room behind us to fight without getting cornered.

Yet none of us move. Delaying the ultimate war that we are so close to starting. Anara may be the one to open the gate, but it's nerve-racking for the rest of us. The Dormant King's first move upon arrival is unknown.

I turn to Anara, whose throat is bobbing up and down and her hands are in a severe tremor. For the first time since I've met her, I feel sorry for her.

It was an unreal experience when she crawled into my bed the other night and comforted me when I had another dream of Jael.

Jael told me she missed me, but not to miss her too much because she was doing fine where she was. In fact, she was happy.

Then, the moment she told me she loved me—the words she hardly ever said but showed—of course I woke up crying. I was pleasantly surprised when Anara showed up at my bedside to offer a comforting hand, and an outlet for my tears until I fell asleep.

Something in her changed. She did something that made her wildly uncomfortable, yet she did it. And in that instant, she became a good friend.

A good friend who is trembling all over, scared out of her mind. I need to return the favor.

"Wet Wench," I say to break the tension to some extent, "it's on you now."

"Thank you for reminding me of my nightmare, Doofus."

Now *that* is the Anara I've come to know.

I step in front of her while her head hangs low and place my hands on her shoulders. "We will be right behind you. Just like last time. You are stronger than you know, Wench."

She holds back a smile as she takes a deep inhale, wringing her hands so hard that I expect one of her fingers to snap from the pressure. To my dismay, she looks behind her to Ender, pleading for his help. He gives her an affirming nod while mouthing something to her that I can't decipher, but something that is no doubt meaningful between the two of them.

Anara loosens her stance ever so slightly, clenching and unclenching her fists.

"Let's get this over with."

Then she moves forward. One step in front of the other.

We follow her all the way to the north side of the island. As she readies herself a few paces ahead of us, so do we.

I unsheathe my sword and allow electricity to run up to the blade, Quill readies his bow, and Ender takes hold of his axe ignited with flames. Our Bennarus, faithful and loyal, adjust their stances, their low growls displaying their hunt mode.

Anara lifts up and extends her hand in front of her. One last time, she turns around to be certain of our presence. She studies Ender in particular, though, insecure and still afraid. All he does is nod at her, the motion of his support. She turns back around, wind blowing her long, bright hair to the side, and focuses on the task at hand.

A black hole opens a few feet in front of her.

And we wait.

Seconds tick by, wasted by simply standing here. The hole remains an empty, black abyss with the blue border moving around it in a regulated stream. We wait, and wait, ready for the unexpected.

Nothing comes out. Not even Dormants.

My heart surges in dread. What if we got the location wrong again? What if he knew of our plan somehow and he's lying in wait somewhere?

"I don't understand," I mutter to myself. "Why is nothing happening?"

I feel Quill's eyes on me, watching me as I doubt everything I know and learned about the Dormant King.

"He's there," he reassures me. "He's just a coward. Like all enemies are."

Bow still held tightly in his grasp, he takes a couple steps forward, attention directed at the open hole.

"Where are you?" he singsongs mockingly. "If you're so powerful, come out and fight us! Coward! What kind of king are you?"

I smile at his taunts directed at the Dormant King. A reassurance that I'm not wrong. No reason to doubt myself.

I find myself following his lead. "Show us what you got, Dormant King!" I scream. "Come on! Hurry up and come out for once!"

Ender stands next to Quill and joins in the taunts. "You coward, Dormant King!"

The three of us are a chorus of insults that all blend together. A mesh of words that make no sense, but ultimately have the same message.

"You stupid!" Ender bellows, thunderous and frightening. "You no good piece of—"

Ender is suddenly thrown off his feet and tossed into a broken stone wall. His body sticks there, unable to move. Flame runs toward him and tries to grab his ankle softly with his mouth, tugging without hurting him too much. It does nothing; Ender can barely bend a finger.

Anara turns and sees this, just as baffled as I am.

Quill is next. He has zero control over a mysterious force that slowly lifts him in the air.

"What the f—"

"Quill!" I scream, leaping as high as I can to grab his ankle and pull him down, but I'm too late. He's thrown at lightning-fast speed toward a palm tree, where he yelps in pain as his back and head make contact with its trunk. He, too, is unable to move. Koa sprints to him, whining incessantly.

Then I'm the last to be lifted a few feet in the air. I scream as I'm hurled toward the depths of the ocean, but come to a sudden stop above the water. My breaths are rapid and afraid for a few seconds while I prepare for my death, but then I'm suddenly flung back to the island and dropped on the wet sand of the shore like a sack of bricks. The impact on the compact sand knocks the breath out of me, just as I see a large oncoming wave. It splashes across my body, which is equally as bad as being fully immersed in the ocean. I'm unable to move fast enough to avoid the contact, and it drenches me.

All I can do is look up at Anara. Nothing has happened to her. She stands in the same spot, keeping the hole open while staring in bewilderment at her incapacitated allies. I feel Bolt's thudding footsteps sprinting my way, then his gorilla hand grasps my arm and yanks me away from the shore.

Then, the horrendous source of the mysterious force emerges from the hole.

His hand locks Quill and Ender in place, his eyes a light purple. His bald head dons a crown of dark, intertwined twigs while the rest of his extremely pale skin is covered in black, baggy clothes that hang loosely at the ankles. The sinister smile on his face exposes his perfect teeth. Centuries spent in another dimension, and he hasn't aged a day. Anara holds the gate open behind him, gazing in disbelief.

This is, in fact, the Dormant King.

I've spent many nights dreaming about this moment. I had a lot of images painted in my mind—what he looked like, what weapons he carried, the kind of voice he had—only to wake up and find that it was all a dream. An unattainable one. I accepted that I would never find him.

But there he is, standing before us in the flesh, crushing every picture I ever created.

He's atrocious.

"Ahh," he breathes out, refreshed and relieved, his voice deep and growly. "It has been so long since I have seen the light of day. And so very long since I have seen the Descendants before me." He turns to Anara, smile widening in the most unsettling way. "Thank you for bringing me back to see it. Pleasure to meet all of you. My name is Alaric. I am the Dormant King."

He lets his hand fall to his side. Quill and Ender collapse to the ground while I attempt to recover myself. The gate behind him suddenly closes.

He curls his other hand and five Dormants emerge from the sand. With glowing eyes, he sends them a message, and they head straight for the Bennarus. One of them leaps for Bolt and tackles him.

"Bolt!"

He roars in its face and rips a tentacle off its body. He may be able to handle this battle, but it brings me such emotional distress that I start crying.

I can't lose my companion.

Kane holds his own, being stuck with these monsters for centuries. He uses his horns to penetrate their bodies and fling them to the side.

"Koa!" Quill shouts in painful distress.

Kane moves to help Koa, who's being held captive by a tentacle about to deliver its final blow. Kane and Wave tear it apart and turn it to dust before it has a chance to kill him. Flame does well to fight the others, but the Bennarus join to help him as a team.

Without them, this will be a losing battle.

"Oh, Kairo," Alaric says in a saddened tone when he addresses Kane out in the distance. "How dare you betray me after all these years."

He turns back to us, his smile creepy enough to induce nightmares. "It brings me great joy that I will see your faces when I finally copy your powers." he says with dripping arrogance as the remaining Dormants have it out with our guardians. He focuses his attention specifically on Anara, which gives us a chance to recover. "You bringing me here has just made my duty as the Dormant King easier."

Anara reaches behind her to grasp her trident, waiting for the moment to strike. I unsheathe my sword quick enough for the Dormant King not to notice. Ender bends down to retrieve his axe ever so slowly, and Quill holds a hand on one of his knives.

Alaric rubs his hands together with a cackle. "I take it you Descendants are here to settle the score? That is a battle you will surely lose."

Before I killed him, Darius was a spitting image of the Dormant King—arrogant, egotistic, and overconfident. He mocked me, relentlessly teased me, and almost killed me. I hated him with every fiber of my being.

That is exactly how I feel about Alaric. The Dormant King.

I can't wait to kill him too.

"No," I respond in a strong voice, "we're here because you deserve to suffer an agonizing death for all you've done." My mouth turns into a snarl as I think about Jael. "You—your Backers—killed my mother and best friend." I motion my hand to Ender and Quill. "He lost his father, and he lost his brother. You've done nothing but bring shame to the Ancestors. We have all suffered at your hand."

The Dormant King's sinister smile converts to an angry snarl, just like mine. I crossed a line by insulting him, but I'm too full of hatred to care. The moment his eyes turn purple again, I know I'm in trouble. He swipes his glowing palm from left to right to push us to the ground, bumpy with debris and rubble that greets our faces with great pain. Then my body is hurled up again, colliding with Ender and Quill, causing our heads to knock together. He propels

Anara from her place to join us, then sets us down as a group. My entire body feels as if I'm wrapped in rope; none of us can move.

"*You* suffered? *You*, Descendant of Lightning?" He clicks his tongue at me. "Pitiful creature, you are. You know *nothing*. I am the one who suffered. *Your* Ancestors brought shame on *me*."

"Bull!" Quill shouts, attempting to stand. "Not possible."

Alaric uses a hand to push him back in place. "Not possible, you say?" he replies, cunning and evil. "Allow me to tell you what truly happened when I lived with your Ancestors."

He leans into our faces, a rabid, angry animal. "All of you," he growls, "your Ancestors never understood me!"

He places his hands behind him, still keeping us stuck together. The purple in his eyes indicates the use of his abilities that somehow only requires his mental energy.

"Imagine spending centuries with the ones who are supposed to be your family," he tells us with a sense of sorrow. "You were supposed to spend every moment together. Create together. Plan futures together. Dream together."

This is all a game to gain our sympathy. It won't work on any of us.

"And through it all—" His tone rises, compressed rage showing its ugly side. "—when that family is supposed to include you, they instead make fun of you. Taunt you. Make you feel worthless. Even going as far as to make fun of your Bennaru." He shakes his head. "I couldn't stand it anymore. So, I retaliated. Copied the Land Ancestor's abilities. Attempted to take over the kingdom until I was banished. *Banished. Me.* The Power Ancestor. With no way of coming back. For centuries thereafter, I perfected my abilities. Transform to keep myself youthful and to create Dormants from the kingdom's creatures. Transmission to command my lovelies at will. Rearranging things to make my new world . . . comfortable, livable, with Manipulation. But, I had no one else to use Usurp on." His evil grin returns. "I'm so happy I saved that for this moment."

Transform has kept the Dormant King completely ageless? It's not just to create weapons and turn animals into evil creatures?

That explains his youthful, albeit ugly, appearance.

He leans in closer to us in an effort to intimidate, his voice a harsh whisper. "None of you understand what I lived with."

His eyes return to a darkness that reflects his soul, and finally we have the strength to move. His story—five hundred years worth of pain—sinks in while I take my time to recover.

Alaric is using the victim mentality. In a way, he *was* a victim. A victim of being bullied. A victim of harassment. A victim of low self-worth.

What he fails to understand is that half of us, the ones standing before him, have felt the same way. We fight against it every day and refuse to let it control us and who we are. We refuse to let it define our future selves. That is how far my sympathy will go.

None of that excuses everything he's done. The lives he's destroyed. Destroying the future of his generations and those of the Ancestors. All because he turned power hungry and fed himself with constant fury.

I tighten my grip on my sword. It's time to end this once and for all.

"No. You're wrong."

I freeze from my plan of attack and slowly pivot to cast a look at Quill. Anara and Ender do the same, as utterly perplexed as I am.

The Dormant King narrows his thick, dark eyebrows in Quill's direction. "What did you say?" he spits out.

Quill comes to a full stand, gesturing to himself. "I know exactly what that's like. That's how I've felt my entire life."

Wait. *What?*

The Dormant King is pleased with this, even relieved. "So, you understand. You know how I have felt for centuries."

Quill swallows hard, his eyes downcast and dark. "Yes. My parents hated me. Made me feel small. And worthless."

This explains so much about him. Why he's so closed off about his past and why he refuses to talk about it with me. He tells me to leave him alone, saying he has a hard time talking about that part of himself, and that it's "still fresh." Yet, despite ferociously pushing me away, it takes no effort for him to relate to the *Dormant King?* The enemy responsible for his brother's death and the whole reason we all lived in hiding?

I am absolutely enraged.

Quill is not the man I thought he was.

I don't know him at all.

CHAPTER 24

I've looked forward to this moment for a long time. Facing the Dormant King head-on and making him pay for my brother's death. However, I never expected him to understand what I have lived with. His reasoning hits me where I'm most vulnerable.

That's part of the reason why I won't open up to Havanna. She can't relate. Her mentor loved her as her own daughter while my parents wished I never existed.

Alaric's reasons for doing what he's doing makes sense.

He steps carefully toward me, his arms reaching in my direction, accompanied by the eyes of an innocent child. "So, you see why I copied your Ancestor's abilities. I snapped. I had had enough of their berating and the torture and hurtful words. I have to prove them wrong, even if they're in the grave. I am fit to rule this kingdom." He peers beyond my shoulder at the rest of the Descendants. "I need all of your abilities. To accomplish what the Ancestors never did. To gain what Halivaara failed to give me."

He turns his attention back to me with purple eyes, staring intensely into mine.

Only you understand me, dear Descendant.

There's no one else around me. The Descendants no longer exist. My tunnel vision singles out the Dormant King, only paying attention to his pleas for sympathy. He understands me. Finally, I've found someone who finds me useful. I have been starving for this kind of friendship for so long.

The opportunity to accept it is right in front of me.

"Quill." Anara's voice acts as a slap to the head. "Snap out of it! You can't possibly be falling for this crap!"

"Of course he is," Alaric responds on my behalf, tampering with a devious grin. "He and I are the same, and he knows it. We both have something to prove to the ones who wronged us."

You have potential, Quill. I believe in you.

Words I have begged to hear my entire life. My brother tried to instill that belief in me, only for my parents to snatch it away again. Perhaps Alaric isn't as bad as he's been made out to be. He has feelings, as the rest of us do. He just needs someone on his side.

"No, Quill," Havanna begs me, holding my bicep in a death grip. "Why are you even feeling bad for him? This is the *Dormant King*! *He's* the reason your brother is dead, remember?"

"Silence!"

He lifts her off the ground, a marionette dangling hopelessly in the air.

Shouts coming from Ender and Anara turn into a dull hum as disbelief sets in in an overwhelming cage. Everything I ever knew and believed in has become convoluted by the daydream the Dormant King put me under. He used Transmission—my own ability, the one he stole from my Ancestor—to force me to succumb to my own pain.

I almost sided with the Dormant King.

What was I thinking?

My whole body weakens just when the Dormant King shoves Havanna above the water, deep enough for her to not be able to swim back on her own. The way he made me feel is eliminated once he drops her in.

"No!"

I force myself to bring strength back to my limbs to help her, only to be stopped by Manipulation. He keeps me standing in front of him, taking full control of my body. Ender and Anara rise from the ground at his will, kicking and yelling, fighting against his strength, but to no avail.

We're so screwed.

Join me, Quill. You deserve so much better.

No. I can't let him drag me down to his level.

I can't let him win.

If I'm going to prove anything to anyone, I'm going to prove that I am stronger than I realize. One more thing Indigo taught me to believe growing up.

I can make you feel worthy.

"No!" I scream out. I shut my eyes so tightly that it gives me a headache. A loud groan bellows from my chest, ripping my throat to shreds, just to focus on anything other than the Dormant King's taunts in my head.

Take revenge on those who wronged you. I can make that happen.

"No!"

Don't let the Descendants hold you back. You do what you want to do, not what they force you to do.

"STOP IT!"

Alaric sighs in frustration. "Well, you have no one to blame but yourself for this."

My feet float upward, still unable to move the rest of my body. He sweeps his arm backward and I'm flung behind him where I fall on my left shoulder in the hardened sand. Ender and Anara remain stuck by the control of his other arm.

I roll myself over while trying to ignore the sharp, shooting pains along my entire arm. The Dormant King's back is facing me, solely focused on Anara and Ender, and completely ignoring the fact that Bolt converted into an eagle to fetch Havanna out of the water. The Bennarus are done with the Dormants and they can now help us.

This is the perfect time to strike.

I grab three arrows from my quiver and place them between my fingers. Carefully, I lift my bow over my head to nock them, but not without examining it thoughtfully.

My brother's bow. The bow Father passed down to Indigo. The bow I kept for myself when he died because it's the only memory I have of him.

He would grab me and shake my body if he knew the Dormant King almost talked me into joining him. That was the most foolish thing I almost fell for.

This is for you, Indy.

An angry scream and balls of electricity head straight for the Dormant King and throw off my aim. They almost reach him as Havanna races to rescue Anara and Ender, but he manages to drop them before forcing the electricity straight back to her. She dodges them just in time as they crash into some trees.

Then, hands spread out to the sides, his fingers curl in with a tremor. Havanna regroups with Ender and Anara as they watch the Dormant King in fearful anticipation.

That is, until five more Dormants that look as if they used to be Gliding Condors break from the surface of the sand. Gliding

Condors are already huge, but the Dormant King managed to make them as big as Ender. In the ocean behind me is a rushing sound, similar to the heaviness of Anara's waterfall. This, though, has a much more ominous presence.

I turn to the source only to find an enormous crab-turned-Dormant rising from the water, tentacles whipping about and legs as long as the trees in Arbol Forest spread wide.

In unison, the Dormants roar at us. An awful, screeching, ear-piercing cry.

Three lumps form in the sand on either side of me. Tentacles whip about as more of his bloodthirsty creatures rise to the surface, sand billowing around their dark and ugly forms. Not only do we have to fight against the Dormant King, we have to fight off a horde of his minions he has at his disposal.

"Turn back now," Alaric announces, "and this ugliness can cease before it begins."

I don't move in fear of the Dormants' ability to kill me in a heartbeat. The ends of their tentacles bloom as a growing flower, flames ignited and sharp forms of ice on the tips. One throw of that in my direction and I'll be the first to die.

The Descendants don't move either for the same reason. Everything has to be done rapidly enough before the Dormant King can retaliate.

My mind scrambles for ideas while the Dormants creep up to their master's side. We need our Bennarus to even make a dent here. There are a few moves we can start with that will unlock us from this position, but it's the outcome afterward I'm having difficulty with.

Without the Dormant King noticing, I redirect my focus.

Ender, create enough wind so Havanna can dry off. Havanna, use Strike on the Dormants. I'm going to tell the Bennarus to focus on them too. Anara, see if you can hit the Dormant King with icicles.

In the distance, Havanna writhes in the sand while letting out a cry of excruciating pain. Her skin is a deep, dark red that indicates severe irritation, and her eyes burn with a fury I have never seen before.

Screw you, Quill.

A brick to my heart. One more person I've disappointed once again. I sided with the Dormant King for a short moment, and that cost me her trust.

It will take everything to gain it back.

Using one of his hands, Ender summons a large gust of wind and sends it toward Havanna, followed by a breeze among the tree leaves that he forces to change direction to continue drying her off. The air is fierce enough to do so within minutes.

Then what? Ender's voice breaks through.

My question exactly. The answer of which still eludes me.

Then we do our best. Be quick.

That doesn't seem to satisfy him, judging by his downcast eyes. That's the best I have at the moment. My entire being is consumed with guilt and fury at myself, eluding my thoughts and focus.

I'm done with all of it. The Dormant King has pissed me right off.

Havanna's breathing heavily on her knees, one hand propping her body up and the other raised to the sky. Anara has her hand subtly reaching toward the ocean and Ender's axe is engulfed in a raging fire.

The Bennarus all come together, standing beside their owners, eyes narrowed in war mode and ready to fight.

We have our army; the Dormant King has his.
The Dormants scream and charge toward us.

244

CHAPTER 25

A lot of events have happened in a short period of time.

We destroyed the Backers Fortress. Havanna and I finished off the ones who almost escaped.

I brought the butt-ugliest being I've ever seen out of his dimension.

Quill was weak and beyond idiotic when he almost sided with Alaric.

He's proven his power within a span of a few minutes.

Now we're fighting him, and it's chaos.

Wave takes a huge bite out of a Dormant and throws it in the water. Bolt pounds another one to death. Flame leaps at the Dormant King only to be swept to the side like he was nothing.

Dormants are flying above us, carrying large fragments of the fortress ruins in their talons to drop on their targets. There's a lot of them—more than the Bennarus can take on by themselves.

I create icicles from the ocean and hurl them at the flying Dormants that dive at the Bennarus. They shatter to dust before their dead bodies can hit the ground.

The Dormant King isn't even close to being fazed by this. All he has to do is curl his fingers inward and summon more of his "lovelies" to replace the ones we kill. Everything we do he seems to cast aside with ease. We're going to be outnumbered. Our Bennarus can only help so much. The only way it will stop is to kill the Dormant King himself.

Havanna may be the one who wants to deliver the final blow, but I might beat her to it.

A large remnant of a ruined watchtower—big enough to make a dent in my head—lands dangerously close to my feet, followed by sprinkles of dust in my hair. I run closer to the shore to escape their attacks and create a wave from the ocean. Frost covers my fingertips and chills both of my hands. My finger-spreading motion sprouts small pieces of ice, sharp as knives. Working at the cabana in Macaphin Village as a card dealer comes into play when I flick shards one after the other, dealing cards at those monsters. It's hit-and-miss as they keep moving, but I don't let up.

The crab Dormant appears much larger than I expected. Even more so when it reaches its pincers out and snaps them threateningly at the Bennarus. They separate from tearing the Dormants apart to dodge the new danger that could easily break one of them in half.

When a flying icicle from a tentacle almost hits Ender in the chest, I decide to focus on protecting him. I cause the water to rise a few feet from the surface—an ordinary wave. I spread my arms and split the wave into two large sections of ice, an effort that causes the chilling sensation to spread from my hands down both my arms up to my shoulders.

A sweep of my arm sends the ice straight to the Dormant King's face. This *has* to be the move that impales and kills him.

I'm very wrong.

They don't even touch him. He is wise enough to have a Dormant shield him from the impact and kill it instead.

How pathetic. He has to have his precious babies be his bodyguard.

Ender slams his flame-engulfed axe on the sand to send a dome of fire toward Alaric. With an expression of boredom, he uses Manipulation to stop it dead and extinguish it by aiming it toward the ocean.

We are truly screwed if this is how this war is going to play out.

Quill creates a moving weapon with a nearby palm tree where the tips of the fronds extend toward Alaric, its roots acting as legs to propel it forward. All he needs to do is use Manipulation to stop the branches and snap them off the trunk. Quill forces new ones to sprout, only to be met with more defeat.

The dust of dead Dormants coats the air. Fire blooms from a Dormant's tentacles to catch the tree on fire. I use Upsurge to take out the fire so Quill can keep fighting with it. The tree continues to work despite its now-charred state, but not as strongly as it started out as splinters litter the area around it.

The tree stops in its tracks for a split second, then changes direction. Somehow, it manages to sprout sharper branches all over. New bark replacing the burned areas, smooth as a youthful and healthy tree. It moves in on Quill with its many knife-sharp branches and tries to stab him instead. He dodges and rolls out of the way, using milliseconds in between blows to try controlling it again.

It's not working. The Dormant King is too powerful.

Quill nocks Pineapple Shell arrows just before he gets stabbed and shoots the roots of the tree. It wobbles on its now unsteady foundation, waving its leaves back and forth. A strike of lightning breaks it down completely, and it finally falls over. More bolts shoot down and hit multiple Dormants for an instant kill. This affects the Dormant King in no way, his stance calm and collected as he summons more and more awful creatures.

Quill then becomes more creative when he hides behind a stone wall and forms pillars out of the sand and shoves them at Alaric. Again, Dormants block their master from the impact as the heavy sand squashes them.

The Bennarus are growing tired by the second. Still outnumbered, they dodge the onslaught of fire and ice, but their strength is meager when tentacles capture their bodies.

Alaric casually strolls away from the scene without a scratch, a greedy smile a clear sign of his victory.

"At least make this a challenge for me!" he bellows.

This needs to be an all-out assault, guys, Quill tells us in a fearful, hurried manner. *Give him everything you got. All at the same time.*

Off to my left, Ender sends fire pouring from his hands straight to the Dormant King, a river that torches everything in its path.

Except the Dormant King himself.

He sticks his hand out and uses Manipulation to build an invisible wall that blocks the fire from coming closer. His greedy smile grows wider. A smile that pisses me off with every passing second.

Alaric summons more of his minions from the water. Ender charges with his axe ready, fire trailing with every swing. The King lifts his hand just as he is about to hit him and a mound of pointed rock springs from beneath the sand to block the impact. Ender keeps swinging and more rocks appear to block his target. Eventually, he stops and uses the breeze around us to build up a forceful tornado. Alaric is laughing hysterically at this point, but I wait to see what Ender is going to do.

With the tornado, grains of sand float upward and join the spinning force of air until it becomes nothing but a swirling cone of sand. Ender moves it so that it surrounds Alaric and impairs his vision. Quill takes this moment to throw knives in the direction of the shroud, hoping one of them will strike.

It clearly doesn't faze the Dormant King. The knives make it through, but they're immediately sent flying back toward Quill. He dodges them and collects them upon landing to put them back in the sheaths on his legs. He looks in Havanna's direction periodically to check on her, and a knife comes flying toward her. My stomach drops at the scene.

Havanna's about to be killed. I'm too far away to save her.

Without a second thought, Quill leaps toward her, arm stretched out in front of her head.

The blade stabs him in the forearm, all the way through. Blood immediately streams from the wound and around the blade protruding from his arm, followed by a bloodcurdling scream.

CHAPTER 26

"Quill!"

My heart drops upon seeing the severity of his wound. Blood covers his arm and his screams of excruciating pain are breaking my heart.

I hate him right now, but I have to help him.

I grab him by his good arm and seek safety behind the wall of a ruined building. Without a second of hesitation, I rip the blade out of his flesh, which makes him scream more as it seems to be a never-ending flow of blood. I whip a bandana out of the pocket of his pants while I press down on the wound with my other hand to stop the bleeding. It takes a little time for the blood to soak my hands and pants, and it seems to get worse as I tighten my grip.

I wrap the bandana around his arm as tight as I can. My hands are sticky, his bandana is already becoming soaked, but I continue to try; I'm trembling in deep fear of losing him.

And losing this battle.

I force Quill to lay on the concrete foundation to keep him hidden, and peer over the edge of the broken wall. The shroud dissipates around the Dormant King at the same time as I spot an enormous portion of a fallen watchtower rising behind Ender with the Dormant King's Manipulation. He can probably maintain a great deal of damage, but an object of that size and weight is going to kill him.

"No!" Anara screams.

She points her trident at the beach and forms a protective wall that she sends in Ender's direction, just as the fallen watchtower soars toward him. She makes a circular motion so the water surrounds him, a strong, heavy wall of security. Gradually, the wave turns into a block of ice, just as the watchtower crashes into it. Ice explodes on impact, landing on the sand as soft as sprinkled sugar.

Ender breaks down the remnant of the ice wall with his axe and escapes, creating huge cubes of ice that Anara can use to her advantage. She forms them into sharp, knifelike weapons to throw them at Alaric, but all that does is stab the Dormants he sends in.

He's such a coward. For centuries, he used Backers to do his dirty work, now he uses his own creations as sacrifices.

Ender charges with his axe slung over his shoulder, but that proves to be a failure when Alaric lifts him up while simultaneously stopping Anara's flinging ice. He throws Ender in the ocean, far enough that it will take him some time to swim back.

"Ender!" she screams, then gives the Dormant King an intense death glare. "How dare you!"

She firmly grips her trident and throws it like a spear with all the force of her petite body. The Dormant King moves at the speed of lightning when he turns and snatches it midair. A perfect catch.

Oh no.

He spins in a circle and throws it back at her, just as easily as he caught it. Anara slides along the sand on her knees and retrieves it. She screams with frustration with every block of her blows with just his arm, simply humoring her.

Nothing we have done has worked since he arrived, and it's pissing me off. Makes me wonder if Arthur screwed us over once again.

I crouch to check on Quill, whose strength is bleeding out with his wound.

"Go," he urges me in a strained voice, "help them."

"Don't you dare tell me what to do," I snap. "I'm staying. We need you."

"I'll be all right. I just need to regain some strength."

I peer back over the wall to see what has transpired so far.

Anara swipes the long end of her trident under Alaric's feet. Once he lands on his back, she goes for the kill. Prongs aimed at his heart. She's ready.

Alaric stops her trident from going farther. No matter how hard she pushes down, she can't get any closer to his chest. He's still humoring her.

He swipes his hand and sends her flying a good distance away from him.

I curse the day Halivaara ever let him exist.

From here, I focus on the Dormant King, pointing my hand at him to use Gridlock. By the way he's suddenly not moving, it's actually working. This is the perfect opportunity for Anara to strike.

She runs toward him as fast as she can. While she charges, I warm up Strike in the sky. I imagine he sees it coming because a Dormant springs up at his side to take the brunt of the blow while another bolt breaks off and hits him. His body unfreezes and collapses forward on all fours, breathing heavily.

Another Dormant crab breaks through the water's surface, along with what I'm assuming is the Dormant form of a Salty Eel. More spring up beside their King, in the form of horses, Niminims,

Winged Wolves, and Swift Dingos. Teeth bared, tentacles rippling from their necks, surrounding their leader in protection.

I've used my abilities more than I ever have, and my headache is weighing down my eyelids. I press my fingers against my temples to ease the aching and take deep breaths. I have to push through. I have to save my friends.

My body shivers from sheer fatigue. My face tenses and tightens as I trudge through the throbbing pulses in my head. I have at least one more Strike before I become depleted, and I pray that it's the one blow that ends this war.

I give it my all.

I scream despite my exertion and throw my hands down. Bolts of lightning hit every single Dormant. They die in one hit, including the ones that just reached the land from the water. Dust fills the air again, fading away with the soft breeze.

The Dormant King gives in to his weakness and falls to the sand. I collapse to my knees, my arms hanging limply at my sides. Like Quill, I need to regain my strength if we are to keep going. Sincerely, I want this to be the last of the fight.

The chaos has died down. Waves arrive on shore in gentle splashes, the calm after a storm. The island looks flatter now, without any standing buildings. Just the broken stones that prove there were once residents among the abandoned civilization.

The Bennarus gather around us, shrinking into their smaller forms and attaching themselves to our bodies. I rise from behind the low wall carefully and I leave Quill to stand on his own. The bandana on his arm is soaked in blood, but the wound itself appears to have stopped bleeding. I only helped him because we need him, not because I was concerned for his well–being. A damaged arm can impede his abilities, and we can't have that happen.

As far as our friendship is concerned, it's over.

All of us are unsure about everything by the way we're glancing at each other as we circle together, tiptoeing toward Alaric. He lays there, motionless, so much so that his entire body is completely limp. Even his chest doesn't move up or down to indicate signs of breathing.

I have a very eerie feeling about this.

"Are you all right?" Anara asks Quill while giving me the side-eye. I don't even care; that's how much I currently hate him.

"Hurts," he groans. "It's going to give me the greatest scar, though."

She rolls her eyes while I gaze at him with all the fire coursing through Ender's body. With the position he put himself in—and us—I don't understand how he can joke like this.

Immature coward.

"Did we do it?" Quill whispers in disbelief, eyeing the Dormant King and us. "Did we really kill him?"

The grunts of someone struggling from the shore prevent us from answering that question. We all twist to find Ender belly crawling through the wet sand, his arms shaking from the weakness of physical exertion. His cape, now drenched, proves to be a heavy weight on his shoulders that add to the struggle. Waves crash and blanket his body and head, his chest heaving with labored breaths.

"Ender!" Anara shouts. The three of us rush to his aid, crouching to his side to grasp his arms. Each one feels as heavy as the Mulhutna pickaxes as we endeavor to pull him out, but he makes it easier when he pushes on with his arms.

Anara huffs in rapid, frantic breaths as she cups his cheek with her hand. "Are you all right?"

"I dying," he groans. "Blaze will be of no use for a while."

Anara rolls her eyes. "So you're fine."

"No." He shakes his head. "I useless. Water hinders Blaze."

"That's all right." Quill slaps his shoulder. "We may have killed him."

Ender rises to his feet faster than I've seen him. "Really? We did it?"

"Only one way to find out," I say.

From the shore, we eye the Dormant King's lifeless body. The only movement we see from this distance is his rags of clothes fluttering with the soft wind.

There's no chance it was that easy. His abilities clearly show that he can't be struck down with just a lightning bolt.

"I don't think he's dead," I say out loud.

"He look dead," Ender simply states.

"He hasn't moved since he collapsed," Quill brings out. "Strike easily could have done the trick."

"I'm surprised to hear you say that about your new best friend," I snap in such a way that could have bitten his head off.

"I just saved you from getting stabbed in the face," Quill argues, emphasizing every word. "You haven't even thanked me!"

"I don't thank traitors." I glare and give him no room to defend himself. "I highly doubt this is all it took to kill him."

"So you don't believe he's dead?" Anara asks doubtfully, then points to Alaric's supposed dead body. "Looking there, right now, you don't think he's dead?"

I shake my head. There's no way. After using everything we had at our disposal, this wasn't the final blow. I just know it. "I have a hard time wrapping my head around it."

Tension and uncertain energy fill the space between us. We're all thinking the same thing, but none of us really want to admit that all it took was a lightning bolt.

Stepping over the rubble of what's left of the island, Anara slowly approaches his body. The pebbles crunch under her boots, noisy enough to alert anyone in the vicinity. But the Dormant King still doesn't react. For all I know, he's still alive and is very aware that we're questioning his survival.

"Anara!" I loudly whisper.

She whips her head in my direction and shuts me up with a finger to her mouth. Quiet as a mouse, she tiptoes on the softer parts of the sand. The subtle breeze moves his black clothing, rippling against his body. His chest remains still, along with his legs, arms, neck, and head. The only time I've seen something this still, such as a creature, is when it's dead.

Did I . . . truly kill the Dormant King? Did I deliver the final blow just as I wanted? Is it over?

Those questions are answered when his hand shoots up and grasps her neck, and all of us jump and scream in shock.

The Dormant King rises from the ground and lifts her off the sand, her feet dangling under her. No sign of thudding paws to indicate any Bennarus coming to our rescue, and all we manage to do is stand in stunned silence.

I knew—I *knew*—something wasn't right here.

Ender charges at him full force, only for Alaric to use his other hand to keep him from coming any closer.

"Did you honestly think you could successfully kill me?" he growls at both Anara and Ender. "You pathetic fools underestimate my power."

Anara chokes under his tight grip. Her hands claw at his wrist and attempt to release herself, but his fingers are so deep in her skin, it's giving her bruises.

"Now I am much closer to my goal," he says in a mischievous way. "Thank you kindly."

CHAPTER 27

As if his grip on me isn't tight enough, he somehow manages to squeeze harder. An odd sensation runs through my body, starting in my feet and tingling along my legs that sends a chill throughout. The ice cold courses up to my torso and chest, and centers to my neck, directly to his palm.

His hand glows a bright purple. Tendrils of the color split into hair-thin pathways under his skin, running through his forearm and his arm, then spreading all the way to his head, neck, and chest. My body feels more and more drained of energy, leaving me limp.

The realization of what is happening hits me like a brick to the head. I feel like a fool for not realizing it sooner. I'm physically exhausted, but still struggle even more under his captive grasp, desperate to make him stop.

He's too strong for me. There's nothing I can do to get out of this. My failing vision blocks my view of the water; I can't use it against him.

He finally lets me fall once he gets what he wants from me. One step closer to ruling this kingdom. One step closer to ridding the kingdom of us Descendants.

I turn to find my friends stuck to a broken wall, straps of sand wrapped around their bodies and ankles to keep them from moving. The Bennarus must be stuck as well if they haven't come to my rescue.

"Thank you, my child," he says to me in a manipulatively saccharine tone.

The Dormant King uses one hand to unwrap Quill from the confines of sand and floats him to his side. "Stay where you are, ally. Move, and I will kill you."

Quill swallows hard and remains frozen. He eyes me with fear, knowing that neither of us can do anything about this situation.

With his other hand, he opens a black hole. Then another. And another.

Oh no.

Havanna and Ender are released from their captivity, only to be set right in front of the portals. Before I know it, he tosses me in with them.

I frantically look for Wave and the other Bennarus. Everything I believed to be in control of is slipping between my fingers. Wave has always been the one stable being in my life; I can't lose him.

"Wave! WAVE!"

The roars in the distance point me to the Bennarus' whereabouts. The Dormant King has them all captive, along with Quill.

He's going to kill all of them.

"No no no no no no," I repeat to myself. I know exactly what's going to happen next, and it's going to be an extremely hard circumstance to escape from.

"No! No!" Havanna continuously screams in sheer desperation. She lunges forward to reach him, only to be held back like a rubber band tied around her body. "BOLT!"

Her incessant kicking sends sand everywhere. It's not going to change what's about to happen. We're not powerful enough to fight back. Ender's roaring from the depths of his throat does nothing either.

"I wish you luck in trying to find each other!" he announces proudly. "I shall never be defeated! Soon enough, I will be the ruler of this kingdom and everything in it!"

I feel a suction pull me into an unknown abyss, and everything goes black.

CHAPTER 28

QUILL

"No!"

I lurch forward as much as I can under the Dormant King's power, but it does little to help me reach my friends.

He copied Anara's abilities and used them against us. One by one, Havanna, Anara, and Ender get sucked into the holes behind them. Sending them to the unknown with no way out. No way for me to find them. The Bennarus, all shrunken and hiding all over my body, squeal at the loss of their owners. Their cries alone are enough to almost bring me to tears of despair. They all know there's nothing more that can be done; he has us under his authority.

I turn into a child having a tantrum. I fight, I kick, I scream, I throw punches, despite the throbbing pain in my arm. But it all catches the air. Alaric remains stoic, calm as can be. Completely ignoring my raging anger, at him and myself.

I'm stuck here, all because he appealed to my weakness for just a moment.

The worst person I've ever known turns to me, a sinister smile playing on his lips. He motions to the blood-filled bandana on my arm. "Looks like you got hurt there."

Havanna took care of me, despite her understandable fury toward me. If she knew the whole story—the emotions behind it—she would feel much differently. I have no one to blame but myself for not telling her.

Alaric steps toward me and lowers himself to his knees, a hand held out for me to take. All I can manage to do is look at it with pure repulsiveness. I refuse to take part in any of his plans. I am in no way going to let him turn me into his weapon, or a Dormant, for that matter.

That impels him to grab my injured arm and yank it toward him. I yelp with the force, but he does something I never expected an enemy to do.

His eyes turn purple; his hand emits a purple glow. The skin of my open wound stretches toward each other and closes the hole. All the damaged muscle and capillaries under my skin move about as they reconnect. The pain disappears and my arm feels brand-new again.

He healed me. With Transform.

He showed me what my own ability could do. Another supposed reminder of all he's done.

"I could have done that myself," I grumble. "You copied my ability, after all."

His only response is a chuckle as he returns to standing. He turns his back to me and spreads out his arms. The exact stance he used throughout the whole battle.

He peeks at me over his shoulder. "Ready to have some fun, ally?"

The worst possible outcome—a living nightmare—comes into play before my eyes.

In the ocean, as far as the coast, little black specks rise to the surface. The number of Dormants he has summoned now pales in comparison to the ones we fought and killed earlier.

They're everywhere. Land and sea.

Water splashes in the ocean as Dormants swim toward the coast. The small black specks climb up the cliffside on their way to land.

Where Havanna's and Anara's villages are.

Where Ender's tribe is.

Where I taught the children archery in Arbol Village.

Where Nyx still lives.

They're going to wipe out the entire kingdom and turn it into a barren wasteland. Lives will be lost for no good cause. More innocent creatures are at risk of becoming Dormants that only know to submit to his authority.

The kingdom of Petros is in grave danger.

No matter what, I will do everything I can to make up for my mistakes, and for bringing the Bennarus into this. I will never let them become Dormants. He will no longer manipulate me. Not under my watch.

I have to stop this. I have to do everything I can to get my friends back.

CHAPTER 29

I fall for what feels like ten minutes, then I land back-first onto something extremely cold.

I can handle the cold, but this is biting, like I've never experienced before. The longer I lie here, the more it burrows into my bones.

The sun shines brightly on my face, but it does little to warm my skin. Not a single cloud dots the sky, increasing the brightness on my eyes.

My mind attempts to comprehend the last few minutes before I ended up here. I got sucked into darkness, falling through pitch-black, then I plopped into freezing-cold land.

White powder covers the flat expanse around me, extending for miles. A gigantic mountain a couple miles away is about three times larger than Montanha Peak. The white stuff converts to water on my skin, dampening my clothes. I come to stand as fast as a bouncing pebble.

Just me, alone, in the middle of nowhere. Quill is held captive by the Dormant King.

Serves him right. He's nothing but a traitor.

Tears collect in my eyes when I consider the fact that I left Bolt behind. I have never been without my Bennaru in my entire life.

Never been far apart. I have no guidance on where to begin searching for him. The mountain ahead is all I have to go on.

I pause briefly. I've seen that mountain before.

I dig in my pocket for the map that is limp from water. I open it gently and look for all the mountains on it. Vulca, Stoneland Hills, Montanha Peak, and Paluso Mountains.

Paluso Mountains. I remember Jael mentioning this place. Which means, the flat expanse of land I'm standing on is Paluso Snowfield.

That's what this substance is. *Snow.* Cold, uncomfortable, and watery.

I attempt to glide my hands up and down my now-red arms to warm myself. The only thing that can help at all is to start moving. My limbs are weak from exerting energy and being cold, and my headache is still so painful that it's affecting my vision.

I didn't expect the war with the Dormant King to go this way. I hoped the fight on Luna Island would be the one to finish this mess. The fight that would end his influence on our lives and all of Petros. Instead, he used Usurp on Anara and sent us all over the place.

I also didn't expect Quill to betray us. That alone enrages me. I'm simply in disbelief that he even felt an inkling of empathy for that menace. He allowed the worst enemy in history to weaken him. To trick him into thinking he has something to offer.

The Dormant King—Alaric—has *nothing* to offer. There's not a single good thing about him. Yet, Quill still found some appeal.

I don't imagine I will ever let this go. Quill was becoming my closest friend. My one true ally. Everything, from the moment I met him till now, has been a lie. Just as it was with Victor. And Lavi. And Arthur.

He refuses to open up to me, but he did it so easily with the Dormant King, a near outpouring of his heart. What does that say about him? What does it say about who I choose to trust?

The betrayal is overwhelming. I knew Quill better than I knew the other betrayers. I thought he was my friend.

Having romantic feelings for him was a complete waste of time. Just as I worried it would be. For once, I thought this would play out better than it did with Victor.

I don't know him at all. He doesn't exist.

I finally come up to a paved pathway that follows the incline of the mountainside. Seeing as this is the only guidance I have, I start up on it.

The scenery is mesmerizing, to say the least. Trees with tiny, prickly, green needles cover each and every branch. The dead brown ones coat the ground and scatter on the pathway. Snow caps all of the trees, leaving the trunks bare. Crunching leaves and tiny animals scurrying up the bark are the only sounds among this snow-covered land. The summit is so high above me; it might take days to reach.

I have nowhere else to go.

The spots of the path that are shaded by the weird-looking trees make the air feel twenty degrees colder. What little sun there is in the sky is actually helping me not drop into a hypothermic state. I'm still exceptionally cold. My fingers can't move. They're numb to the bone. No amount of breath I blow onto them revives them. At this point, I could be attacked by a Swift Dingo and I wouldn't have the strength to fight back. My fingers can't grip my sword. The chances of surviving out here are slim if this doesn't go anywhere.

This path better lead me to a warm place.

The incline isn't steep, yet my legs are running out of strength. The dampness of my clothes makes the chill that much more intense. A tree branch scraping against my skin hurts more than it would under living temperatures.

The Dormant King did well in putting me in a place that could kill me. What a stellar man.

Around a rock protrusion, away from the paved path, I see the smoke of a fire, followed by a lovely aroma. Whatever is being cooked is bringing my stomach to intense grumbles. I need a hot bowl of soup, some hot water to drink, and super-thick blankets. Anything to bring me back to life.

I don't care if I'm out of strength. I sprint farther up the mountain, straight toward the smoke. The hope of food and warmth is the only thing that keeps me moving.

I round the corner, where the source of the smoke is. There is, indeed, food cooking over a fire. But there is also a man sitting by it on a wooden bench in front of a log cabin. Small lanterns on both sides of the door and the windows brighten the space, along with the wraparound porch.

The man sees me and freezes. His thick jacket adds bulk to his already steady build, a fur-lined hood covering the majority of his face. Snow attaches to his gray beard like honey.

He stands slowly. That's when I notice the hilt of a sword sticking above his shoulder. His right hand twitches in preparation to grab it, staring me down as a predator does its prey.

"Who are you?" he asks in a gruff, threatening voice.

I lift up my hands to somehow ease the situation. "I'm lost," I tell him in a shaky, desperate fervor, my mouth so dry it reduces my voice to softness. "Can I just stay here and get warm? I will leave as soon as I'm done."

He scoffs. "I've heard the same sob story for the last ten years." He unsheathes his sword and waves it in front of him. Something about the sword, and the way he's using it, seems familiar, but I can't put my finger on why. "Get off our property."

"I promise, I'm not dangerous," I plead further. "I'm just so cold, I can barely move—"

He comes at me before I can finish my sentence. I get my sword out just before his blade slices my head in half. I use all my mental power to force my arm to move and to block his attacks, but I'm not moving as fast as I need to.

I refuse to let my story end here.

"Please," I beg him, tears falling and freezing on my skin. "Please stop. I mean no harm."

This does nothing. He keeps striking. My energy depletes with every blow. It's only a matter of time before he wins this match.

A door closing beside me grabs my attention. A woman comes out of the cabin, looking on in horror at this fight. The strips of blonde hair escape the confines of her hood, arms folded.

I know her.

I haven't seen her in many years, but I know her from somewhere.

The distraction of it all leads to the man knocking the sword out of my hand. My heart drops at the thought of what is going to happen next.

"Distraction doesn't look good on you."

My heart drops, but for a whole different reason.

I've heard those words before.

I was ten years old, back in Cal–léa. My childhood friends watched me and my father practice sword fighting in the backyard.

He was the only one that ever said that to me. He always said it when he knocked the sword out of my hand.

I know him.

" . . . Papa?"

Thank you for reading *The Call of Allies*!

The Descendants' journey will continue in book three of the *Hidden Heroes* series. Will the Descendants be able to gather an army for the ultimate war? Will Havanna and Quill finally admit how they feel about each other?

You will soon find out.

Want more of the Hidden Heroes? Get your copy of *The Call of the Lost King*, the backstory of the Ancestors and the Dormant King, at www.sarahblynnewrites.com!

Are you enjoying the Descendants' journey so far? Leave a review on Amazon or Barnes & Noble!

Follow me on -
Facebook: Sarah Blynne Writes
Instagram: @sarahblynnewrites
Tiktok: sarahblynne

Acknowledgements

It took me about two years to cultivate and start writing the *Hidden Heroes* series. It felt like such a huge accomplishment to create something that brings me so much joy, and I carried that with me into this book as well. All I can hope for is that you were able to immerse yourself in this world and the story, and even become attached to one (or more) of the characters.

First, I want to thank all my readers. This is my third book overall, and I'm still new to the author world. Thank you for following my writing journey and being willing to give my books a chance. You have no idea how much an indie author like me appreciates that.

My editor, Kasey Kubica, deserves a mention. Your advice and expertise are invaluable, and I'm so grateful for all your hard work on my books. Thank you, truly.

Thank you, also, to my closest friends and family for being so supportive of me as I've delved into this journey. I really don't know what I would do without you. I love all of you so much.

I'm going to single out my mom for a moment. Much like the Descendants, she's a hero. Always has been. She amazes me in so many ways. Mom, I want to be like you when I grow up. Thank you for being my mom.

And, as I usually do, I conclude my thanks with a note to my husband, Cody. He may not be much of a reader, but he's the best cheerleader, and that's all that matters. I love you, dude.

I'll see you in book three!

SB

ABOUT THE AUTHOR

Sarah Blynne resides in Renton, WA with her husband and fur child, Gracie. In her spare time, Sarah likes to read, cook, play video games, go on walks, drink coffee, and spend time with her loved ones. *The Call of Allies* is Sarah's third novel, and the second installment of the Hidden Heroes series.